RANSOM RUN

RANSOM RUN

MARTIN DIBNER

1977

DOUBLEDAY & COMPANY, INC., GARDEN CITY, NEW YORK

Library of Congress Cataloging in Publication Data

Dibner, Martin.
Ransom run.

I. Title.
PZ3.D54815Ran [PS3507.I215]   813'.5'4
ISBN 0-385-12242-X
Library of Congress Catalog Card Number 76–18341

For
Walter Bradbury

RANSOM RUN

PART ONE

CHAPTER ONE

Autumn in Maine that year was unseasonably gentle. Elsewhere in the nation, temperatures plummeted. Icy rain launched floods in the Midwest, sweeping homes and families to ruin. A hurricane belted the midriff of Florida, killing cattle and devastating crops before it slackened and died in the Gulf. Surprised Montana sheep froze like pewter statues in the hills and plains. An eerie earth tremor made a shambles of eighty square miles of ticky-tacky east of Los Angeles. Yet Maine's air, untroubled and serene in tender blue skies, blessed the astonished people.

Cool days and honest New England sunshine coddled the red russet and gold yellow in the oak and maple treetops. Mighty Katahdin towered like an inland Gibraltar over the vast secret forests, a snowless eminence imperious against the fierce sunsets of October's end.

Too bad for the hunters, the people reflected. But in their hearts they welcomed this gift of time before the icy grip of winter. The nights turned cold but never cold enough for frost. Trusting their luck and the *Old Farmer's Almanac,* the good Maine folk kept the lettuce and pole beans and squash in their gardens well past harvest time. The orchard slopes hung heavy with ripe dark fruit. It was a chancy game, but the daft weather had got into the people like good elderberry wine and made them lightheaded. They laughed about it and made love more often and felt simply wonderful and gave thanks for the unusual streak of good weather. As far north as Moosehead Lake and Desolation Pond, the weather held and the people marveled.

They could not have dreamed of what was soon to come.

CHAPTER TWO

It began on a soft Sunday in Cambridge, outside of Boston. A young man in fancy cowboy boots was kicking the new Michelin tires on a brown Mercedes-Benz 250 SC. Grogan, the used-car-lot owner, caught sight of him and, cursing under his breath, hurried over. Grogan was plagued daily by the unshaven long-hairs and Harvard Square hippies who drifted half-stoned along Mass Avenue kicking his tires and sometimes slashing them just for the hell of it.

"Look here—" he began in a bluster. Seeing the young man close up changed his mind.

"Just looking," the young man said, smiling.

Grogan relaxed. After a decade or more in the bloody arena of used-car dealing, he fancied himself a lion among Christians, a connoisseur of human flesh. A rare morsel, he thought, looking the young man over. His eyes took in the smooth deerskin jacket and the western-cut whipcord jeans tucked into the boots. He admired those boots. Grogan had survived an army hitch in Texas some twenty years ago. Handmade boots like those the young man wore went for a C-note then. At today's prices—? Michael Xavier Grogan, d/b/a Madman Mike Motor Sales, Inc., turned on the charm. His smile was pure altar boy emeritus.

"I can see you're familiar with the Mercedes. And this cream puff is ready to roll."

The young man touched the gleaming finish. "She's a beauty, all right."

Grogan liked his cheerful face and the genteel quality of his spoken words. He led him to the driver's side of the car, away from the right door panel which had been completely rebuilt and painted. Glancing toward his office, he saw that his salesman was back from lunch. He offered to take the young man for a spin. The young man declined.

"I have a car, thank you."

"We can trade." Grogan looked out front for the young man's car. "What are you driving?"

"An XK-E."

He said it almost apologetically. Grogan could scarcely repress his delight. A rare one indeed. A real money cat.

"What year XK-E, may I ask?"

"She's a '74. Gun-metal gray, V-12 convertible, power steering, power disks, four-speed, AM/FM stereo tape, factory air, five wire wheels, and black genuine leather interior."

"You sound like a man trying to sell a car," Grogan said.

"Not my Jag. I've owned her since Mile One."

"Where is she?"

"Having her regular checkup."

"I mean, *where?*"

"Foreign Imports in Watertown."

Grogan in torment near ecstasy had trouble holding back. But the years of used-car dealing had thickened his hairless white skin to scar tissue. "You're not from around here, are you?"

"Oh no."

"Texas—?"

"Why do you ask?"

"The jacket and jeans. Those boots. And you don't talk like one of us Bostonians."

"I travel quite a bit. Drove my mother here a few days ago. She'll be staying on, visiting her aunt. Her grandaunt, really. Which makes her my great-grandaunt."

Grogan who never before had fathomed the distinction between great and grand in family relationships, was dazzled. "Here in Cambridge?"

"Salem," the young man said. "On Chestnut Street. One of the older homes. Do you know Salem?"

"I'm from Lynn." It seemed to explain everything. Grogan was uneasily aware that the conversation had shifted away from cars and wondered how that had happened. "I'm prepared to give you a once-in-a-lifetime trade on this Mercedes."

"Actually," the young man said, "I'm interested in transportation. Until my Jag's out of the shop. Something for my mother to drive after I've gone. A smaller car. Less sophisticated."

"Got just the thing, sir. A clean '71 Chevelle. Automatic, power steering, low mileage. Sold it new to the sisters over to the Holy Cross Armenian Church. One owner, you might say—"

"Sounds interesting."

"Like for you to see it, try it—"

"I really should discuss it with Mother first. She'll be driving it."

"Won't cost a dime to look. It's just across the lot. Okay guaranteed. Clean as a hound's tooth."

"I'd be taking up your valuable time."

"What I'm here for, isn't it?"

They walked between the tight rows of brightly painted cars under flapping plastic multicolored pennants in crisp November sunlight. In the street the traffic rumbled and clattered. An ambulance raced by, siren wailing.

"Cradle of Liberty," the young man murmured, watching it go.

"Beg pardon?"

"Faneuil Hall."

"Fresh fruits and vegetables," Grogan said, somewhat confused. "You don't want to miss it." He stuck out his hand. "Michael Grogan," he said.

"A pleasure," the young man said and shook Grogan's hand.

"Tell me something," Grogan said. "Why do people kick car tires?"

The young man laughed. "That's very funny."

"I'm serious. Don't mean to offend, y'know. But they come around, they look at a car, they kick the tires. It doesn't mean a goddamn thing—" He saw the tightened expression on the young man's face. "I mean, you can't tell a thing about a car by kicking the tires, can you? Yet nine out of every ten people come looking, they kick the tires."

"I like to kick tires," the young man said.

"Why?"

"Feels good." He smiled, slow and easy.

Grogan unlocked the door of the Chevelle. The young man looked inside. He swung the door. It clunked just right. He got in and started the motor and listened for a few moments and shut it off. He walked around the car and kicked the left front tire and grinned. "Oops, sorry," he said and Grogan grinned back.

You got to hand it to these western types, he thought. Straight as arrows. Polite and honest and death on swearing. Not like the run of Lynn and East Boston and the wrong end of Cambridge. Good people. Salt of the earth.

They talked price and terms. The young man said it would be a cash deal, no trade. But he'd want his mother to have a look first.

"When'll she be back from visiting the aunt?"

"She's staying there. Aunt Agatha—well, it's terminal."

"Sorry to hear that." Grogan considered crossing himself. His own aunt's terminal road had been lined with empty gin bottles. "A matter of days? Weeks?"

"There's no telling. But this Chevelle, well, it seems to be just the thing. If Mother could see it—"

Grogan's antenna shot up. He had been here before. He had heard it many times. "If you're asking me, sir, to let you have the car to run up to Salem just so's your mother can see it—uh-uh. Nothing personal, y'understand. It's a strict company rule."

"I had no such thought in mind, Mr. Grogan. Like I said, a cash transaction, but not until Mother approves. Also, I'd like my mechanic in Watertown to check her out."

"Could you post a deposit, Mr. ah?"

"How much of a deposit?"

"Say ten per cent of the sale price."

"No problem." He reached inside his breast pocket. "Of course you'd want to wait until an out-of-town check cleared, wouldn't you?"

"That's the usual procedure."

"Too bad. Mother'd want it right off." As he spoke, the checkbook came out, along with a plastic accordion of credit cards. Its fawn deerskin cover matched the jacket. Grogan could have swooned. "Tell you what," he said, his lips dry as dust. "Just for the deposit, maybe we can make an exception. I'll accept your personal check."

"That's very kind of you." The checkbook hovered. "Now what if Mother disapproves, then what?"

"Your deposit's promptly returned, no questions asked." Over my dead body, Grogan told himself. "Unless of course you choose to make another choice."

"Fair enough," the young man said.

"All there's left to do, sir, is step into my office and we'll write it up."

"What I'd prefer to do, Mr. Grogan, is hold off until after lunch."

"Join me for lunch, sir. I was just about to go."

"Thank you. That's most generous of you. But I'm already late for an appointment back at the hotel. Old college chum."

"Where are you staying?"

"The Copley Plaza." He produced a large hotel key from the patch pocket of his jacket and turned it to read the number. "Room Ten Twenty-six, Mr. Grogan. I'll come by later for the car, say about three."

Some of the love was gone from Grogan's voice. "And your name, sir?"

"Tatum." The young man spelled it. "Gary Tatum."

"Now look, Mr. Tatum, may I suggest you leave the deposit check. Like in escrow? There's no telling two minutes after you're gone, who'll come along and snap up this one-of-a-kind clean automobile. That way, leaving the check, I can reserve it for you until you get back."

"It'll be here," Tatum said.

They shook hands and parted. Grogan went to his office. He had an urgent phone call to make. Tatum strolled back across the lot and, passing the Mercedes-Benz, dug the tip of the hotel key hard into its side as he walked by, gouging the finish its full length.

"Shit-colored cars," he muttered.

He walked down the street toward Harvard Bridge and the river. At a nearby bus stop, he chatted animatedly with a huge old woman until the bus arrived. He helped her up the steps and to her seat. She was red-faced, arthritic, and profusely grateful. Tatum waved off her words. "You remind me of my mother," he said and took a seat further on.

"Such a dear young man," the old lady wheezed to her seat neighbor. "They just don't make 'em that way no more."

Grogan was on the phone to Foreign Imports in Watertown. "Erich?"

"Speaking."

"Grogan in Cambridge. Listen. Do you by chance have an XK-E in for a check-up?"

"We got several, Mike."

"This is a gun-metal gray '74, belongs to a guy name of"—he fished around in his mind—"Tatum?"

"Brought in yesterday, Mike. A nice vehicle." He hesitated. "Don't tell me it's hot?"

"No, Erich. Leastways, I don't know. But he was in looking at a Chevelle. For his mother, he said. I was just wondering."

"About the Jag? You mean to trade?"

"No. I don't know. Like I said. There was something—look, I got no reason to question—"

"He's getting some fancy carburetor work and a tune-up. She's a clean Jag, Mike. Arizona plates. Registration's in the glove compartment—"

"No sweat, Erich. I was just checking."

"You think he's okay for the bill?"

"He flashed a deck of credit cards is all I know. How much is it going to run?"

"The things he wants done—over a hundred, hundred ten, maybe. He still there?"

"No." Grogan was angry at himself for letting Tatum get away. "I'll give him a ring at his hotel. I'll give him a deal on the Chevelle he can't refuse."

CHAPTER THREE

Some fifty miles north of Madman Mike's vandalized Mercedes-Benz, David Briggs, fourteen and freshly expelled, sat sprawled in the cab of his grandfather's pickup. His expression was alternately sullen and devil-may-care. It froze to a stony stare when students en route to the Academy dining room for their noon meal turned to look at him. Actually he was sick at heart and close to tears. In the weeks he had been at the Academy, there were few hours when he was not wishing and scheming to be away from it. Now that it had happened, he felt abandoned and humiliated. It was not at all as he expected it would be.

He had loaded his foot locker and loose gear in the body of the light truck. It smelled strongly of the cow dressing his grandfather had hastily shoveled out when the call had come. David watched his grandfather yacking with Harkness, the headmaster. He wished he would hurry.

He stared across the smooth lawn at the two older men. What the hell was there to yack about? He'd been kicked out, period. Harkness had made that quite clear. There wasn't a thing Grampa Kimball with all his charm and legal clout could do about it. Which was just dandy with David. He had been ready to kick ass out of here a month ago. To split for keeps. He'd had all of the Academy he could stomach. He wished his grandfather'd wind it up and get rolling, before he puked on three square feet of the Academy's precious manicured grass.

David detested the neat lawns and Keep Off signs. The endless putt-putt of the multi-rig riding mowers day in, day out, almost drove him out of his skull. He'd be sitting in a classroom trying to absorb whatever it was the teacher was saying and the mowers would be putt-putting back and forth across his brain like hot irons. When his name'd be called to give an answer, he'd have no idea whatever the hell the question had been. Those goddamn mowers kept the whole hundred acres looking like a paint-sprayed, G-rated Walt Disney wonderland and David's mind like a dark pocketful of broken glass.

Harkness himself was an asshole. He stalked about in his baggy, shaggy tweeds with those useless suede elbows, scolding and smirking, robbing the kids of peace and privacy. Harkness the Hard-on, they called him. It was the one subject on which David and the rest of his freshman class agreed.

A few yards away in the sun-filtered shadow of the Academy's two revered oaks (planted by John Greenleaf Whittier's cousin's niece in 1895), Abner Harkness III frowned at the weathered, white-haired old gentleman in smelly farm clothes who had come to fetch David Briggs. Harkness had never met Alonzo Kimball and had, in fact, mistaken him for a hired hand, a blunder which gave Kimball considerable edge and much satisfaction.

The previous half hour spent inside had made it quite clear to Kimball that Harkness was a pompous, pontifical bore, full of stale homilies and meaningless caveats. Kimball showed him no deference and Harkness was somewhat put out. He had expected the boy's father, Sydney Briggs, to pick up David. He had virtually demanded it over the phone. He had been looking forward with keen pleasure to meeting Briggs again. Briggs had been an Academy classmate and big-man-on-campus, and Harkness an obscure plodder. The opportunity of lecturing wealthy, successful Sydney Briggs on how Academy alumni are expected to rear their sons would have afforded him the added gambit of displaying his own success in his career. Now he felt cheated and chose to vent his displeasure on this odd country gentleman from Maine.

"Why isn't David's father here to pick him up?"

Kimball's smile was bleak. "Sydney Briggs is a very busy man."

"I made it distinctly clear to Syd how urgent it was for him to appear in person to pick up the boy."

"Sorry you didn't convince him. Would've saved me a trip."

"What about Mrs. Briggs? Certainly she—"

Kimball's indulgent smile faded swiftly enough to stop Harkness right there. "It would have been inconvenient for my daughter at this time."

"Convenience, Mr. Kimball, is hardly a consideration at this point in time. David's a sick boy. Expulsion can be a traumatic, a shattering experience to a fourteen-year-old boy."

"You really think so?"

"I certainly do. My twenty years—"

"David tells me he can't wait to get out of here, Mr. Harkness."

"It's Doctor. Dr. Harkness."

"You practice medicine?"

"No, I'm a—"

"Psychiatry, then. You treat the mentally ill?"

"—doctor of philosophy. Ph.D. No matter." He peered more sharply at Kimball's bland face. "Now if there are no further questions—"

"There are, Doctor. When my son-in-law called me from Boston to pick up David, he was tied up in some business negotiations and neglected to tell me why David's being expelled."

"Infractions of Academy rules. Sydney knew that. I told him so in no uncertain terms."

"Would you tell me?"

"Delighted to tell you—"

"Yes. I see that."

"Eh? Well. Beginning with last September a week after school opened. David ran away—"

"I hadn't heard."

"We dealt with the matter right here. He ran off and was picked up by the state police who notified us."

"What was he doing wrong?"

"Hitchhiking. The trooper arrived with lights flashing. An embarrassment to me personally and of course to staff. And a blemish on the Academy's escutcheon."

"I beg your pardon?"

"Academy boys do not run off, Mr. Kimball. They consider it a great privilege to be here."

"Where was David running off to?"

"He refused to say. He was most difficult. I suspended him, of course. For a week. Then a month ago without provocation he attacked another student—"

"Raped him?"

"—and blackened his eye and bloodied his nose. The prefects

broke it up almost immediately. At that point in time, David should have been expelled. Second offense. I called Sydney and told him so. He persuaded me—actually begged me—to give David another chance. Which I did."

"Why'd he attack this other boy?"

"He would give no reason. Clams right up."

"And the other boy?"

"Taken completely by surprise. Couldn't understand why—"

"Witnesses?"

"Now look, Mr. Kimball, this is no court case."

"As the boy's grandfather, I'd like to know."

"There seem to be no witnesses."

"Did you suspend the other boy?"

"Of course not. Since he was the victim."

"What else did David do wrong?"

"Possession." Harkness's eyes lighted up. "Possession alone, Mr. Kimball, is grounds for dismissal. Here at the Academy one infraction of the rules means suspension. Two are cause for dismissal. I should like to point out that the decisions are not mine alone. A student/faculty council hears the case and makes recommendations—"

"But the final judgment is yours."

"Yes. So there you have it. Running away. Fistfighting. Possession of marijuana." He ticked them off on his fleshy fingers like crimes of passion. "Expulsion by the unanimous decision of all."

He glared at Alonzo Kimball and wondered what it was about the man that intimidated him. He recalled that Sydney Briggs's parents had been well-to-do and had lived in a perfectly respectable suburb of Boston somewhere on the north shore. He had heard through the alumni columns that Sydney had done well, had in fact made something of a name for himself as a financial wizard of sorts while he, Harkness, was groping through the lower echelons of his ivy-festooned career. He had read the announcement of Sydney's marriage to a Maine girl. Maine was all right, Harkness conceded. The Academy enrollment included several boys from Maine, carefully selected, of course. Harkness had not expected the likes of this Kimball. No parent had ever driven into the immaculate Academy grounds in a beat-up pickup truck, wearing a soiled dungaree shirt and Levi's and boots redolent of cow dung.

"One more question, Dr. Harkness."

"A brief one, then. I'm late for luncheon." His insides gurgled and whined in Pavlovian obedience to the years of ritual institutional feeding.

"Did David have an opportunity to defend himself?"

"Defend *himself?* My dear man. We've had to defend ourselves against *him!*"

"I mean, defend himself against the charges."

"We don't run a kangaroo court, Mr. Kimball—"

"It's Justice Kimball."

"Justice?"

"Of the Maine Supreme Judicial Court. I'm sure you don't run a kangaroo court, Dr. Harkness. You run a nice school for nice boys. That being the case, you should have notified David's parents when he ran off—"

"We usually notify parents in such matters. However—"

"It's required by law, Dr. Harkness, in disciplinary matters."

"Such laws," Harkness snapped, "are not for us. They apply to the public schools. The Academy is a private institution and as such—"

"Your academy, Dr. Harkness, has a library built five years ago with federal funds. Your academy right now has an application with HEW in Washington for funds to construct a theater arts complex on a matching basis with the community here. That being the case, your students are entitled to certain protection against suspension and expulsion for disciplinary reasons under the Federal Civil Rights Act."

"I refuse to believe—"

"*Goss* versus *Lopez.* Go to your library and look it up. It was decided by the Supreme Court of the United States in January 1975. Any student suspended for less than ten days must be given oral or written notice of the charges against him. Was that done for David, Dr. Harkness?"

"I'd—have to check. It was some time ago."

"Under the same statute, the student is entitled to an explanation of the evidence if he denies the charges. Did David deny the charges?"

"I told you. He clammed up."

"The statute also provides that he be given an opportunity to present his side of the case."

"Well, he certainly had the opportunity. He just did nothing about it."

"That was for suspension, was it not? What about his expulsion? The law is quite clear. *Wood* versus *Strickland*, February 1975. The highest court in our nation, Dr. Harkness, decided that in expulsion proceedings, it is mandatory—I repeat, *mandatory* —that any student being expelled for disciplinary reasons secure counsel, confront and cross-examine witnesses, and call witnesses to verify his story. Did you, or did your student/faculty council, meet the requirements of that statute?"

"David readily admitted his guilt—"

"We aren't discussing guilt, Doctor. We're speaking of his rights."

"He had the marijuana right there in his desk. I don't see that anything else matters, one way or the other."

"I find that a surprising statement from an educator who presumes to devote his life work to the character-molding of young people."

It took Harkness several moments to digest what Kimball had said. Then he did a strange thing. He stamped his foot and his voice shot out of control. David, sunk into the seat of the pickup cab, sat up and craned his neck to stare.

"We have no room for troublemakers here," Harkness shrilled. "David Briggs in two months has caused more trouble than I've had to deal with in my entire career as a headmaster. And I'm not about to undergo more of the same from his grandfather or anyone else. You tell Sydney Briggs his son is through here. Finished. I never want to see his face again. Or yours, sir."

"On the subject of troublemaking," Kimball said mildly, "may I remind you of John Hancock and Patrick Henry and John Adams and several of their buddies. Much depends on what tyranny it is that troubles the troublemakers."

"I must go," Harkness said, ashen. He glared across the clipped green to David. David stuck out his tongue as far as it would go.

"No need to consult your attorneys," Kimball was saying. "I'm sure David won't sue the Academy. He's happy to be free of it. But Sydney might. Sydney's a pathological plaintiff."

"You don't have to tell me the kind of man Sydney Briggs is. We were Academy classmates."

"Then you know Sydney. He'll be expecting a rebate on the unused portion of his son's tuition."

"It isn't Academy policy to return tuitions in expulsion cases."

"Sydney will like that. He loves a challenge."

Harkness turned away with a sour look. "I'll see that the matter is given some attention." He paused. "Ah yes. The balance of David's spending account." He handed Kimball a small manila envelope. "To be returned to the parent, of course."

"It's been a pleasure doing business with you," Kimball said. "At this point in time."

CHAPTER FOUR

Kimball drove the pickup north along the Maine Turnpike at a leisurely speed. There was plenty of time now. David beside him spoke little. Kimball was eager to hear the boy's view of the matter but held his questions. There would be time enough later.

The call from Sydney Briggs had come early that morning. Kimball was in the orchard spreading the winter dressing around his fruit trees. Briggs's words were urgent and dictatorial. That was Briggs's style. He was also explicit. Pick up David before noon. Drive to the cottage at Moosehead. Wait until Briggs's arrival, scheduled for eight o'clock Monday night.

Kimball hung up and swore aloud and went out again and spread the rest of the load and headed south. He did not bother to change. An accurate indication, he reflected with sour pleasure, of his attitude toward snob prep schools like the Academy.

Had I kept the full load in the pickup, he comforted himself, I'd be carrying coals to Newcastle.

He resented Briggs. He detested his son-in-law's thoughtlessness and lack of consideration in using people like chattel. He would have told Briggs to go to hell. He had done so on other occasions. Only his devotion to his daughter and grandson kept him from doing so now.

He wondered why Briggs had chosen the cottage at Moosehead for the meeting place. Kimball's farm in the Kennebec Valley and the Briggs mansion in Bangor were both more easily accessible. But it was not Briggs's style to make things convenient for others. Could he possibly have chosen the cottage deliberately to flaunt the supposed dishonor David's dismissal had brought to the family name? Briggs hated the cottage, an enduring symbol of four generations of Kimball tenacity and achievement. He had listened too often to the hogwash about the original log cabin built a century ago of whole unpeeled cedar logs, cut, adzed, notched, and fitted by Alonzo's grandfather who had come barefooted from Perth across the St. John, carrying his new boots in his hands, to court a river logger's daughter.

David's was the fifth generation and David sole heir and last of the line. Was his expulsion Briggs's small triumph over Kimball's proud bloodlines? Was that the way Briggs wanted it?

Kimball glanced at David preoccupied, his eyes searching the woods for wildlife. School discipline must have been hell for the lad, Kimball reflected. And now what? Another school? Another rebellious disaster?

It was a marvelous Sunday. The tourist hordes dispersed and the perennial lovers of autumn foliage long gone. Kimball swung the pickup off the turnpike at Falmouth and drove north on the old road through Yarmouth. They stopped for fish chowder and chunky lobster rolls en route and continued on to Freeport. David's glumness had diminished somewhat and it occurred to Kimball that a visit to the L. L. Bean establishment might restore the lad's normally buoyant spirits. His hunch proved sound. A new pair of hunting boots did the trick, the leather-topped, rubber-bottomed style for which Bean's is famous. He had given David the manila envelope and David insisted on paying for the boots himself. They quit Freeport in high spirits and picked up the turnpike at Gardiner. Conversation was easy now.

"Care to talk about it, David?" David nodded but looked away.

"That headmaster—did you get along with him?"

"Harkness?" David shrugged. "I hardly ever saw him."

"How come?"

"He stuck around his office mostly. Except to snoop on the kids. A lot of the time he was off on business trips or raising money, stuff like that."

"Couldn't the boys just go in and talk to him?"

"He was always too busy. You know, like Dad. Unless you were hauled up front for discipline. Even then it was the duty prefect who handled it, or one of the teachers."

"Harkness had some pretty nasty things to say about you."

"Harkness is a shmuck, Grampa."

The phrase startled Kimball. It was big-city street slang, alien and obscene. "Where on earth did you ever hear that word?"

"One of the new kids. From New York." David looked pleased. "I got along fine with him."

"That's a terrible word, David."

"All the kids use it."

"Do you know what it means?"

"Course. It means an asshole."

Kimball stared straight ahead. The world will never be the same, he thought. He felt rather bleak for a moment. "Dr. Harkness gave me his three reasons for expelling you. Care to hear them?"

David shrugged.

"First offense was running away. Did you run away?"

"Yes, sir."

"Knock off the sir, David. We're old tentmates. Let's just level with each other, eh?"

"Sorry, Gramp. Sure. I ran away."

"Why?"

"You wrote me Mom was at this place, the Acres, for me to write her a letter, and I looked up the town on the map. It was only thirty-eight miles from where I was. So I decided to go and see her."

"Did you ask for permission to leave?"

"I asked my prefect—"

"What exactly is a prefect?"

"A senior in charge of a dorm group. Todman was his name. Lolly Todman. A faggot. He said to ask Harkness for permission. I didn't."

"Why not?"

"I'd be wasting my breath."

"So you took off on your own."

"I wanted to see Mom."

"Why, David?"

"I was worried about her. I missed her."

"A holiday was coming up. You could have gone then."

"I wanted her to get me out of that damned school, Gramp. It's a lousy place—a kindergarten for stinking rich kids from Boston and Connecticut and New York—"

"Never mind that. Second offense was taking a swing at one of the boys. Did you?"

"I did better. I slugged the hell out of him."

"Why, David?"

"Something he said."

"What did he say?"

"I can't tell you that."

"You promised we'd level with each other."

"I didn't promise anything."

"We agreed then. What could a boy possibly say that would make you want to—slug him?"

David remained silent for several moments, staring straight ahead. How much, he wondered, do you tell that will hurt an old man you love?

"David?"

"Can we go on to the third offense, Gramp, huh? The grass in my desk. You want the honest truth, right? Okay. The honest truth is, I don't know how it got in my desk. I didn't put it there. I don't smoke pot. I hate the smell of it. When they told me they found grass in my desk, I thought they were joking. They're always pulling practical jokes on us new kids. Maybe it was a joke. Maybe the lousy kid I slugged put it there. But who told Todman to look in my desk?" He turned to face his grandfather. "That's the truth. If it was a joke, it sure backfired. On me. Well, the hell with them. I'm glad it happened. Because here I am."

He turned away, lips pinched, eyes misty. Kimball let the matter rest. He had shared mishaps and joys with the boy enough times to know he spoke the truth. In spite of the boy's bravado and seeming indifference, Kimball realized the dismissal had hurt David deeply. He reached over and rumpled the boy's long hair, unable to speak the words of comfort he felt.

He left the turnpike at Newport and drove through Dexter and Guilford toward Greenville and the big lake. David was cheerful again. They passed through farm country and small towns and villages, alert to the signs of nature they so loved to point out to each other. Where deer had passed. A partridge in silent flight to deep cover. The patient artistry of beaver in the dammed brook beyond a bridge they crossed.

In Greenville, Kimball paused long enough to pick up groceries for the next few days. He had no idea of how long Briggs intended to stay or if Briggs would arrive when he had said he would. David remained in the truck, hunched down, hoping none of the townspeople who knew him would see him.

In the store, Kimball chatted with the locals. They were surprised to see the old judge this time of year. Something up? they wondered. Warm for November, he said. Ayuh, they said and let it go at that.

Eddie Michaud, a local bush pilot, helped Kimball with the grocery boxes and stowed them in the truck. His cheery hi to David went unnoticed. Was it possible the boy had not heard? It puzzled Michaud. Kimball climbed in and drove off. Michaud watched them go, then crossed to the telephone booth on the opposite side of the street. He had an urgent call to make. To Gary Tatum. At the Copley Plaza in Boston. Collect.

They left the blacktop and followed the woods road to Kimball's Point, the family compound at Beaver Cove on the east shore of Moosehead. David helped with the groceries and carried his own gear to the A-frame nearby. He had built the A-frame that summer. Seeing it refreshed his dampened spirits. He rejoined Kimball in the cottage and got a fire going. He loved the old place. I'm home, he told himself. Where I belong. . .

It was a simple, sturdy structure of weathered shingles, a hundred yards down from the woods road, on a secluded point of pine and cedar, facing west. The paneled living room, flanked by the kitchen and bedroom wings, centered on a huge fieldstone fireplace, the work of a Finnish stonemason long gone. The furnishings were well used and comfortable, the walls of smooth pine darkened by time and wood smoke.

After a light supper, Kimball led the way to the shore to watch the sunset over Squaw Mountain. "Our orders are to lay around here until your father shows up. Which will probably be some time tomorrow night."

"Where is he?"

"Boston. A Sunday business conference and a closing tomorrow some time."

"What's a closing?"

"A polite gathering of hostile lawyers armed to the fangs with small print. Never fear. Our hero, Sydney Briggs, will emerge triumphant."

"He never loses, does he?"

"Not if he can help it." Kimball felt guilty, speaking of Briggs to David. He could not trust himself to hide his true feelings.

Briggs's marriage to Martha Kimball had made a private hell of her life.

Kimball sniffed the night air. "Freaky weather," he said half to himself. He did not feel the slightest hint of winter on the wind and it troubled him. They walked back to the cottage.

"Can I take the boat across to Caribou Point tomorrow?"

"The motor's put up for the winter, David."

"I mean the skiff. To row. May I?"

"It's a long pull."

"I've done it before. It's my last chance to look for Kineo flint and Indian spear points. Please, Gramp?"

"Okay, then. If the weather's fair." He regarded the boy fondly. "And we can talk later about what it was that boy said to you." David turned away and said nothing.

"It might help get a load off your mind."

"Don't ask me again. Please."

They went inside. Rosy embers flickered in the fireplace. Kimball added a chunk of birch and settled into the soft cushions. "No self-respecting Indian summer'd have the bad manners to hang around this late in the year."

"I read somewhere the seasons are changing," David said. "Longer summers, shorter winters. Maybe someday we'll have no winters at all."

"Maine'd never be the same." Kimball saw that David was admiring his new boots. "Feel comfortable in 'em?"

"Super." He ran his hand along the leather tops.

"You're going to have to go to school, you know."

"Can't I get a job?"

"Against the law. And what kind of job could you get, anyway?"

"Work in the woods. Cut pulp."

"At fourteen? Come on, Davey."

"*You* did."

"I had to work or starve. Be damned glad you don't *have* to work for a living. Not yet." He yawned. "Was the Academy so bad? Wasn't there anything you enjoyed?"

"The woods out back. Really wild. But it was off limits."

"No regrets about leaving?"

"Only about being kicked out. That wasn't fair."

"You broke the rules, slugged a classmate—"

"Damn it, stop bugging me!" He was out of his chair and stood irresolute.

"Sorry, Davey." Kimball went to him.

"I'm *okay*." But he did not resist when Kimball put an arm around him until things were under control. Loneliness, Kimball thought. Cancer of man's spirit.

"We're both bushed," he said gently. "It's been a long day."

"I didn't do a damn thing wrong," David mumbled. "I swear it."

"I believe you, son." He was having difficulty himself with words. "Let's get some shut-eye."

He watched the boy go, flashlight beam bobbing, up the path to his A-frame twenty yards in a grove of young cedar. Work in the woods, he mused, proud. Fourteen and no more meat on him than last year's fawn. And wiped his eyes and went to bed.

CHAPTER FIVE

Michaud spoke for several minutes to Tatum. When he hung up, his spirits had flagged. Tatum's reaction to the collect call was less than enthusiastic. But he would drive up anyway, he said. For old time's sake. He said it with a funny laugh that puzzled Michaud. Michaud agreed to meet him later that night and arranged the room reservation.

He was too charged up to go home for supper. He drove his rusting blue Wagoneer past the closed Moosehead Theater and up the hill to the Greenville Inn. It was full of hunters. Michaud splurged. He bypassed the salad bar, had two whiskeys and a juicy steak with french fries, and a slice of fresh blueberry pie with coffee. He smoked a cigar in the lounge, uncomfortable and faintly defensive in the presence of well-dressed strangers. Some time after dark he drove out of town along the winding blacktop from Greenville to Rockwood.

Eddie Michaud was an experienced pilot in his early thirties, a Vietnam veteran, slight of build and balding, a tangled man reliable drunk or sober behind a wheel. This time he was barely sober and in an awful hurry.

Michaud was president and vice-president of Michaud's Sportsflying Charter Service of Greenville. He was senior (and only) pilot, chief aviation mechanic, navigator and weatherman, and a registered Maine guide. The only title he did not hold was company treasurer. His wife, Doreen, handled the finances, which included the charter fees and the fuel and parts bills. And the petty cash, what there was of it.

She had learned in the ten luckless years of their marriage, Eddie was no hand at running a business. Doreen was smart with all kinds of figures except her own. She booked the reservations by mail and phone for the hunters and fishermen who came to try their luck in the Moosehead region. And carped at Eddie when he drank, which was too often. Early on, she was fed up with Eddie's faults, but Doreen loved him too much to leave him.

Beyond Rockwood he slowed along the short stretch of the Moose River between Brassua and Moosehead lakes and swung off the road into the gravel drive of the Northern Lights Kottage Kamps, a haphazard compound of white clapboard cabins with green shutters and red-painted chimneys. An odor of fried grease mingled with the good wood-smoke smell. Eddie parked as close as possible to Number Nine and crossed the gravel strip, looking for Gary Tatum's gun-metal Jaguar with the Arizona plates. He did not see it and wondered what Gary had traded for. The window blinds were drawn in Number Nine. Michaud knocked on the door.

"Come right in, Eddie."

Tatum looked up with a lazy smile from the double bed where, propped up against two pillows, in stockinged feet, he had been reading. Several books and magazines were neatly stacked on the night table. "And what's doing with Nanook of the North these days?"

Eddie always grinned when Tatum spoke like that, to hide his irritation. Though he rarely understood what Tatum meant, it made him feel foolish.

"Just fine, Gary, just fine. Hey! Where's the Jag?"

"Unloaded it in Boston." He avoided Eddie's eyes. "Too conspicuous." He looked down at Eddie's boots. "You forgot to wipe your feet, Eddie."

Michaud went back and obediently scuffed his clean worn boots on the mat inside the door. Somehow, Gary Tatum did not seem the same without the Jag. "Like I told you on the phone, Gary. *They're here.*" Local French accents tinged his speech when he became excited. "This could be it, Gary. The big chance."

"Relax, *mon ami.*" Tatum's voice was faintly mocking. He put aside the magazine and swung easily off the bed. He was slender and fair, with a pleasantly attractive look about him; a young man under thirty with light brown hair neatly trimmed and parted on the side. His eyes were blue and guileless in his smooth tanned face. The smile he fixed on Michaud seemed somewhat indulgent. He wore a bright Pendleton plaid wool shirt over a yellow turtle neck, and hip-hugging jeans. The deerskin jacket hung from a hook in the open closet. The high-heeled, hand-tooled cowboy boots that Grogan had admired lay in a box near the foot of the bed. Eddie Michaud, beset most of his life with endless frustrations, envied carefree clever Tatum, who smiled so much.

"Not too bad a room, Gary, on such short notice."

"A fleabag, Eddie, and you know it."

"Then how's about a nip?"

"You've already had a few, Eddie."

"Just one? To celebrate old times?"

"Like being seasick on Moosehead Lake?" Tatum got up and smoothed the bedcover and went to the dresser where several cans of soft drinks, a cardboard bucket of ice, and clear plastic glasses were neatly aligned. "You know my house rules, Eddie. Root beer or ginger ale?" He dropped ice cubes into two tumblers and poured drinks for the both of them. He gave one to Eddie and sat in the one chair provided, brushing its white plastic seat almost absently before sitting and stretching his legs. After an uneasy glance at the smooth bed, Eddie remained standing, an elbow on the oak bureau.

"Okay, Eddie," Tatum said, "step by step."

Reciting like a schoolboy in class, Michaud told how he had stopped that afternoon for cigarettes at the supermarket in Greenville. Judge Kimball came out carrying a carton of groceries. "Just for a couple of days," Michaud pointed out to Tatum. "Not like he was digging in for a long stretch of hunting." Kimball had greeted him. He had known Eddie Michaud a long time. Michaud described how he went along to the parking lot and helped Kimball stow the groceries. That was when he saw the boy slouched in the front seat, looking miserable.

"It struck me queer," Michaud said. "The kid's a real smart-ass, Gary, always nosing around the hangar, yacking, you know? So I told him hi and, damn it, he never even looks up." Eddie also thought it strange Judge Kimball would be here in November. He had quit hunting deer years ago.

"Does the kid hunt?"

"Hunt? When the little bugger was nine or ten, he shot him a twelve-point buck. One round from a thirty-thirty, and the big bastard dressed out at two hundred eight pounds. It was in the Bangor newspaper. But he hasn't done much hunting lately."

"Why not?"

"The old judge, I guess. He's one of those conservation nuts. Hung up on this ecology thing about no more killing. The old-timers, though, they tell of back before the war, the old gent he took his share and more of deer, bear, moose, whatever—"

"The boy still attends that private school, doesn't he?"

"Supposed to."

"No vacations until Thanskgiving, are there?"

"Hell, Gary, how would I know?"

"Schools are in session now. Everywhere. What's the boy doing here?"

"Could be he messed up." Michaud grinned. "Davey's radical. Him and schools don't mix. They tell me he used to give those grade school teachers up to Bangor a hell of a hard time. Sassing them. Running off. Playing hooky in the woods—"

"You know that to be true? Or just talk?"

"His old man himself once told me." The smile faded. "Before the sumbitch screwed me."

Tatum winced. "You've got a filthy mouth, Eddie."

Michaud shrugged. "Anyway, it figures that's how come the kid got sent away to this private school."

"Where he presently is not."

"So he must've blown it."

"How well does the boy know you?"

"He used to drop by the hangar and, yeah, I flew him once, just him and his mother."

"Where?"

"Allagash Lake."

"For salmon?"

Eddie would have scoffed at anyone else making such a remark. Tatum had revealed his ignorance of the Maine woods before. But Eddie needed Tatum. He needed Tatum's brains and Tatum's money. Forgiveness for such a trifling gaffe came easy. "Just to run the river, is all."

"What about the husband?"

"Sydney's the big-city type. Hates the woods. That lazy sumbitch keeps a butler in Bangor just to wipe his ass. Begging your pardon."

"Pretty risky, canoeing the Allagash, isn't it? A woman and a boy alone?"

"They've done it before, those two. We lash the canoe to a pontoon and drop them off with their gear at a campground close-by Allagash Lake. That cuts out a big piece of paddling, were they to put in at Northeast Carry on Moosehead, or even Chamberlain. A truck picks them up at Allagash maybe ten days later and brings them and the canoe back to Greenville."

"Still a risky run, isn't it?"

"Not in the fall of the year. There's not much white water. Rocky, sure, but it's not too bad."

"When was this, Eddie?"

"A year ago this summer. Just before Martha, that's the kid's mother, took sick. Nine long years, Gary, after that sumbitch Sydney screwed me out of my grandfather's farm."

He waited for Tatum to say something. After a heavy pause he could wait no longer. "It's our big break, Gary. Nothing's changed. You're right. Labor Day would've been better, sure. But now—here we got the kid and the weather's right—"

"I don't like it."

"What don't you like?"

"Just for openers, the Briggs kid knows your voice, Eddie."

"What d'you mean?"

"Your accent."

"I said I'd keep my mouth shut. You do the talking. I fly the plane. The way we worked it out, Gary, remember?" He drained his glass, sullen now. "What else is bugging you?"

"I checked Briggs out. You're right, Eddie. He's loaded. But can he come up fast with enough ready cash to pay the ransom?"

"That sumbitch pockets forty, fifty thousand cash every day, Gary! Just from his damned Yankee Trader cigarette machines."

"During the summer season maybe. That was what we counted on. But this is November, Eddie. No tourists."

"There's the kickbacks."

"What kickbacks?"

"I got this pal, Dubord, Jimmy Dubord? He subcontracted the plasterwork on Briggs's first two shopping centers. Maybe two hundred grand in all. Jimmy had to kick back almost fifty thousand of it. It pissed him off but it was the only way he could get the bid. And he's not the only one. There's the plumbers, electricians—"

"When was this?"

"Eight, ten years ago."

"I don't know, Eddie." He picked up a magazine and flipped a few pages.

Tatum's indifference began to rattle Michaud. Fear that the lone opportunity of his lifetime for a financial windfall might vanish, overcame his fawnishness. And he had learned to his surprise that with Tatum flattery could get him everywhere. "Can I have a refill?"

"Be my guest."

Michaud poured himself more root beer. "It's a master plan, Gary. Foolproof. Perfect. You worked hard on it. Remember the time we flew the route to Depot Lake last summer? Remember your driving with a stop watch to Skowhegan? And that fancy restaurant where the woman has no head? Waterville, was it? Jesus! The way you timed each move, each mile. Even that newspaper clipping with Sydney Briggs's picture, so you'd know what he looked like. Everything on the nose. It's got to work."

"A mere exercise in discipline," Tatum said, but Michaud saw that he had scored. Tatum yawned. "It's a long shot, Eddie. On such short notice. A dangerous gamble."

Aah, the teasing bastard, Michaud thought. Wanting to be coaxed. Wanting me on my knees, tongue-lashing his asshole. He looked at Tatum's clean, fresh face, the college-educated face he envied and admired. "You're right, Gary. It's too damn risky. And I wouldn't want to take you away from those tit 'n' pussy pictures."

Tatum managed a cool smile. "You've a stupid, filthy mind, Eddie. You know zero about art and less about life."

"I know a good thing when I see it, Gary. And I don't mean pictures of naked broads. Grabbing the Briggs kid for two hundred thousand bucks is what I mean. And I'm ready to go. On my own, if I got to."

Tatum laughed. "You wouldn't have a Chinaman's chance without me."

Michaud tried hard to look pensive for a few moments. "So you want out, eh?" He spoke softly, craftily, watching Tatum's eyes.

"That'd be the smart thing," Tatum said.

"Okay, Gary. Would you mind if I go it alone?"

"Not at all, Eddie. Go it alone. Be my guest. Yes, sir. Good luck to you, *mon ami.*" He got to his feet, scowling. "You dumb Canuck! You think I'd allow you to mess it up? After the brain-work and the time and money I've put into it?"

"It was my idea, Gary, originally—"   •

"*You* came to *me*, Eddie. *You* begged *me* to work it out. And I did. To perfection. And it would have worked if that miserable plane of yours had been ready to go last Labor Day."

"It's ready to go now."

"Sure. Two months too late." He finished his drink and rinsed the tumbler and put it aside. "Let's you and me get a few things straight, Eddie. Right now."

"Okay."

"You know very well you can't handle this alone. You ought to be ashamed of yourself, even mentioning it. I've been around capers of this kind enough times, Eddie, to know the mechanics, to pull it off without a hitch. In L.A., in Vegas—"

"Sure, Gary. Sure. You told me. You're a real pro."

"So I call the shots. Is that clear?"

"Sure, Gary."

"You say your new engine is checked out, inspected, everything. Right?"

"A-one, licensed. The works."

"Where's the equipment?"

"Equipment?"

"My musette bag, stupid. The stuff I left with you when you blew it."

"Oh, *that.* It's where we left it Labor Day weekend, stowed in a corner of the hangar. It's okay—I checked."

"When?"

"A couple of days ago."

"You still on the sauce, Eddie?"

"Now look, Gary—"

"Last time, Eddie, you took a few drinks that day, remember?"

"To steady my nerves."

"And tonight before you got here? How many, Eddie?" He did not wait for an answer. "You know the rules, Eddie. Not a drop of booze until this job is over."

"Okay, okay." Eddie drained the rest of his root beer and sucked on a shard of ice and set the glass down and wiped his lips. "I swear to God on my mother's grave."

Tatum was silent for a while. Michaud's oath rang unpleasantly in his ears. It made his stomach queasy. Michaud fidgeted. "We got to act fast, Gary. The kid's here now, tonight. By tomorrow he may be gone and so will a couple hundred thousand bucks."

"I want a few hours to think it over," Tatum said. "I'm still not sure. If I decide to go ahead, I'll be at your place early in the morning. If not"—he gestured—"*c'est la vie*. That's French, Eddie. You should know that."

"I'm half Indian," Michaud muttered. "You should know *that*."

Tatum grinned. "Okay, Big Chief. Just you be sure that plane of yours is ready. If your wife should ask, I'm hiring you for a few days to fly me to Depot Lake for the deer hunting. That's the whole story. Like last time it was for the fishing."

"What car you driving, Gary?"

"A '71 Chevelle, dark green with Mass plates. Remember now. I'm here for the deer hunting. That's all anyone has to know. You're flying me in and guiding me, and when I get my deer, we fly back. An open-end charter." He reached into a zippered pocket of his valise and handed a sheet of paper to Eddie. "That's the old schedule. Same as we planned. Sit down now and study it so you know it by heart."

"Hell, Gary, I already know it—"

"Two months ago you thought you knew it. And you didn't. Refresh your memory again."

"If you say so, Gary."

"Because I'm burning it after you read it and we go on memory alone."

Eddie sat in the white plastic-covered chair and obediently read the instructions. Tatum sprawled on the bed and picked up the magazine. The only sound in the room was Eddie Michaud reading his instructions.

"I'll pick up a red jacket and cap in the morning," Tatum said. "Do you have a rifle for me?"

"Just the old Krag thirty-forty I keep in the plane. She shoots okay and there's near a full box of ammo." He cackled. "Be funny as hell if we jump a deer."

"Forget it," Tatum said.

"What about a hunting license? The wardens check, you know."

"I'm all set."

Eddie was studying the boots in the box on Tatum's bed. "You figuring to wear those fancy cowboy boots in the woods, Gary?"

"Those boots," Tatum said coldly, "are original handmades by Tony Lama."

"They're beauties, Gary, sure, but—"

"What I intend to do with those boots, Eddie, is none of your business."

Eddie shrugged. "I guess where you won't be doing any hunting anyway, it doesn't much matter."

"Get going," Tatum said.

"Just one thing," said Eddie at the door. "The water in Depot Lake."

"What about the water in Depot Lake?"

"When we flew over it last summer there was plenty. But it's been a dry summer and the level's dropped way down."

"What of it?"

"Landing's going to be kind of risky."

"What are you suggesting, Eddie?"

"There's this abandoned camp on Ross Lake. It's bigger than Depot and half the distance. We can keep the kid there—"

"No more changes, Eddie. The plan is set."

"With that low water in Depot—I don't know."

"That should be no problem to an old war ace like French Eddie Michaud."

"It could be a problem, Gary. Depot Lake is full of deadwood."

"That's your problem, Eddie. Work it out. I've got enough to worry about."

"One last thing, Gary." Tatum's look of annoyance hastened

Michaud's words. "It's just this one job for me. To get back the dough that sumbitch Briggs screwed me out of."

"Make your point, Eddie."

"I don't want the kid hurt is what I'm getting at, Gary. No killing. Nothing like that."

Tatum's smile was generous. "Never fear, *mon ami*. Trust your Uncle Gary, eh?"

He was into the magazine again and Eddie quietly closed the door.

CHAPTER SIX

Michaud drove home in high spirits. A drink was what he
needed now, but Tatum's stern warning was too fresh in mind.
Eddie whooped his joy to the chill night air. The deal was on
again.

It had been a lucky break for Eddie Michaud, meeting up
with the affable Tatum. Michaud had been in Boston then, the
weekend guest of a grateful client whom Michaud had guided to
a six-point buck, a three-hundred-pound black bear, and Yvette,
a hairy-legged chippie from Quebec City. They had been drinking in the downstairs bar of the hotel, the client loudly bragging
about the deer, omitting the detail that Michaud had to shoot it
for him. Tatum, seated nearby, joined them and bought drinks
all around. Tatum's good looks and smooth banter attracted
girls. In no time there was a lively party going with Tatum the
amiable host in his three-room suite. The girls amused him. He
treated them like ladies, being polite and solicitous and not handling them coarsely, the way the other two men did. His courtly
manner slowed Michaud at first but Tatum urged him to get into
the swing of things. He enjoyed parties most that way, he said.
Watching others having fun.

Michaud was more than eager to oblige. He loved his Doreen
but her affectionate displays at times were stifling and he needed
a change. By one o'clock, the client had passed out, Tatum had
retired, and Michaud spent the night in the extra bedroom with
one of the girls. Before the weekend was out, Michaud in a eu-
phoric haze had invited Gary Tatum to Maine come spring for a
week of flying and fishing as his personal guest.

It was not all goodness of heart on Michaud's part. There was
an aura of easy living about Tatum: his clothes, his car, the plastic accordion of credit cards. The smell of rich had rubbed off on
Michaud and he liked it. He was smart enough not to ask questions. Tatum had modestly implied, without actually saying so,

that his business connections in Chicago, New York, Las Vegas, and Los Angeles amply took care of his needs.

After the good time in Boston, Tatum had gone south for the winter. Eddie Michaud, resigned to a life of small defeats and failures, believed it would be the last he would see of his cheerful, free-spending young friend. To his surprise, there was a card from Palm Beach in late April and Tatum in person in mid-May soon after the ice was out. After the dreary winter, Michaud was delighted to have the opportunity to reciprocate for the weekend in Boston. He promised to fly Tatum to some of the finest trout and salmon fishing in Maine. Doreen packed lunches and hot Thermoses of tea and went along.

Tatum proved to be a clumsy fisherman, plagued by insects and vulnerable to nausea in small boats. His lack of real interest after a few hours of cold, wet, and fruitless trolling for salmon and his ineptitude surprised Michaud, since Tatum did everything else with effortless grace and style.

What Tatum enjoyed most, it seemed, was to lie back in the boat's bow on the inflated cushions, while Michaud or Doreen handled the rods and rowed or ran the outboard. Tatum quoted the classics or reminisced casually of his underworld connections and exploits. Eddie Michaud didn't understand the classics but he possessed an insatiable imagination and a vicarious curiosity about violence and crime. He believed in Tatum's escapades. The names. The places. The lawless capers (Michaud loved the word). It all rang true. This was no counterfeit rerun of a Jimmy Cagney classic, a Kojak episode, or a rip-off of *The Godfather*. Tatum was the real McCoy. It was not long before Michaud felt he could speak freely to Tatum about his secret grudge against Sydney Briggs.

It was a sad, rambling story. The Michaud homestead in Aroostook County lay in the heart of the rich potato-growing country near Masardis, northeast of the Oxbow. Farms had flourished there half a century ago but had since fallen on hard times. Most were abandoned now, or a few acres were worked at a near-poverty level. The first Michaud had come down from Acadia almost a hundred years ago and settled on a five-hundred-acre tract. As a boy, Eddie's father, Ami, swam in the Aroostook River and worked on the big log drives and dug potatoes at harvest time with the other children. But his true love was trapping. At eighteen, he left his father's farm and built himself a solid cedar log cabin at the edge of the wilderness on Depot Lake.

Ami married a soft shy Micmac girl and in 1940 was drafted into construction work at the Limestone air force base. Eddie was born that year, the only child of three to survive. After the war, Ami tried to run the potato farm. There were good years and bad. He missed the woods too much and went back to trapping and part-time logging. The boy Eddie went with him wherever he worked. Ami drowned with a peavey through his thigh in a river drive in 1960. Eddie's mother leased out the farm land, buildings, and equipment, and moved Eddie and herself into a rent with her widowed sister in Greenville Junction. Eddie grew up there, tried a couple years of high school, but soon gave it up. He, too, was a trapper at heart. He put a new roof on the cabin at Depot Lake, replaced the rotted floor timbers, and hauled up a big potbellied stove. He spent many hours there. Like his father, he loved the woods, but he needed work.

He hired out as an apprentice to Pete Ellis, one of the area's veteran charter plane pilots. Eddie read the aviation magazines and flying manuals and picked the brains of the motor mechanics across the bay at the state forest ranger's flying base.

After a couple of poor potato years, the farm lease ran out. Eddie's mother died while Eddie was flying attack bombers over Vietnam. He was given a hardship discharge and came back to Greenville and married Doreen. After the funeral expenses and lawyers' fees, the remainder of Eddie's accumulated flight pay paid off the back taxes on the farm. He drove to Masardis with his new bride to see how the old family place had fared. It was a discouraging sight. The board sides of the huge barn had caved in under the snowload of several winters. The gambrel roof of the potato house sagged badly and needed repair. The contents of the farmhouse had been vandalized. The shed was infested with bats, rats, and squirrels. The broad potato fields sloping down to the river, once the pride of the Michauds, were buried under a wild tangle of witch grass and weeds and the beginning black growth and hardwood.

A visit to a nearby neighbor on the Oxbow road offered a

glimmer of hope. Abandoned farm land was being bought by a syndicate hoping to raise beef cattle in the area. "They must be out of their minds," the neighbor said, "but just the same, it's cash on the barrelhead."

That was how Eddie Michaud met Sydney Briggs. Briggs looked over the old Michaud place and was sympathetic but not encouraging. He told Michaud he was into acreage far deeper than he had planned. He'd never get his money out. Michaud pleaded. He wanted out. Briggs finally gave in, ". . . because you've served your country, Eddie."

A deal was made for the farm buildings and land at forty dollars an acre. Twenty thousand dollars was more money than Eddie had seen in all his life. Half of it went at once for a down payment on a Cessna 180 on amphibious floats, and another thousand on a lavish belated honeymoon for Doreen, who loved every minute of it but hated to see the money go.

When the newlyweds returned, Michaud learned that the going price for old farms on both sides of his land was at least one hundred dollars an acre and hard to find at that price. He also discovered that in the last six months the Briggs syndicate had quietly picked up options on fifteen thousand acres in the area. The Michaud farm was the key piece needed to complete the spread. The waste from the Briggs-controlled potato processing plant would furnish the silage to feed the thousand head of white-faced Herefords Briggs had grazing east of Ashland. Michaud ran back to Briggs.

Briggs shrugged off Michaud's demands for more money. A deal, he said, was a deal. Michaud begged. A fair price would mean he could buy his Cessna outright without a mortgage on it. Briggs relented. He offered to carry the paper at a percentage point lower than the banks offered. Michaud told him to go to hell.

He leased a piece of lakefront in Greenville and built himself a hangar and workshop. He fixed up the two-room apartment with a kitchen and bath above the small office, and Michaud's Sportsflying Charter Service was in business. He worked hard to make a go of it. He flew sports to wild game, ferried supplies to trackless places, hauled canoes and backpackers to out-of-the-way holes in the wilderness. He could barely stay ahead of his payments and expenses. Doreen nagged and sulked. The Briggs deal rankled. Eddie drank. His grudge against Briggs festered and swelled for ten hard years. Now his time had come and no one was more sure of it than Eddie Michaud himself.

It was past midnight when Michaud got home. The apartment smelled of bacon grease and fumes from the kerosene heater. Doreen was waiting for him, her hair in rollers, her cheeks glistening with night cream. She sat in a red-flowered housecoat with her elbows on the scratched Formica of the kitchen table. She had just eaten Michaud's cold supper and was tearing idly at the crusts of bread. A half-empty Coke bottle and cigarette stubs littered the table. Doreen had been pretty and vivacious not too long ago. Living with Michaud had drained it out of her. She did not look up.

"Where've you been, Eddie?"

"Rockwood, sweetie. Drumming up business." He bent to kiss her head. The rollers turned him off. He put an arm around her. "How come you're still up?"

"The phone is how come."

"At this hour?"

"Not ten minutes ago. I took a sleeping pill and the damned phone woke me out of my first real sleep—" Doreen began to sniffle. "I thought maybe you had an accident—"

"Jeez, I'm sorry, Doreen."

"Well, I booked you a charter party, first thing in the morning."

His thoughts whirled. The possibility of a conflict with Tatum's plans churned inside his mind. He began to protest. "You shouldn't have—"

"It's with that dude from—California, was it? The one drove that racing car you two fooled around in—?"

"Tatum?" The relief oozed out of him.

She nodded. "He left early Labor Day weekend, remember? He's the one hated the fishing so last spring." She giggled. "Some sport! He couldn't catch cold with a ten-foot dip net. He said maybe five days. Not a bad charter, Eddie." She wiped her face with a paper napkin, smearing grease with tears. "A hell of a nerve, calling decent people after midnight."

"At two hundred fifty bucks a day, Doreen, I'm not complaining. Tatum, eh?" He chortled and Doreen looked up sharply. He smacked a loud kiss on Doreen's bare shoulder. *Oh that Gary Tatum!* "I'll take him to Depot Lake. Where's he staying?"

"He didn't say. But he'll be here first thing in the morning." She sniffed. "Lucky thing you don't already have a booking. That's awful short notice."

"He mentioned when he left Labor Day weekend he'd be up for the deer hunting." He fondled Doreen and kissed her cheek, avoiding the plastic rollers, testing. Doreen did not resist. He kissed her lips, which she parted from habit, and his tongue slipped in. Doreen leaned back and closed her eyes. But it was not Eddie's tongue that made her breathe more rapidly. It was the quick arithmetic of two hundred and fifty dollars times five. Twelve hundred and fifty bucks. It would just about take care of the past-due fuel bills.

She pulled away abruptly, leaving Eddie sucking air. "I don't dig that what's-his-name, Tatum, Eddie."

"A playboy, Doreen. What's there to dig?"

"He isn't a—you know—queer, is he?"

"A nice-looking guy like Gary Tatum? Hell no!" Remembering Boston, he wondered. "Why?"

"He never looked at me twice. After all, Eddie, I'm not that bad-looking, am I? Dressed up to step out, all made up, I mean. All that time he was hanging around here, I never saw him once so much as give another girl a tumble, even the real rich summer ones."

"He's a gentleman, Doreen. Gentlemen don't screw around."

"With their own kind, they do."

His hands were on her heavy breasts. "Whose kind are you, sweetie?"

"Yours, Eddie." Twelve hundred and fifty bucks, she thought, and another bank payment due. Peanuts. She pushed him aside, pulling the housecoat close around her body.

"That's the trouble. I'm all yours. And where does it get us, Eddie? Where?"

CHAPTER SEVEN

When Eddie Michaud had gone, Tatum moved about putting things in order. He unpacked a leather kit of toilet articles and his pajamas. The soft drinks had come from the office dispensing machine. Tatum could have done with a taste of cognac but he knew the depth of Eddie's craving and had decided against it.

There was no phone in the room. He went outside to the lighted booth and called Michaud's Sportsflying Service and, after a few words with Doreen, made the reservation for the plane. He jiggled for the operator and placed a credit card call to his mother in Scottsdale, Arizona. After repeated ringing, he heard her voice, dreamy and cultivated.

"Hi, Mother."

"Darling boy! Where are you?"

"Maine. Deer hunting."

"How perfectly marvelous for you! Hold on while I get a cigarette." She reached down with her free hand and caressed the blond head of curly hair snug against her thighs. "Light me one, darling," she whispered. Then to her son: "Have you caught one yet?"

"You don't *catch* deer, Mother. You shoot them."

"How ghastly! Now then: Wasn't it Maine you were in last time? Fishing for tuna?"

"Salmon, Mother. They fish for tuna off Nova Scotia. I think."

"Salmon, darling. Nova Scotia salmon."

He listened to her breathing. "Are you all right, Mums?" Someone with her. He could tell by the languid throatiness of her voice. And high. Spaced out or stoned on whatever newfangled drug she and her circle of sick tweedy fags were into. "Mums? You there?"

"Here, Gare." She gently moved her lover's head aside and exhaled a blue cloud. "Will you be coming home soon?"

"When you say home, Mother, just exactly where do you mean?"

"Don't snarl at your mummy, darling. I mean right here. By your loving mother's side."

"Last year it was Taos and two years ago—" He clamped his lips.

"Gare, darling, whatever are you saying?"

"Sorry, Mums." Helpless tears. Damn her.

"After all, I'm your mother—"

He fought rancor and outrage, wiped his eyes, and said in a controlled even voice, "I'll be heading back in a few weeks; a month, no more."

"Do you hear from your father?"

"Not really."

"You *are* getting your allowance?"

"The first of every month, like clockwork." Orange, he thought.

"It was part of the settlement, you know, until your thirtieth birthday, Gare. I insisted on it."

"I know, Mums. You've told me." Many times. Many, many times. He drew a deep uneven breath. "That's what I'm calling about."

"Your birthday."

"Not exactly, but—well, I'm short again."

"You mean he didn't send you your allowance? Don't tell me he's welshed on *that* too?"

"No, Mother. You see—"

"But it's only the fifth—or is it the sixth of the month, Gare. And it's all gone? Twenty-five hundred dollars shot? What on earth are you spending it on? Or should I ask on whom?"

"Nothing like that. If you'll listen—"

"You listen. I wired you—was it five hundred?—not two weeks ago, to tide you over, you said, until your father—Gare, you haven't run through that, too, have you?"

"Well, actually, there was the car payment, and the hotel in Boston. I'd run up a few expenses in the hotel, you see, and now American Express—"

"What about dear American Express?"

"They're not honoring my credit card. Some foul-up with their stupid computers. It's a matter of a few hundred, Mums. Until I get my first salary check."

"Salary? What salary?"

"I've this prospect, you see. A sure thing, Mums. A terrific opportunity to go into partnership with a sports flying service here. Very successful outfit. Lovely people. Eh? Oh no. Salary *plus* a percentage. I'll be in charge of operations, manage the entire business. Sales, trip planning, publicity, scenic tours, club scheduling, that stuff. And with my contacts . . . No, no investment at all. They *like* me, and they're crazy about my promotion ideas. Year-round tourism in Maine. From Europe and Canada. The foreign exchange balance, you know? They want me with them badly. And you know how well I run things—"

"Yes, my darling. Only too well. The snorkel school fiasco at La Jolla. A mere thirty thousand before they drowned you. And that racing car rodeo in Palm Springs. Now you listen to your wise old mother, my handsome son: This had better be the real thing. Because they've been here, asking about you, about the grand prize, that smoky Jaguar you were so in love with, that never materialized at your rodeo in Palm Springs. Who was asking? The police, my dear. All the way from California. I mentioned nothing. Not even the changed license plates, my love. So you'd better the hell straighten out because I will not go on forever pulling your chestnuts out of the fire. Where should I send the check?"

"A postal money order'd be better, Mums."

"How much?"

"The limit's three hundred and it costs forty cents, plus the air mail envelope. Send it to General Delivery, Greenville, Maine. The zip is 04441. And I promise you—"

"The only promise I want from you, Gare, is to stay out of California. This time it could mean real trouble. They're out looking for you."

"Sure thing, Mums."

"Promise?"

"You got that down? General Delivery, Greenville, Maine, zip—"

"Promise, Gare?"

"Promise." *Get off my back, damn it.*

"Your Mums loves you, Gare." She made kissing noises.

"'By, Mother." Just before he hung up, he put his lips close to the phone. "Wh-o-o-re," he whispered.

CHAPTER EIGHT

In the morning sun of Monday, David spread his sleeping bag to freshen on the stony jut of Kimball's Point. He had risen early, unable to shake the foredoom of his father's coming. Kimball stayed late abed, wearied by the long drive and himself uneasy at the prospect of his son-in-law's arrival. Later, in a wool robe and slippers, he sipped hot black coffee on the unscreened veranda and watched David casting from the rocks.

If he could only help the boy. He had observed David's retreat to reticence, his sulky yet polite withdrawal into self. Kimball could guess the reasons. He knew the father well and too often had witnessed the swift eruption of Sydney Briggs's temper. All he could do now was sit here with something to read, sip his coffee, and wonder how and why his snug family world had gone to pieces.

He watched David casting and retrieving, a study in grace and skill. His pride in the boy welled. He thought of the boy's loneliness during the past year, and the damage it had done. Kimball at seventy knew all about loneliness. What was it like at fourteen? The boy had suffered enough. It was time now for gentleness and understanding. And yes, love. Sydney Briggs would hear about that tonight, number one on the agenda.

David, swearing, gathered up his lure and skipped over the rocks. He said hi to Kimball as he passed. Kimball's shrewd eye did not miss the boy's strained smile or the forlorn look about him. David put up his rod and puttered about the A-frame. He passed the rest of the morning stacking stovewood and kindling, clearing brush, and raking the dead autumn leaves that had swirled and clung in crisp spiraled heaps about the cedar posts.

Never quits, Kimball observed, pity mixed with wonder, pride, and love.

After lunch David rowed the skiff to Caribou Point. He combed the shore line, found no relics, and, gathering an armful of dry-ki, rowed the piled twists of driftwood back to the cottage beach where Kimball helped him spread them to dry through the winter to silvery free forms.

It had been a hard pull, a mile each way, against a quartering wind. The boy was exhausted. Kimball ordered him to rest. He prepared hot cocoa and sat with David on the veranda facing the island across the bay. A truce had grown between them and with it a reaffirmation of respect and trust.

That evening after supper they sat by the fire awaiting the arrival of Briggs. David had slipped a red wool hunting shirt over his T-shirt. Kimball, wise in the ways of interrogation, released his casual questions like decoys. Subtly coaxed and perhaps softened by the lovely sunset, David had begun to talk, eager to unscramble his troubled thoughts.

"Will I be sent to another school?"

"I'm afraid so, Davey."

"Why? When I hate it so much."

"It's the law."

"Laws get broken, don't they? They're unfair lots of times. You know that."

"I also know that if you quit school now, you'll never forgive yourself."

"How can you be so sure?"

"I've sat in enough courtrooms and I've heard it enough times to know it's true."

"I'm grown-up—"

"In some ways, yes. But not in others."

"Remember the canoe, Grampa?"

"I remember a lot of canoes."

"The last time we ran the Allagash. When we made the portage from Chamberlain into Eagle Lake?"

Kimball remembered. David had begged to make the canoe carry unassisted. It was man's work and Kimball wagered he could not handle it. David lashed the paddles to the thwarts in a carrying yoke, turned the canoe on its side with its bottom to him. He grasped the center thwart with one hand and the upper gunwale with the other. He shoved his knees against the bottom and pulled the canoe upward in a swift rolling motion. He ducked his head into the carrying yoke and settled the canoe on his shoulders.

Kimball had done it many times. It was a technique that required less strength than skill. He was astonished that David had done it the first time alone. He followed the boy, carrying the rest of their dunnage on his back. It was more than a hundred yards to the other side of the portage. David easily deposited the canoe at the water's edge of Eagle Lake. The pleasure it gave Kimball was well worth the five-dollar bill it cost him.

"Sure, David, I remember and I was proud of you."

"I'm a year older now. I've learned a lot since then."

"It was skill then, David, not learning. Learning goes deeper."

David slumped lower in the chair. "Why can't I live alone like you do and do what I want, not what they tell me to do?"

"Living alone's not easy, Davey. People need people."

"I don't need people. I got things I want to do. Things I don't like being told I can't or shouldn't—"

"Trouble is, you're a loner. So was I until I met your grandmother. After that I never had a chance." He grinned. "Not that I minded one bit."

"What was she like?"

"A firm-chinned, saucy Quaker gal with a will of her own and fire and brimstone in her violet eyes."

"How'd you meet her?"

"In New York during my law clerk days. She was arrested during an antiwar demonstration—"

David sat up, pleased. "Arrested? For what?"

"Kicking one of New York's Finest in the shins. I got her off and married her and brought her to Maine. I suspect she married me not in gratitude but because she was determined to make me give up tobacco and the slaughter of wild creatures."

"She did, didn't she?"

"In time. It was the subject of many a winter evening's conversation. However, after picking up pieces of my shipmates in the kamikaze attacks in the South Pacific, I saw the wisdom of her views and joined the club."

"How'd she die?"

"Quietly. Without complaint."

"From what?"

"Cancer."

"How old was she?"

"Fifty."

"She must've been super. Wish I'd known her."

"You do. Your mother's just like her."

"Being a loner, Gramp, doesn't mean I can't love people. I love Mother and you—"

"And Dad."

"Yeah. Dad, too. But he sure doesn't make it easy, like you and Mom."

And later:

"I'm scared, Gramp. I don't know what to tell him when he gets here. Every time I do something to please him, something he wants me to do even if I hate doing it, I end up in the doghouse. He always finds fault. Sure, sometimes I goof. Lots of kids goof. But a pat on the back could go a long way to make a kid feel better. Now I'm kicked out of his stupid Academy. He warned me it was my last chance. I swear to God I don't know how that grass got in my desk. But sure as hell he'll take Harkness's crummy word over mine. What'll I tell him?"

"Tell him the truth," Kimball said.

David sat in his mother's chair, uneasy, hoping his father wouldn't make it, missing a plane, a turn. . . . His grandfather dozed. Looking at him, David thought of a time to come when he would sit there, a grandfather himself, with his own grandson. The thought gave him great comfort.

Briggs arrived about ten that night in a mood as dark as his crumpled sharkskin suit and black city shoes. The moment he stepped through the door, Kimball's hopes for a tranquil family discussion evaporated. He had seen the look on Briggs's mottled face before. He prepared himself for the worst.

Without a word of greeting Briggs dropped his overnight bag, threw his topcoat and bulging briefcase on the sofa, and plopped down beside them. David got to his feet as he had been taught to do when adults entered a room. He started toward his father, hand extended. Briggs jumped up and with both hands shoved the boy hard. David, stunned, fell back into the chair.

"You will sit right there, young man, until I'm through with you." He went to the dry sink Kimball used for a bar and splashed whiskey into a tumbler. Kimball began to protest. Briggs cut him short.

"Shut up, Alonzo, or go to bed. This is a private matter between David and me."

In the hour that ensued, interrupted only by trips to the dry sink, Briggs, chain-smoking, dredged up the details of every escapade and blunder in David's brief lifetime. It was a blistering tirade distinguished by a remarkable memory for exact times and places, as though his sharp mind had marshaled the facts during the long trip from Boston. He dismissed Kimball's protests with the blunt reminder that it still was none of his damned affair and he might as well retire. Kimball, with no choice short of some physical action, had to hear him through. Knowing Briggs's temper, he actually feared for David's physical well-being. When the unreasonable anger, the tensions and pent-up venom had run their course, he would take over. But to do so before that time would risk disaster.

David's thoughts were less prudent. A slow rebellion grew inside him. He sat at first in stunned silence, responding sullenly and almost inaudibly to his father's harsh questioning. He had decided to speak the truth, and if that was not enough, to admit wrongdoing and failure (because, hating the Academy, he had not really tried). He was prepared to accept punishment. Anything to get the inquisition over with. He had been dealt punishment in the past but not like this. Never with such cruel swiftness and blind rage, never without respite in which to explain his actions.

The hurt drove deep. Injustice, live and feral, buries itself in the cave of a child's mind and, like some dangerous and forbidden pet fondled and nursed in secret, never forgotten, turns one day without warning and strikes back.

The hour approached midnight. Briggs ranted on. The boy's patience ebbed. His mind drifted. The image of his absent mother filled his thoughts. David clutched it like a security blanket against the terror of his father's words. It gave him strength. This was her chair and this was her cottage. In time it would be his cottage and his children's, as it had always been with the Kimballs. This ranting bully, his father, who chose not to share this good life and worse, held it and all it meant in low esteem, had become the enemy, threatening all David held dear. It was no secret to David that the marriage of fifteen years had foundered and his mother now suffered because of it. Now more than ever he loved her and missed her sorely. His fingers gripped the arms of the chair. All through his childhood he had watched her, serene and lovely in this chair, weaving the bright-colored squares that grew into the handsome afghans her friends treasured.

Where was she now that he needed her?

Silence from his grandfather dismayed him. He had counted on Kimball for moral support. *Nobody cares.* He bent to hide the helpless rush of tears, his face half lost in the thicket of hair that fell over his eyes and shoulders.

"Sit up," his father snapped. "I'm not through with you."

All at once David was out of the loved chair.

"Sit down, damn it!"

David ran across the room of finned and furred trophies, pained in passing by the shocked look he saw in his grandfather's blurred face.

Briggs rose, whiskey spilling. "Stop right there!"

"Fuck off, Dad!"

Briggs grabbed for him, swung out, caught the boy a glancing blow. He tried to follow but stumbled and almost fell. The boy ran free.

Hunched down in his old easy chair, the judge winced, sighed, sore at heart but not displeased with what the boy had done. Spunky, he thought.

On the porch the screen door slammed. The boy plunged into the night. Blackness surrounded him. No moon. Slivers of light filtered through the cottage curtains. David Briggs in the stillness trembled, smelled wood smoke and balsam, breathed hard, fighting tears.

The skiff he had used that afternoon was pulled up on the beach of pebbles. He thought of escape. The boat, the woods . . . He knew the woods. He would make out a hell of a lot better in the woods than he would in the morning face to face with his father's anger. If he took off now . . .

He kicked a few pebbles, glanced up the path to the A-frame and back to the cottage. He could go back and apologize and face another hour of bullshit . . .

The hell I will. He's dead wrong. He doesn't know a damned thing about what happened at his crummy school. He doesn't give a damn. He doesn't give a good goddamn about anything but money. Money and himself and his good name. *Shit on that!*

Why the hell didn't Grampa Kimball say something when Dad was pouring all that booze into himself and running off at the mouth? Grampa knew what had happened at the school. He could've said something before it was too late, before there was nothing to do but run. One word from Grampa and I'd have stayed and taken all the bullshit Dad could deliver.

Slaps. Blows. Curses. Some father! Too busy to take a kid fishing. Or just rap. Too damn chicken to climb Katahdin or run the Allagash. The hell with him! Let him find somebody else to slap around. I've had it. I've had it to here.

He scaled a flat stone against the inkiness of Moosehead and listened to its splinks and fading splashes. Voices from the cottage broke the night stillness. No use, he thought miserably, to go back in there. Things'll be brighter in the morning. Grampa always said that, when something went wrong on a camping trip. The thought cheered David. He decided to turn in.

The A-frame lay twenty yards up the path toward the woods' road. The boy was bone-weary. The troubles of the last two days had crippled his spirit. His lean body ached from the hard row to Caribou Point. His cheek still stung. It will be nice, he told himself, to slide into the old sleeping bag and curl up and forget my troubles. He started up the path to the A-frame.

He never made it.

CHAPTER NINE

Inside the cottage the judge rose, knees cracking. "I'll have a few words with the lad."

"Words!" Briggs mopped at wetness, drained his glass, fumbled for a cigarette. "A good belting's what he needs."

"You've belted him enough, Sydney."

"You hear the way he cursed me? Where the hell does a kid learn words like that?"

"I can't imagine."

"I'll knock that stubborn streak out of him. Breaking the rules —rules, hell! Breaking the law—"

"He says no."

"Who's lying, damn it? A headmaster I've known over thirty years or a fourteen-year-old hippie—"

"You gave him no chance to explain."

"Explain hell! He smoked pot and was caught and got his ass kicked out."

"Still no cause to treat him like that."

"Goddammit, Alonzo. I get this emergency phone call. Your son's expelled! Pick him up! On a Sunday! In the middle of a two-million-dollar deal! So I grab a plane and race up here—"

"Why Moosehead, Sydney? Bangor would have been easier."

"Never mind why—"

"You needed your shabby triumph in Kimball country. Wasn't that it? Wasn't that your sick selfish way of punishing Martha and me?"

"Bullshit. David's the one I'm punishing. Your conscience is bothering, you sick old goat."

"I'll talk to him," the judge said, abruptly rising.

"No, damn it. Let him sulk." Briggs crossed the room and splashed more whiskey into his glass. Kimball settled back, then suddenly stiffened. Briggs glared at him. "What now?"

"I heard something."

"Like what?"

"A kind of—yell." He went to a window, stared into blackness.

"It figures."

"What do you mean?"

"The kid's looking for sympathy."

"Not David." He left the window reluctantly. "That was a real yell I heard."

"So the kid's letting off steam. Pissed off because I slapped him." Briggs drank some of the whiskey. "Spoiled rotten. And no wonder, the way you and Martha coddle him."

"Not Martha. It's your own damned fault."

"The hell it's my fault, you old meddler." Briggs lurched to his feet. The glass in his trembling fingers spilled whiskey. He could not stop now, the words like razor blades between his lips. "Why the hell isn't his mother here? When the kid needs her?"

Kimball could have hit him. He started for the door. "I'm having a look."

"The hell you are." He lurched close to Kimball. "Leave that damned kid to me."

Kimball stared at Briggs's mottled face, fleshy and swollen. He felt no pity now, only contempt for Briggs and concern for the boy. He strode past Briggs and stepped outside. The screen door squeaked until it closed. He listened to the night sounds. Inside, Briggs's curses. Outside, the slap of wavelets along the skiff's smooth hull. November's wind sifted the pine boughs. Somewhere in the depths of memory the sweet sadness of Martha's voice blended with the wind and water sounds. We all need you, he thought. Father, husband, son.

The A-frame loomed dark, silent. Should he check? David had certainly yelled. Anger? Defiance? Or, as Briggs had said, just letting off steam? Kimball could not shake his feeling of uneasiness. But it was Briggs, drunk and unpredictable, crashing about, who needed help more than David.

Kimball went back inside. Briggs was sprawled on the big braided rug staring morosely at the ashes of the near-dead fire. The contents of his open briefcase were strewn in disorder about him. He gestured loosely—"Two million bucks"—and looked up. "The kid okay?"

"I didn't go over." Kimball had no more to say about it. He moved toward his bedroom. "Good night, Sydney."

"Nightcap?"

"No, thanks."

"Mad at me, huh?"

"Something like that."

"Sorry I blew my top. Where do I sleep?"

"Martha's room." He caught the quick hurt look, like a slap across his son-in-law's face. No more than he deserves, Kimball thought in cold anger. He did not regret it.

"Thanks for fetching David," Briggs said.

"You might go over and say good night to him."

"A hell of a lot of good that'd do."

"In my opinion it would."

"Save your opinions for the bench, Mr. Justice."

"Good night, Sydney." You poor benighted bastard.

"I've seen better."

Sleep no longer came easily to Alonzo Kimball. When he did sleep, it was a thin veil of slumber, a watchful dozing. Now he lay on his back under his mother's old crazy quilt, his eyes open, the ceiling overhead a shadowy screen for his thoughts. He sat up once, hearing a car motor start, and listened. Nothing. He sank back. Getting old, Alonzo, he muttered. Hearing things.

He had heard enough this sorrowful night. Had he failed David? Yes, yes, he had failed the boy. But Briggs drunk could be ugly and dangerous and not responsible for his actions. Kimball had seen it happen before. David had endured enough in the past two days to shake up any fourteen-year-old, but David was young and resilient and could take it. He would sleep it off. In the morning things would be brighter. Briggs, though . . .

He heard Briggs stumbling about in the adjoining room. Flung shoes, a coarse belching, thick curses. If I knew how to hate, Kimball mused, there is the first man. But the years of judgment and the discipline gained in dealing justly and wisely with human frailties (listening to testimonies, weighing right versus wrong, deciding and sentencing) had drained him of hate. Hatred was a luxury forbidden him in his line of work.

Through the fifteen years of his daughter's marriage, he had observed the rise of Sydney Briggs with deep concern. Essentially decent, Sydney Briggs had, early on, yielded to the enticements of quick profits through sharp practices in his business dealings. The drive for wealth and power now possessed him to a degree that pre-empted his responsibilities as a husband and father. His brute force, his contempt for wise counsel, his impatience with reason, convinced Kimball that Briggs was a pathologically sick man, morbidly and irrevocably bent on his own destruction. His senseless course left in its wake a bewildered and hostile son and an unloved wife with shattered nerves.

Kimball believed that Briggs probably loved his wife and son. It was tenderness he lacked, and time and understanding. And he was unable to communicate his true feelings in a visible or even meaningful way. Kimball had sat in judgment before hundreds of family cases. He had never dreamed he would face it one day in his own. He regretted the circumstance which had brought this disagreeable man into his family. His daughter's infatuation and Briggs's aggressive courtship had swept the matter from his hands. Yet he could not totally condemn it. It had given him David.

David again. He stretched his bony legs and sighed and closed his eyes. David's expulsion did not surprise Kimball. He thought it remarkable that David had lasted two months. The drugs and fistfights were part of his rebellion. His long hair was his battle flag. The Academy was a fusty old institution, steeped in Victorian traditions and only recently beginning to consider mid-twentieth-century teaching concepts. Its curriculum of social snobbery (ties and jackets at mealtime, compulsory chapel, an annual cotillion) and academic asphyxia (four years of Greek or Latin, required Bible studies) and the low-key intramural athletic program were hardly designed for a boy like David. He was there because his father had gone there. Period. How many young minds were warped and lives wasted, Kimball mused, because of the blind loyalty of parents to their alma maters?

He had earned his own way through the University of Maine and the law school at Yale at a time when learning was respected and ethics sacred. But values were changing in a violent way. Was any university education today meeting the *real* needs of our changing society? What had higher education done for Sydney Briggs, snoring away in the next room? How had a genteel New England upbringing and a proper college education turned this bachelor of arts into the ruthless son of a bitch he was? And how much of his wild blood will seep into his son's veins? How much, via those artful genes inside those cunning chromosomes, or through good old osmosis, had David absorbed already? It was too gloomy to contemplate.

Briggs's outburst about Martha had startled Kimball, not alone by its loudness but in its callous disregard of the truth. Briggs alone was the cause of her breakdown. No one else. Now Martha's recovery was proceeding remarkably well. If she improved at the same rate through her period of convalescence, her doctor at the Acres seemed confident she could be discharged and home in a week's time. It would be cruel to tell her the sad news about David, and to bring her home because of it, sheer madness. It was stupid of Briggs to suggest it. And typical.

He pounded on Briggs's wall and the snoring subsided. He rolled over, envying the man's deep sleep. There was little else he envied in Briggs, whom he had disliked from the day Martha, starry-eyed, had brought him to the Kennebec Valley farmhouse. When she told him she loved Sydney Briggs and wanted to marry him, Kimball had not the heart to dissuade her. He loved Martha more than life. His objections would simply have made matters worse.

Briggs. An absurd man who evaluated social status by the sum total of available cash, conspicuous possessions, and a wallet full of restricted club memberships. What was it that drove men like Sydney Briggs, already burdened with more money than he could possibly spend in his lifetime, to their inescapably disastrous ends? A popular type these days, Kimball reflected. Men who find no joy in life equal to the accumulation of wealth and the pursuit of power. Kimball had dealt with men like that, corporate business types, civic leaders, administrators of other people's wealth, long on cunning, short on compassion, driven and hard driving, in love with money, and lousy in bed. He had known them. He had listened to the grievances of their wives and mistresses. He had sentenced plenty of them. The ones who, like careless trout, did not get away. One trait ran true in all of them—abuse of nature and a ruinous contempt for the balanced order of things.

The new breed. Made in America. The wheeler-dealers. The paper money men, the addicts of push button and plastic. Thoreau is dead, Kimball thought, drowsy now. God is not.

Thank God. He dropped off to sleep, still troubled because David in the dark outside had cried out and he had not gone to him.

Sydney Briggs in the high double bed beneath a mountainous comforter twitched and moaned, tortured by guilt feelings. Why do I do it? What the hell is it drives me to hurt the boy? Martha? Is it Martha? Or her old man? Here in his wife's bed he ached for the solace of her womanly flesh. *A half-empty bed is twice as empty as an empty bed.* Fighting nausea and lust, he fell into deep troubled sleep.

At forty-two, the danger signs in Briggs were ominously evident. Hypertension, shortness of breath and temper, sagging flesh, a nagging obesity. He seemed not to care, driving himself cruelly from deal to deal as though his life depended on it.

With a liberal arts degree, two years of Korea, and several failed business ventures behind him, he discovered Maine's cheap land and dormant economy and moved in. In ten years his ruthless skill in assembling land parcels and negotiating complicated development deals brought him wealth and a host of bitter enemies. He paid a large staff of lawyers a small fortune to keep him out of the courts. He moved from the construction of shopping centers into land deals, the ownership of vending machines, and a potato processing plant in northern Maine. He drove a white Continental Mark IV to work and a loving, bewildered wife to distraction.

Harkness's call from the Academy had disrupted the multimillion-dollar land deal. His rage en route to Maine built up and burst on arrival into the vicious tongue-lashing he had dealt his son. He had been known to treat bungling business associates and hired help in the same manner.

Behind a wall of drunk sleep, his train of jumbled dreams rattled and careened in mad disorder. Distorted images of David, Martha, and Kimball overlapped that of his prim office secretary in Bangor. Profiles of his Boston business partners passed like warped frames in a surrealist stereopticon. He writhed and groaned, guilt-laden, self-pitying, helpless to escape the nightmare horror. David bleeding. Martha in chains. Kimball dead in a Dorchester alley, crumpled like a bloated, frozen deerskin. His

Brahmin partners in outrageous drag dancing a lively jig atop the oval conference table, urinating ecstatically into each other's bustles. His naked secretary astride him and headless. Himself beseeching his sphincters, unable to perform.

It was a familiar nightmare with variations. Sometimes Kimball bled and his secretary peed. Often it was David in the shadows, aloof and disapproving. Sometimes at the end of the garbage-strewn alley, beyond Kimball's corpse, a narrow place of light and joy beckoned. He would move toward it, hand in hand with his lissome wife and stalwart son, himself immaculate and radiant with pride. The light, still beckoning, would teasingly recede with each step, and in sleep his pained cries of frustration died throat-clogged within him.

These were torments of his own making. Decency at the core was Briggs's true nature. Ironically, it was the only part of himself he refused to believe in.

CHAPTER TEN

An hour before midnight, Eddie Michaud landed the plane in Lily Bay. He taxied the Cessna as quietly as possible to a secluded mooring in Mathews Cove. Minutes later, he was driving the green Chevelle on dimmed lights through the silent darkness south along the woods road. Gary Tatum alongside him sat erect, staring straight ahead. He wore his western boots, having switched from sneakers while Michaud moored the plane. The last-minute change puzzled Michaud but he said nothing. Tatum seemed tense and too nervous for small talk and Michaud had no wish to risk more of his sharp sarcasm. He was jumpy enough.

He peered down through the woods to the Briggs cottage as they passed. "Jesus, a light's still on," he said, surprised.

"Keep your voice down," Tatum muttered. "And eyes on the road."

"They're still up, Gary. It don't figure."

"Keep driving," Tatum ordered.

Michaud drove about a hundred yards to an abandoned gravel road thick with weeds that curved down to Beaver Cove. "This is it," Tatum said. Michaud swung in a few yards and cut the motor and lights.

"Why'd you tell me they always turn in early?"

"They're never up this late, Gary. I swear, the place is always dark by ten."

"It's past eleven-thirty. I spotted the old man's pickup but who belongs to the white Continental?"

"That'd be Briggs."

"You told me there was just the boy and his grandfather."

"Something's wrong if Briggs is here. He hates the place. I'm scared, Gary. Maybe we better—"

"No backing off now," Tatum said in a cool voice. "I'm going down for a look." He reached for a navy blue musette bag on the back seat. "If the boy's asleep in his A-frame, I'll grab him. If he's not, I'll hang in there until he is." He opened the door gently. "You wait here. I'll get back to you. Stay out of sight and don't panic."

He slung the musette bag over one shoulder and stepped with great care along the edge of the deserted road. A few yards from the Briggs entry he cut through the woods, treading carefully, feeling his way slowly from tree to tree. A faint murmur of voices came from the cottage. He cautiously circled the A-frame. Inside, the boy's sleeping bag on the narrow cot was empty. If he's not here, Tatum told himself, trembling, he's got to be in the cottage. And if he's not in the cottage I'm going to wring one clumsy-minded Canuck neck. He heard the voices clearly now, a man's voice, loud and angry, the other, a young voice. He glanced at his watch. Eleven-fifty. He slid the musette from his shoulder and removed a leather-covered billy club. He leaned the bag against the trunk of a stubby cedar close by the A-frame and crouched low in the deep growth to wait, unable to control the trembling in his limbs.

Eddie Michaud on the road above fidgeted in the eerie darkness. He needed a drink. He grudgingly admired Tatum's coolness under pressure. That's experience, he reflected. That's what it takes. Michaud's element was swift flight and open space. Alone here, waiting for Tatum in darkness and doubt, he no longer felt the affinity of his youth for deep woods and silent places. Softly he cursed his poor luck. He had stowed a pint under the dashboard of his Wagoneer. But Tatum had switched to the Chevelle at the last minute. The Wagoneer was too easy to recognize, he had told Eddie. Eddie knew differently. He knew that Tatum did not trust him, and hell, you couldn't really blame him.

They had flown north to Depot Lake early that morning, taking Tatum's valise and carrying along a sleeping bag and food. Tatum's plan was complicated but sound. They spent the day at Depot going over the final stages of the kidnap plan and ransom route. Now the plane was back on Moosehead, secured to the rickety boat dock in Mathews Cove.

The plan called for Tatum to pick up the boy and for Michaud to fly him back to Depot Lake drugged, blindfolded, and bound.

Tatum would remain on shore to make the ransom run. He would rendezvous with Michaud at midnight for the hop back to Depot and the final procedure for the boy's release.

Michaud and Tatum had disagreed over the amount of the ransom. Michaud could not believe a tightwad like Sydney Briggs would ante up $200,000. Not even for his own son. Not even for himself, Michaud argued. Briggs'd rather die. But Tatum held firm. He wasn't in this for peanuts, he said. If Eddie wanted to run a two-bit operation, he was welcome to run it himself. Without the brains and expertise of Gary Tatum. So Michaud went along with the $200,000 and prayed that Briggs would raise it.

Michaud was getting worried, just sitting there. What the hell was holding Gary up? He would have liked to get out and have a look, but Tatum's last word had been to stay out of sight. Michaud snorted. Out of whose sight? What that Arizona playboy didn't know about the Maine woods'd fill a book. And those cowboy boots!

Just the same, you had to hand it to him for style and nerve. He was down there, wasn't he? After the kid? Or whatever. Eddie shivered. He needed that drink now more than anything else in the world. Tatum had been gone over twenty minutes and the strain was beginning to tell.

Angry voices erupted. A screen door slammed. Michaud froze. *What in hell was going on down there?*

Tatum in his hiding place heard the screen door slam. He saw a figure run from the cottage. A girl, he thought. Damn! The dumb Canuck had told him nothing about a girl. Moments later he realized his mistake. It was the first time he set eyes on David Briggs. Eddie hasn't said anything about long hair.

Tatum, crouching and tense, scarcely dared to breathe. His eyes followed the boy's movements. To the skiff, along the shore, scaling a stone. He saw David turn quite suddenly and with resolute strides march up the path toward the A-frame.

Panic seized Tatum. This was the moment on which everything so painstakingly prepared, depended. Whatever he had learned from the books he had studied, from lurid newspaper accounts of abduction and murder, slaughter and gore in Hollywood Technicolor, from the horror and violence on the TV tube in abnormal color, now mattered very little. This was the real thing. It was happening to him. Now. He fought back a strong urge to run. Eddie was up there, waiting. In two minutes they could drive off and be gone from the scene, no one the wiser. The incident would be passed off as a frustrated robbery attempt. If noticed at all. But Eddie waiting was a challenge in itself to Tatum. He'd rather die than lose face and suffer the humiliation of Eddie Michaud sneering.

The boy was approaching. Tatum tightened his sweaty grip on the billy club. It was too late now to run.

David passed within a foot or two of Tatum, who rose suddenly, reached a hand over the boy's mouth, and swung the billy club at David's bobbing head. In that split instant David heard the swish and rustle and ducked. Tatum's sweaty fingers slipped. The boy cried out. The billy club grazed his cheek, caught his shoulder a glancing blow. There was no time to cry out again. Tatum in swift panic brought down the weapon once more in a short vicious arc. David dropped senseless at his feet.

Tatum shrank into the bushes, overcome with horror at what he had done. He crouched over the boy's still body and hoped to God he wasn't dead. For all his boastful talk to Michaud, Tatum in all his life had never struck anyone with anything more lethal than his open hand. Down at the cottage, someone must have heard the boy's outcry. He waited, poised to run.

After a few tense moments, he groped about in the musette, breathing heavily, whining, until his fingers found the hypodermic. He tore away the protective cap, pushed up the boy's shirt sleeve, felt for the deltoid muscle, and plunged the needle into his arm.

David moaned, stirred feebly, and fell silent. Tatum slung the musette on a shoulder, lifted David under the armpit, and began to drag him through the woods. The screen door of the cottage squeaked on its hinges. Tatum froze. He saw the gaunt shape of Kimball on the open porch. Tatum sank to the ground. Kimball peered about and seemed to stare directly at Tatum for several moments. He went inside. Tatum left David where he lay and made his way as quietly as he could to the car.

Eddie Michaud's frightened face stared back at him.

"Gary? What the hell happened to you?"

"I'm here, stupid."

"Where's the kid?"

"Out like a light. Why didn't you tell me he had long hair?"

"I never thought of it."

Tatum waited until he was sure of his voice. "Open the trunk."

"The light'll go on." Michaud said.

"It's unscrewed, stupid. Hurry now."

Michaud got out and fumbled with the trunk key. "I heard a yell."

"Shut up and open the trunk and follow me." Tatum's legs were wobbly. He leaned against the car, breathing noisily. He led Michaud through the woods to David. They carried the boy to the car, settled him into the trunk space, and lowered the lid cautiously until it clicked shut. Tatum got behind the wheel. He eased the car onto the road and drove back the way they had come, four miles to the plane mooring in Mathews Cove. He was composed now.

"Suppose the kid comes to?" Michaud asked.

"He won't."

"You're sure the shot'll hold him till I get him to Depot?"

"You're shivering," Tatum said.

"It's damn cold," Eddie said.

"Not just scared, Eddie?" Tatum's voice carried an edge of scorn.

"No more'n you were, running out of those woods." Eddie snickered. "Looking like you pissed in your pants."

They lifted David from the trunk. "He's still out cold," Michaud said.

"Is he breathing?"

Michaud bent over the boy and listened. "He's breathing okay. He's supposed to, ain't he?"

They bound his wrists and ankles with thick short wide leather straps, and wrapped wide strips of tape across his mouth and eyes. Tatum fumbled about in the boy's pockets.

"What're you doing?"

"Taking his wallet."

"Why?"

"Shut up and grab hold."

They carried David to the dock in the clearing where the plane was moored, nose in. Eddie freed the lines and stepped onto the starboard pontoon and opened the door and tossed the lines into the cockpit. He jumped to the dock and with Tatum's help eased the boy into the copilot seat and buckled him in. Tatum stuffed a spare shirt and socks in his musette bag and passed it to Michaud, who stowed it under the rear seat. He climbed into the pilot's seat and lowered the window. His voice was sullen. "Swing her round, so's I'm headed out."

"You sound angry, Eddie."

"You shouldn't've swiped the kid's wallet."

"It's part of the plan, stupid."

Tatum pushed against the wing tip, turning the plane until he could reach the tail assembly. He swung the horizontal stabilizer and headed the plane into the lake. Michaud cursed under his breath as he buckled himself in. The wallet business still troubled him. So did Tatum's contempt for him. Where the hell would he be without a pilot and a plane?

Calm and steady, he told himself. Like the old piss-and-vinegar days in Nam.

Tatum came forward. "Start her up, Eddie, but don't take off for a while."

"How come?"

"I'll need a few minutes to get away. Somebody hearing the engine might come by for a look and spot me."

"Roger," Eddie said, still sullen. It made sense for Tatum, sure. What about his own skin?

Tatum held on to the wing tip. "You know when we rendezvous?"

"Tomorrow midnight, right here."

"Don't talk to the boy. Not a word. Keep him blindfolded. Check his bindings every few hours."

"Cri'sake, we've been over all this, Gary—"

"You're doing fine, Eddie." Tatum could not contain a shrill note of elation. "Good luck," he whispered. He reached up. Eddie reached down. Their fingertips grazed. Tatum instantly regretted the show of intimacy and pulled back. "Get going," he said sharply.

"One thing, Gary."

"What?"

"The rendezvous?"

"What about it?"

"You'll be here, won't you?"

"Of course, stupid. Why ask?"

"Just, you know, be here."

"Why, Eddie? What's worrying you?"

"We're in this together is why," Eddie said softly. "Don't you forget it."

Tatum's foot gave the plane a hard shove. "That's stupid, Eddie. Real stupid. Just do as you're told, will you?"

Eddie touched the starter key. The plane's motor roared to life. Eddie throttled her to a quiet idle, glanced once at the unconscious boy, and settled back to wait.

Tatum walked to his car and drove off.

At the junction with the main road he turned south toward Greenville and parked off the road near Beaver Cove. He opened the car trunk and removed his boots and exchanged them for his sneakers. Moments later he heard Michaud's plane rev up, distant and clear. He searched the sky over Sugar Island and Lily Bay, hearing the plane take off but not seeing it. He sat for several minutes until the tenseness was out of him.

The damned Canuck had him fooled. Michaud must have given a lot more thought to the alternatives than Tatum had given him credit for. He must have considered the possibility of Tatum disappearing with the ransom money, leaving the pilot holding the boy and the bag.

Tatum snickered. He too had given it some thought. Plenty of thought. And if there had been any way he could have gotten away with it, it would have been good-by, Eddie Michaud. But all Eddie had to do was to fly back with the boy and make himself a hero with some cock-and-bull story about being forced at gun point to help Tatum abduct the boy. They'd believe Eddie. Eddie was a home town boy, a war veteran, and his record was clear. And the sheriff would be in touch with the FBI and the FBI would be on his tail in no time and that was just about the last thing Gary Tatum wanted right now.

No sense in rushing things, he told himself. There would be plenty of time to deal with Eddie. He smiled, pleased with himself, pleased with the way things were going. He started up the car, put David's wallet on the dashboard, and headed for Greenville.

CHAPTER ELEVEN

Michaud waited ten minutes, then taxied the Cessna into the wind and gave her full throttle for an effortless lift-off and climb. He picked up Mile Light, passed over Mount Kineo and Little Kineo, and set his course at 355° for Depot Lake. The country beyond Moosehead lay in pitch-blackness. No power lines ran that far north. It did not matter to Michaud. He had flown the course many times. He could fly it in his sleep.

He settled down, glancing once or twice at David. The boy had not stirred since take-off. Michaud did not know that Tatum had slugged him. He knew only what Tatum had told him—that the shot would last long enough to get the boy into the cabin at Depot Lake.

He looked below where a few scattered lights fringed the lake. Hunters, probably, stiff with booze and bragging about the deer they killed and the women they screwed. Michaud envied the life-style of the overdressed sports on whom he depended for his barebones living. But he envied them only for the money they had to spend. Their loud lies disgusted him. It was Michaud who tracked and shot the game they tagged. They paid him well and hauled their trophies back to places named Scarsdale and Teaneck and Westport and Lynn, places he had never seen and only rarely heard of. Their carelessness with their weapons appalled him. Their clumsiness and stupidity in the woods scared the hell out of him.

He no longer enjoyed what he did. Each year the deer were fewer and harder to track in the thick swampland where they herded. The last hunting season had been so poor, the Fish and Game commissioner in mid-November cut it short by a week. One party of hunters from Chicago, whom Michaud guided, demanded a deer apiece or no pay for Michaud. They looked nasty enough to mean it. He hadn't the guts to tell them to go to hell. A thousand bucks for a week's work is hard to come by. He shot them their deer. Two were spotted doe fawns too innocent to run. Killing them sickened him. It was like slaughtering children.

Michaud glanced at David Briggs, dead to the world. Serves his old man right. Tough on the kid, but who's to blame but Briggs himself? Sydney Briggs wasn't thinking of any kids of mine when he screwed me out of the land. The worst that could happen to a kid like Davey Briggs was to end up like his old man. A hard-nosed, big-city bastard squeezing the last cent like good red blood out of plain decent people.

The kid, he thought. Davey Briggs was a hell of a lot smarter than his old man. Woods smart, and with too damn much free time on his hands. He had got himself a reputation around Greenville as a mischief maker, a kid you had to keep an eye on every second. This past summer had been the worst. The mother was off to a loony-bin. The judge was working his Kennebec Valley farm or down to Portland hearing final appeals. His old man, Sydney, never showed his face, and David spent most of the summer alone, letting his hair grow long, taking off to the woods on his own for week-long stretches at a time.

Rich oddballs, the Briggs crowd, letting that kid of theirs run loose all summer. Nobody felt too sorry for his being alone so much of the time. He always had money to spend, more in his pocket than some men earned in a week in the woods cutting pulp.

Trouble was, the little bugger was full of beans. Like the time he took off from Sawyer's Marina one hot July day in a spanking new fiber glass outboard with a seventy-five-horse Evinrude with maybe ten minutes' running time on it. They caught up with him an hour later and only because he'd run out of gas. The boat owner was mad as hell but wouldn't press charges. The boy was Alonzo Kimball's grandson. Alonzo Kimball had done a lot of good for local people afoul of the law.

Another time, he was caught shoplifting in the Indian Store. No charges made, but the manager laid him over his knee on the steps alongside the new savings bank where the whole town could see and walloped his bare backside. There was nothing to tell the police. It was a matter of local pride.

That was how the summer went. It must have taught David a

lesson. Late that summer he started to build his A-frame. One of
his grandfather's old fishing buddies, a retired carpenter named
Mert Emery, helped him cut and fit the glass and hang the
door. That was all the help David had and all he needed. By
Labor Day, folks were saying hi to him again. He was a likable
kid when the mood was on him, and with his mother or grandfather around, they remembered, he could be downright lovable.

It's as though he does those mean things, Michaud reflected, to
attract attention. He thought of the time he flew David and his
mother to Allagash Lake, the mother lean and full of grace,
blessed with the judge's wise smile and the same deep love of
the woods. Only her eyes were different. The judge's eyes twinkled. Hers were full of sadness and searching. Easy to hurt, it
seemed to Michaud, with all that trusting and warmth.

On the flight north, an easy half hour, the boy had been helpful with the gear and very savvy about unlashing the canoe and
loading it. They got off in good shape, David in the bow seat,
Martha Briggs paddling stern. He would have liked to join them,
to spend a few nights by a dying campfire along the banks of
that wild tumbling river, listening to Martha Briggs's soft refined
voice, drinking in her soft beauty, daring to kiss her good night,
maybe while David slept.

It was too bad about the kid, rattling around by himself all
summer. David had stopped by a few times at the hangar, asking
for summer work, for anything to keep himself occupied. Michaud had nothing for him. Michaud had trouble enough getting
grocery money together and paying his hi-octane bills. But no
one would hire him as long as there were local kids looking for
summer work. And Michaud was not about to be helpful to the
kid whose father had used him so badly ten years ago in the
farm deal. It wasn't the kid's fault. It was just that anything that
had to do with Sydney Briggs left a sour taste in his mouth.

He began checking course, speed, and altitude. According to
his watch and instrument panel, he should be following a strip of
the St. John River with Daaquam Gate an even nine miles to the
west. He reached for his scratched Bausch & Lomb night binocu-
lars, cumshawed twenty years ago from a crashed navy fighter
plane at Danang. He steadied the glasses. The lights of Daaquam flickered into focus. He began a gradual descent. At five

hundred feet he switched on his landing light and picked up the choppy black waters of Depot Lake. He welcomed the visible chop. It pointed up the surface. He circled the wooded point where Ami's old cabin stood and made his approach, guiding on the west shore.

Bush pilots and boatmen avoid Depot Lake, a shallow and treacherous wilderness pond. Much of its broad surface is pierced by branches and dead tree trunks. Though it is considered hazardous for both air and surface nagivation, Eddie Michaud had landed there many times. He knew where the channel lay—a deep strip of black water along the west shore, barely wide enough for his Cessna.

He landed smoothly, swung the plane around, and taxied to the dock and tied up. He carried David into the cabin and settled him on the sagging bunk where he had passed so many winter nights of his youth with his father. For the first time he discovered the large swelling on David's head. He cleaned the wick of the kerosene lamp and lighted it and hung it from a spike in the cabin's central beam. He took a closer look at David's bruise. A small clot of dried blood showed through the boy's matted hair. He wondered what Tatum had used to raise a bump as ugly as that. If it was a pistol butt, Michaud wanted to know. Tatum had reassured him there would be no weapons, no violence of any kind.

He checked David's blindfold and bindings. After some hesitation he removed the gag. Suppose the kid yelled? All he could scare were the spruce partridge. Michaud would have relaxed the leather straps as well but Tatum's orders had been not to touch them.

He loaded the iron wood stove with kindling and a few sticks of pine, checked the chimney, and in moments had a fire going. He went out and checked the plane, securing it for the night. From the woodshed he carried back an armload of firewood and stacked it near the stove.

He opened the carton of food and supplies they had brought with them that morning. Using his pocket knife, Michaud carved a chunk of sharp Cheddar, known locally as rat cheese, and wolfed it down with a hard Baldwin apple and shards of broken biscuit.

He sat in the broken-down armchair that had been his father's. Chewing noisily, tilted back with his feet on the wood box, he felt better than he had felt in a long time.

He was where he loved being most, in the cabin of his childhood, deep in the north woods, secure and at peace. Snug as a bug in a rug, old man Ami used to say.

It was up to Tatum now. Michaud chuckled. How dumb did Tatum think he was? If Tatum goofed and didn't pick up the ransom money, or got himself caught, Michaud had his story ready-made. All he had to do was fly the kid back the same night, drop him in a safe place, and return to Depot and sweat it out for a few days as though nothing had happened. If they wanted to know where his charter party was, Michaud would tell them Tatum had cut his trip short and he had flown him back days ago. What Tatum had been up to since then was none of Michaud's business. But if Tatum *had* the ransom money and took off— Just don't try it, Mr. Gary Tatum. I'll have the law on your ass before you can say another goddamn *mon ami*. . . .

And if everything went off according to plan— Michaud squeezed his thighs together. He could scarcely bear the thought of all that money.

He stretched and yawned and set the alarm for eight, the hour Tatum had scheduled for David's first food. He covered David with a thin moth-eaten blanket, fed the fire and banked it, and slid into his old down sleeping bag. In a few minutes he was asleep.

CHAPTER TWELVE

Tatum spent the rest of the night in a motel a few miles north of Skowhegan. He locked his car and locked the door to his room and turned the thermostat up to eighty degrees. He undressed and showered, hot and long, and stretched out steamy and naked on the bed with the damp towel across his loins.

The night's work had drained him, yet he was too charged emotionally to sleep. In his mind he retraced the day's events. So far, so good—except for Eddie's surprising remark just before take-off. *The nerve of that dumb Canuck, practically accusing me*—Tatum tittered, giggled. Eddie was all right. He just hadn't given Eddie credit for honest cunning. Eddie had always seemed the simple, trusting yokel and Tatum had bought it. A cheap lesson, Tatum reflected. Sure, it was Eddie's scheme and it was Eddie's plane, but the brainwork and the details, the timing and expertise—all pure Tatum genius. He had misjudged Eddie Michaud and Eddie would bear watching. Because there were surprises in store for Eddie Michaud when the time would come.

The wallet, for instance. It wasn't in the planning, but no need to tell Eddie why. Tatum had driven into Greenville after the plane was aloft and headed north, and he had tucked the wallet behind the state road sign pointing the way to Jackman. After he'd removed the seventy-two dollars, of course. Can you believe a fourteen-year-old carrying seventy-two dollars in cash in a two-buck wallet? What's becoming of this younger generation?

David Briggs. Tatum mouthed the name softly. Tall for fourteen and skinny, but nothing frail about him. His dead weight had surprised Tatum when he dragged him through the woods. And his long hair disgusted him. He looked at his watch. Eddie should be at Depot by now and the boy still knocked out.

What had really scared Tatum was the shot he had given the boy. The veterinarian in Boston had told him it would take a couple of cc.'s of hypodermic Nembutal to knock out a fair-sized dog. Tatum had to be sure. "Gretchen's a Saint Bernard," he explained.

"How much does she weigh?"

"A hundred pounds."

"It might take four cc., then, to be safe."

"Will that keep her quiet, sir, until I pull out the splinter?"

"Is the splinter deep? Easy to get at?"

"Once she's knocked out, sir, I can handle it. I just couldn't stand her suffering any more pain."

"Well, she'll be like dead for eight hours." The vet caught the anxious look in Tatum's blue eyes. Poor lad, he thought, taking it so hard. "You're sure you can't bring, ah, Gretchen in?"

"No chance, sir. I'm traveling south, you see," Tatum said, "on urgent family business."

"I'd have you on your way in less than an hour, son."

"That would mean going back to the kennels, sir, fetching poor Gretchen here, then driving all the way back to I-95." He lowered his eyes, bit his lower lip, shook his head slowly. "I know that would be best, sir, but I've got to keep driving all night. My mother's in Montclair, waiting for us. New Jersey. She's not well. Terminal, sir, and Gretch and I are all she's got."

"Tell you what," the vet said. "I'll give you three ampoules to take along. Four cc. each. One's all you're going to need but we may as well play it safe." He prepared the small kit and handed it to Tatum. "Just be careful, son. An overdose can be fatal."

"But you said four cc. for a hundred-pound dog is okay?"

"Sure is." The doctor smiled to reassure him. "Some people panic if the animal comes out of it sooner than expected and they jab another shot into him."

"I won't be doing anything as stupid as that." Tatum's eyes glistened with gratitude. "I'm paying cash, sir."

"Your personal check will do." His eyes twinkled. "I've a sister-in-law in Montclair. Full of the right people."

"Cash it must be, sir. For your valuable time and the ampoules."

"You've administered shots before, I suppose?"

"Oh yes. Navy corpsman duty, Vietnam. Morphine Syrettes, mostly, but I'm familiar with the procedure."

The doctor folded and pocketed the money. "Hope your

Gretchen pulls through." He shook Tatum's hand warmly. "And of course your mother—"

"I'll drop you a card," said Tatum. "That's a promise."

Well, Eddie had the boy now and he hoped Eddie was on the ball and off the sauce. As far as he could figure out, Eddie was nowhere near a bottle unless he had stashed one away a long time ago in the cabin at Depot Lake. Tatum had thoroughly checked every other possibility.

He had to think now about the morning, about Briggs and the old judge finding the boy gone and what they would do about it. And he had to get a call to them before they really began to worry and brought in the law. From what Eddie had told him of the boy, he often took off mornings for a hike in the woods or to fish one of the nearby streams. It was odd, too, the way the boy had come bouncing out of the cottage after the loud angry words Tatum had heard. In the morning, the boy'll be missing. Would they buy the boy's running away?

It would be a lucky break if they thought he had run off. It would give Tatum an extra margin of time. And when he would phone to tell them he had the boy and wanted ransom money— would they risk going to the police? Briggs was a hardheaded businessman, Kimball a softhearted judge. How would they handle it? Pay the ransom or call in the law? The FBI?

Once the police were in, they'd be all over the place where he had trampled the brush and dragged David through the woods. They would dust for prints and seal random hairs in plastic. They would ask about the stifled scream and make molds of the tire tracks and the deep narrow heel marks of his cowboy boots. They would comb the lakeside community to find someone who had heard anything odd during the night. A car motor stopping and starting, a plane taking off or landing.

Tatum had questioned Eddie thoroughly on that point. Eddie had held firm. Private planes landed and took off day and night. There was no law to stop them, no one to check on them. It was a wilderness frontier. Besides the federal customs and immigration officers, there were the state Fish and Game wardens and the forest rangers, the Border Patrol, the county sheriffs, and the local police. They all flew planes and patrolled the roads and highways in the Moosehead region. Their hands were full with smugglers and lost hunters, with mishaps on the lake and accidents in the woods. Hundreds of charter planes and private planes, both local and out-of-state, landed and took off, carrying hunters and fishermen round the clock. If they weren't smuggling or lost or in trouble, the law couldn't care less. They were on their own.

Tatum got out of bed and carried the damp towel into the bathroom and took a fresh one and crawled under the covers. The next steps were clear in his mind. At 0800, the phoned instructions to Sydney Briggs. At 0830, the Indian Store. At 1700, the Bangor House. At 1830, the Silent Woman. At 2100, the South Solon Meetinghouse. At midnight, the rendezvous with Eddie Michaud.

He did not care to plan beyond that. Too much depended on what happened between now and then.

Eddie, for example. If Eddie opened his mouth, the Briggs boy would know his voice. Once the word was out that it was Eddie Michaud who flew the kidnap plane, it was curtains for both of them.

The room had become excessively hot. Tatum did not mind. Cold depressed him. He lied often about the childhood years of desert living in his mother's cactus-rimmed hacienda. It had thinned his blood, he would explain with a wry smile. Ah, Mums, he thought, you smooth-bellied loving whore-mother. If you only knew what a delicious CARE package I have in store for you. Your darling little Gare will be coming home, Mums, loaded with gifts from Cartier and Gucci, pockets crammed with thousand-dollar bills. He thought of the fortune, the child of his brain, and his damp body filled with a delicious longing between the sheets.

The postal money order was on its way. The whore-mother never failed him. Once he had the ransom money, her chicken feed could rot in the Greenville post office forever.

The thought of being stranded without money terrified him. It had terrified him most of his adolescent life when he depended on the arrival of allowance checks at the schools and camps he attended; where, many times, the checks were late or did not arrive at all. He would not forget those summonings to the head-masters' offices (or deans' or directors')—the fishy eyes and false smiles, the stony ultimatums for unpaid tuition. Until the arrival of his mother, always charmingly vague, or his father in icy anger. And the hard looks and the hassling over rebates and refunds, enough to make him queasy and more than once throw up, hopefully on a priceless antique rug, the cherished gift of some misguided alumnus.

Ah well, he reflected, we each have our own lives to live. In a matter of a day or so—hours, really—he would never again have a money worry as long as he lived. He would travel. He would be generous, admired, loved. He would write a book and dedicate it to Mums. He'd show her. . . .

He curled up, drowsy, snugly fetal, the covers a comforting womb round his damp smooth body, his head under the soft pillow. And soon slept.

CHAPTER THIRTEEN

The boy in drugged sleep dreamed of the wilderness river, his runaway canoe swept along by raging flood waters, he helpless on the ribbed bottom between varnished gunwales. His head seemed ready to burst with pain. He thought desperately of escape, of safety. His limbs strained for freedom. He could not move. He could not understand what held him.

Where were the others? How had he gotten here? How much longer could the good White canoe take the awful pounding before it piled itself and him on the rocky shore?

In this dream his terrified eyes watched the rolling blue sky above swing crazily into the dense green growth along the shore for brief moments, first this side, then that, he supine, stricken with fear, aware only that his body, stretched along the canoe's bottom, made ballast and lessened the chance of capsizing.

He wanted to live, not drown.

With skin rubbed raw, muscles seeming to tear, he worked himself an inch at a time toward the stern until his head touched the strut and rested there. With failing strength he raised himself and searched the shore. He saw his mother waving gaily as the canoe plunged and tossed past the clearing where they had made camp that day. She wore the bright plaid shirt he loved and waved the black iron skillet. She was shouting (he thought), shouting words he could not hear. To his astonishment, he saw the good White canoe pulled up on the bank, the canoe in which he now raced to disaster. He could not believe his eyes. He yelled with all his strength. No sound came forth. His head throbbed. His teeth and belly and limbs and heart ached. He strained but could not turn his head for one last look at his mother before he was swept from sight.

Where was his father when everyone needed him? Why does he do this to us?

And screamed and screamed, surfacing from his dream, awake and eyes wide open to blackness (My God, I'm blind!) as Eddie Michaud's large rough hand stifled the scream.

PART TWO

CHAPTER FOURTEEN

"Sydney." Kimball shook him. "Get up."

Briggs snuffled, tried one eye. It opened gummily.

"On your feet. Come on now."

"Wha' for?"

"David's gone."

Briggs turned to the wall. Kimball ripped back the comforter and flung it across the foot of the bed.

Briggs sat up shivering. "What a lousy thing to do."

"Up, Sydney."

"Head's splitting," he whined. "Feel awful."

"Coffee's on. Get dressed."

"What time's it?"

"Seven o'clock."

"My *God* . . ." He rolled back on the pillow.

Kimball tossed Briggs's rumpled trousers and stained shorts on the bed. "If you're not out of that bed and dressed three minutes from now," he said, "I'm dragging you under a cold shower."

He went to the kitchen and dropped two slices of bread in the toaster and poured two mugs of steamy black coffee. Briggs appeared minutes later wearing heavy wool socks and a faded robe too long for him.

"I said dressed, Sydney."

"Can't."

"Why not?"

"You've no idea what someone's done in my shorts."

"Take a pair of mine."

"Too small in the butt." He sniffed. "Is that coffee I smell?"

"Sit right down."

"I'm so glad I married you."

Kimball grinned in spite of himself. "Drink up, Sydney. We're going after David."

"He's run away before."

"This time—"

"Damn it, Alonzo, I've got a two-and-a-half-million-dollar deal about to go on the rocks because of that kid. I've got to get on the phone—"

"You've got a fourteen-year-old son, Sydney, who's been gone all night and no sign of him."

"So what?" He sipped his coffee noisily. "You know David. He's gone fishing or bird watching or whatever the hell it is you outdoor types do in the wee hours."

"His sleeping bag's untouched. The clothes he wore last night aren't around. Frankly, I'm worried."

"He's pulled this stunt before. He's pissed off, like I said last night." He bit into a piece of toast. "A true Kimball. Spoiled rotten."

"You don't know your own son."

"I know human nature, Judge. An eye for an eye. That's also Solomon's Law."

"Not David's."

"Come off it, Judge. Your grandson David's sitting on a rock somewhere within hollering distance, getting his revenge."

"You heard him yell last night, didn't you?"

"I didn't hear any yell."

"You were blind drunk." Kimball reached for his wool shirt. "Eat up and get dressed. We're losing time."

"Got to call Boston."

"You've got two hours before any of your fine city friends show up at their teak-paneled trade salons."

"I call 'em at home."

"Obviously, Sydney, you don't give a damn about your son. All right. Sit on your ass if you want to. I'm looking for David." He buttoned his shirt and jammed an old poplin fishing hat on his head and started for the door. Briggs rose groaning and followed him, chewing a piece of toast.

"Alonzo."

"Go to hell."

"That's what David said. In a four-letter word." He gripped Kimball's shoulder. Kimball shook loose. Briggs grabbed his arm and held him. "Goddammit, will you listen to me? You're wrong. I do give a damn about David. A thousand damns—"

"Then do something about it."

"Sit and listen."

Kimball sat, frowning and angry. Briggs paced, waving his arms. "You hurt me when you said what you did. I love the boy. You know damned well I love him. Sure. I lose my head sometimes. My temper. Okay. I run too much. I drink too much. Okay. But don't ever tell me again I don't love David. Or his mother. They're all I've got. I make so damn much money, I don't even know what I'm worth. And I make it for them, every damned cent of it. And one day it'll all be David's. For his wife. His kids. My grandchildren. Your great-grandchildren, old man."

"No need to shout, Sydney. I hear you quite well with my pocket ear trumpet."

"I've been wanting to get this off my chest for a long time, so shut up and listen. That kid's going to be sitting on top of four or five million bucks someday, and he better the hell learn how to handle it. I'm not about to let a son of mine piss away his life climbing mountains and running wilderness rivers and scorching hot dogs over campfires. He'll have plenty of time to do those silly things after he gets the kind of education he's going to need. I'm not about to knock everything Martha and you taught him. It has its good points; but there's a limit. You can't run a four- or five-million-dollar estate rubbing two Boy Scouts together. Most of the world doesn't live in the woods, Mr. Justice Kimball. Most people have jobs and businesses and face up to adult responsibilities of society. Like you. And me. And don't tell me Henry David Thoreau was anything but a nature freak, a sour misfit who ended up in jail. I want David Kimball Briggs to survive in the real world. To cope with real problems and deal with hard facts and he's got to go to school to do it, get a university education, the kind of education it takes to handle the responsibility of four or five million clams. And I don't mean art history or music appreciation. Or how to cook a woodchuck. I mean mergers and interlocking directorates and stock options. I want him to be able to read a fiscal statement and know what it means and if it's worth bothering with. All I want for my boy is his happiness. So get off my back, old man."

"I don't believe my ears," Kimball said.

"Clean 'em," said Briggs.

"Your views, both personal and corporate, are commendable, Sydney. I'm delighted at long last to hear *something* from you that isn't bitter or sarcastic. I will just say this about the woods. Anyone who's content to get along with a sharp knife and a few matches, and finds his fulfillment in being close to nature, isn't going to need four or five million dollars."

"Bullshit. You romantic idealists give me a pain in the ass. Happiness is bucks, and the more bucks, the more happiness. Now if Your Eminence will wait five seconds, I'll get out of this ratty robe of yours and join in the search for the alleged missing heir."

"You amaze me, Sydney. That pretty speech."

"Thanks. Remind me to send you a silk robe from Sulka next Christmas."

"Make it L. L. Bean and all wool and you got a deal."

Kimball poked about in the underbrush close by the A-frame. "Something went on here."

"Sure. Davey threw a fit of pique."

"The way the brush is matted down. See? Deep heel marks here. These broken twigs and branches. Fresh breaks, Sydney. As though he crawled up this way into the woods."

"Or was dragged."

Kimball was startled. "Exactly," he frowned, "but I'm not joking."

"Come off it, Judge. You've been hearing too many criminal cases. Or watching too much TV."

With Briggs shivering in his topcoat and reluctantly tagging behind, Kimball studied the slanting course along which Tatum and Michaud had carried the boy. The woods were deeper here, further from the A-frame. "Up to here," Kimball pointed out, "he dragged himself along the ground. Above this point, there are fewer broken branches. He must've gotten up and walked. Or been carried."

"And when you come up with the blunt instrument and bloodstains, I'll listen." He patted Kimball's shoulder. "Carry on, Sherlock. I'm putting in my call to Boston."

"He was wearing a new pair of L. L. Bean boots. We bought

'em Sunday. His prints go from the beach almost to the A-frame and stop."

"He's probably in the kitchen having his breakfast. I'll check his boot prints."

Kimball followed the trail through the woods to the abandoned road where Michaud had parked the car. He returned a few minutes later, his seamed face a shade paler, his keen eyes under shaggy brows troubled. "I'm calling the police."

Briggs looked up from the table crammed with legal-looking business papers.

"What the hell for?"

"David's in real trouble." Kimball reached for the phone. Briggs clamped his hand over it. "Now wait a minute—I'm expecting a call."

"I'll have that phone, Sydney."

"Damn it, Alonzo, you're going off half-cocked. Let's talk about it a minute."

Kimball restrained himself with an effort. "All right. One minute." He sat across from Briggs, his fists clenched. "A car parked last night not a hundred yards from here on old lady Tibbets's road. She died two years ago. The estate's in probate. Nobody's been down that road since. There are tire tracks, a short way in and out. Some footprints. A man and maybe a large woman, judging from the deep heel marks. Those tracks from the A-frame lead right to it. But there's no sign of David's boot prints."

"So he wasn't there."

"What the hell's wrong with you, Sydney? Last night he yelled for help. Today I find strange tracks all over the place. And this." He removed a small torn bit of plastic from his shirt pocket and tossed it on the briefcase. Briggs poked it with his finger.

"What's it supposed to be? A condom wrapper?"

"It could be the plastic cap they use to seal drug ampoules. I've seen hundreds of them in evidence. To inject a hypodermic, you simply remove that protective cap."

"Where'd you find it?"

"In the underbrush near the A-frame. We missed it when we first looked."

Briggs smoked quietly for several moments, his hand still on the phone. Kimball waited, his patience ebbing. "We're losing valuable time, Sydney."

"Who are you calling?"

"Junior Tuttle. He's the town chief of police."

"The Tuttle kid?"

"He's thirty, has a college degree, is married, and has two kids. You're behind the times, Sydney. I'll take that phone now."

He reached for it the moment it rang. He heard a stranger's voice. "It's for you," he told Briggs. "Make it short."

"My Boston call." Briggs picked up the phone and settled back. As he listened, his face turned ashen. He tried twice to interrupt, but stopped in midsentence. He glanced wildly at Kimball, then shouted into the phone. "Just a minute, now. Will you repeat those instructions?"

Tatum had already hung up.

CHAPTER FIFTEEN

David screaming in blackness caught the muzzling thrust of Eddie Michaud's rough hand against his mouth. Instinctively, he drew back. The hand followed, not quickly enough. David's head shot forward. His teeth sank into the soft mound below Michaud's thumb. Eddie howled, a pained profane outburst incredibly sweet to David's ear. *Sweet,* he thought, *the taste of flesh.* He was alive. Blind, perhaps paralyzed, he did not know. But *alive.* He had bit savagely, splitting skin, drawing blood. It was no nightmare, no dream. Whose hand? he wondered, waiting for a blow, a rain of blows and more obscenities.

No words came. He dared not speak. Coarse fabric across his eyes told him he was not blind. He listened to movement, boots on boards, a chair scraping, steam hissing, familiar smells. Cedar bark, balsam, dank rot, a wood fire, rat cheese . . . crankcase oil?

"Grampa? Dad?" Voice cracked and throat dry.

The rough hand held his chin now, thumb and forefinger firmly gripping, cheese at his lips. He turned his head. The strong fingers forced his lips apart, pushed the cheese between. He chewed cautiously, a throb of head pain with each chew.

Silence. More cheese. A mug with a cracked rim poured sweet steamy tea, a swallow at a time. He choked on words. "Where am I? Damn it!" Sitting up suddenly, his chest flinging hot tea, mug and all. A muttered curse. He realized now he was bound hand and foot. "Loosen me up," he croaked. "It hurts."

Steps again, moving away. Rattle of utensils. Water sloshed in a bucket. The woods, all right, but where? Fingers loosened the ankle bonds a notch. A calloused hand massaged his skin. No loosening at the wrists, but more brisk massage. His blood coursed, a warm glow inside him. He wanted to scream his frustration. No use, he thought. A waste of strength. Rest. Listen. Something will happen. Things take time.

He tried to remember what had happened. Confused images. Scaling pebbles. His father's anger. The A-frame . . . *the A-frame!* But he could not remember what had happened at the A-frame. He lay still in sore pain, gathering strength.

Eddie Michaud wrapped the chunk of cheese, sipped his tea noisily. In a sour mood, tea-drenched, he sucked at his gouged flesh. Twice now the goddamn kid had caught him by surprise. He should have clobbered him. How do you hit a kid who's tied up hand and foot? He hoped David had not recognized his voice. Gary had been pretty damn positive about that one point. Well, what the hell. One word. No need to tell Gary. Right now, let's see, Gary's on the phone giving Briggs his instructions. That puts the rendezvous time sixteen hours away.

Sixteen hours! All that time to kill.

He thought back to the years he had spent in this cabin with his father. No worrying, no hurrying, and all the game to kill a man could want. He would never forget what his father had told him, his father who in some ways was more Indian than white man, who adored his Micmac wife and lived much of his life according to her Indian beliefs and customs. "The white man kills for sport," old Ami once told him. "Not the Indian. The Indian kills to live."

When Michaud was eight, his father took him along on snow-shoes which his mother had made for the boy. They spent much of the winter trapping the country around Depot, working the trails over a forty-mile stretch in below-zero, blizzardy weather, with winds to fifty knots. They were away before dawn each morning with empty packs and fresh bait, and back by dark loaded down with frozen carcasses of beaver, otter, mink, and fox. They would hang the animals until they thawed and skin them quickly so they wouldn't go bad. Then they would stretch the hides on wood frames to dry. Eddie ate deer meat, bear, and moose before he was ten, spruce partridge and wild duck when-ever he could get them. He slept under old blankets and smelly hides close to the banked wood fire on the rude bunk covered with boughs, curled snugly against his father's hard body, the earthy male smell familiar and reassuring. Northern lights fright-ened him. Until he learned what made them he truly believed it was God at play.

They would bring back the hides in March, when the trapping season closed, to a fat Yankee trader in the back of a Greenville sporting-goods store. The trader owned a fine new pickup each year and smelled of choice whiskey and cigars. He would pinch the boy's cheek and give him a quarter and send him out. He would get Eddie Michaud's father drunk on cheap whiskey and cheat him outrageously on the price of the furs. Sometimes Eddie would sneak back early and sit in a corner pretending to read the old sports magazines, feeling helpless and ashamed of the Indian in him. When his father had the cash and it was time to go, it was Eddie's job to get his father home before he spent it all.

The things you remember . . .

He looked across the room at David. The little smart-ass was being quiet. Too damn quiet, Michaud thought. Cooking up some scheme to make me open my yap again. He sucked at the torn skin and thought of the whiskey in the glove compartment of his Wagoneer a million miles away.

He got up, yawned, and stepped out for an armful of stove-wood. A heavy thump inside the cabin brought him running. David had rolled from the bunk to the floor, screaming curses. Michaud went to him, lifted him, and heaved him onto the bunk. David thrashed and tossed like a helpless epileptic. His shrill cries pierced Michaud's ears like hot needles. He jerked about like a caged rat, desperate and trapped, half-crazed with frustration, hands clapped to his ears.

David continued to scream.

CHAPTER SIXTEEN

Sydney Briggs went to the dry sink and poured a shot glass full of whiskey. Kimball took it from his shaking fingers and set it down.

"What instructions?"

"Some young punk says he's got David and I'm to go to the phone booth—" He took the glass from the dry sink and tossed the whiskey down. "If David put somebody up to this—" He looked at his watch. Kimball took him not gently by the shoulders and sat him down.

"What phone booth, Sydney? For God's sake."

"Outside the Indian Store. I'm to go there and wait for a call."

"How soon?"

"Twenty minutes."

"Whoever it is knows the driving time. Let's go."

"If this is David's idea of a joke—"

"We'll damn well find out. Come *on*."

Briggs drove the seven miles in ten minutes. The big Continental spewed dust clouds all the way. He never stopped talking. "It's a rip-off," he insisted. "David's screwball idea of revenge."

Kimball hoped it was nothing more serious than that. The unfunniest practical joke in the world would be better than the real thing.

"Why did you say the caller was a young punk?"

"The voice. You heard him. Trying to sound gruff and tough. It cracked once. Not a kid's voice—someone in his twenties."

"A Maine voice?"

"Hell, no. More—well, sharp and big city, like."

Briggs parked the car nose in, facing the Shaw Block building. The phone booth was around the corner. "I'll go along," Kimball said.

"Stay where you are."

Briggs got out of the car. Kimball watched the sag of shoulder,

the shuffling gait. For the first time since he had known Sydney
Briggs, he felt sorry for him. He sat with his big-knuckled hands
helpless in his lap. A kidnaping in Greenville, Maine. Who
would ever have believed it?

Sydney Briggs sat on the wood bench alongside the phone
booth. He had brought a memo pad and ball-point pen and jot-
ted down the phone number, not knowing why. The time was
several minutes before eight-thirty.

Sydney Briggs in his black vicuna coat over his midnight-blue
sharkskin suit, in his narrow black shoes, sat facing the main
drag of Greenville, loathing its backwater plainness. Hunters in
their bright orange reflective gear stared at his city clothes and
wondered what curious circumstance would bring a type like
that to a place like this. Briggs read their thoughts, quite aware
of his image in this unplanned, unfinished corner of the world,
relishing its impact, not giving a damn. All he cared about was
getting to the bottom of this incredibly crazy thing with David
and back to Boston to close the deal. He had to close that deal.
More depended on it than anyone but Sydney Briggs knew.

He wondered where his brains had been when he fell in love
with Martha Kimball, when he turned to jelly and junked his sin-
gle-minded ambition to be a millionaire before he was thirty.
Now he was saddled with a wife who climbed mountains and a
son who smoked pot and paddled down wilderness rivers. And
ridiculed him for scorning such insanity. And there was the
crusty old father-in-law who sanctioned their madness. Such a
waste of energy, time, and money, he thought.

He stared at the steady traffic of hunters in their jeeps and
rust-rimmed sedans bristling with gun barrels and wished fer-
vently they would all shoot each other dead. Not that he loved
deer and detested this annual violence on wildlife. Not at all. It
simply represented a way of life counter to his concept of what
life was all about. Progress, depicted by acres of planned
cement-girdled shopping centers, was Sydney Briggs's dream for
America, soon to be realized when all this nature nonsense
would go. . . .

The booth phone rang. Briggs grabbed it. "Hello," he shouted.
"This is Sydney Briggs."

"Listen carefully, Mr. Briggs. I'm not repeating the instructions."

"Who the hell are you? Where's my son?"

"Scream again and I'll hang up." The voice was even, the words crisp and clear. "You've been watched from the minute you got to the phone booth. One word to the police and you'll never see David again."

"What d'you want?"

"Two hundred thousand dollars in twenties and fifties."

"Where the hell—"

"From your vending machines. You take in—"

"*No!* I'm asking where the hell's my son. You don't get a goddamn dime until I know where he is."

"Park your Mark IV at the Bangor airport. Pick up a dark rental car, Chevrolet Impala. Be at the public phone in the vestibule outside the lobby of the Bangor House, five o'clock tonight. Have—"

"Slow up, damn it. I'm writing it down."

"Have the cash in a knapsack in the rental car trunk. We'll phone instructions."

"Don't hang up! How do I know you've got David?"

"You don't, really, but he's safe."

"I demand some proof."

"Look across the street, Mr. Briggs. See that road sign? David's wallet is wedged behind the Route 6 and 15 arrows."

Briggs began to shout but the line went dead. He slammed down the receiver. Two hundred thousand—at the worst possible time. *Son of a bitch bastards*. He crossed the street to the road sign and retrieved the wallet from its hiding place. Kimball opened the car door. Briggs slumped into the driver's seat. "They've got David, all right." He tossed the wallet into Kimball's lap.

Kimball looked inside. "They robbed him, too." His voice was dry and tight. "He had over fifty dollars in it yesterday."

Briggs snorted. "Chicken feed. They want two hundred thousand in small bills. Today!"

Kimball nodded in the direction of the town's one-story municipal building. "Let's get word to the police."

"Not yet," Briggs said.

"Why not?"

"I need time to think."

"This is a kidnaping, Sydney. Don't waste time."

"They're watching us, Alonzo. I swear to God. One move to the police and David's done for."

"They said that?"

"Just let me think," Briggs begged.

"Coffee?"

"You go on over. I'll wait here."

"I'm not leaving until you come round to your senses."

"Meaning I go to the police and let those maniacs kill David. Right? Isn't that exactly what you're asking me to do?"

"I don't believe anyone's watching us. It's part of their game." He put the wallet in his pocket. "Come on over to Knowlton's. We'll talk about it over a cup of coffee."

Briggs was silent for several moments. "If I took off now, Alonzo, you'd get a ride back to the cottage, wouldn't you?"

"What the hell are you talking about?"

"I've got to handle this on my own."

"What do you intend to do?"

"That kidnaper bastard told me what to do and the first thing is to say nothing to the police."

"You're making a grave mistake, Sydney."

"We'll see about that."

"Don't be a fool, Sydney. One word from me to Junior Tuttle, and no matter where you're headed the state police'll pick you up."

"On what charges? I'd sue the ass off them." Briggs looked at his watch. "For God's sake. Get out," he said in a thick anguished voice. "I'm losing precious time."

Kimball opened the door and slowly got out. Briggs started the motor and raced it. "I'll phone you," he shouted. He glared angrily at a pair of hunters who had stopped to watch him. "Mind your own damn business, you clowns," he snarled.

"What about Martha?" Kimball asked, holding the door.

"For Chri'sake, how can you think of Martha at a time like this?" He threw the gear lever into reverse.

Kimball slammed the door. Briggs backed out, swung the car around, and, burning rubber, headed south.

Kimball crossed the street. The manager of the Mobil garage was gassing up a Dodge station wagon loaded with five fat hunters from New Jersey. He waved to Kimball. "You look beat, Judge."

Kimball straightened up and walked with a springier step into the driveway where the police chief's car was parked. The desk clerk smiled up at him. "Morning, Judge Kimball. Can I help you?"

"Junior around?"

"Chief Tuttle, sir?" She nodded. "He's back in his office."

"I'd like to see him, please."

Junior Tuttle drove the patrol car with the ominous rack of blue lights and sirens carefully down the lake road.

"No way to stop him, Judge, without some kind of a violation or suspicion of something."

"He drove off like a madman."

"Was there a ransom note or some piece of evidence we could go on?"

"I showed you that plastic hypodermic cover."

"Could be off of a toothbrush, Judge. All there really is to go on is, Davey's missing and your word there was a phone call—"

"Two phone calls."

"Right. The one to the cottage and then over at the phone booth by the Indian Store. That's all there is. Not that I doubt for a minute your word that it happened, you understand."

They arrived at the entrance to the Briggs compound. "Park up here," Kimball said. "So we won't mess up any tracks or anything."

He led Tuttle down the drive and showed him the footprints around the A-frame. "Those pointy ones look like a woman's shoe," he said. "With that deep heel."

"Could be," Tuttle said. He was a solid young man, built to wear uniforms. His manner was reserved, softly polite, but Kimball knew better. He had seen Junior Tuttle knock heads together when the occasion demanded. And drunken woodsmen or insolent hunters provided frequent occasions. Kimball was one of the few men who knew that modest young Tuttle had been at the head of his police academy class. Tuttle crouched close to the embedded prints. "Could be a doggin' heel," he said.

"What's a dogging heel?"

"On cowboy boots. Slants in to get a better grip. We'll send for a police lab technician to make a cast." He stood up. "What else?"

Kimball showed him the drive where the kidnapers had parked the car. Tuttle studied the area carefully but did not seem impressed. This time of year, hunters trespassed everywhere. They went back to the cottage. Kimball warmed up the pot of coffee and they sat in the big room near the fireplace. Tuttle made some notes in a small memo pad.

"You didn't take those phone calls, did you?"

"Just the first one. It was for Sydney and all I did was to say hello."

"Wasn't Davey's voice, was it?"

"Not at all."

Tuttle groped for the right words. "Not meaning to offend, Judge, but that grandson of yours is a damn hellion."

"I'm aware of that."

"Nothing criminal, understand—"

"What're you trying to say, Junior?"

"Do you reckon David put someone up to it? After what happened last night?"

"That's what Sydney thought at first." Kimball smiled bleakly. "I know the opinions of indulgent grandfathers aren't exactly objective ones, Junior. But David's not like that."

"He's played some pretty odd tricks around town, Judge. Practical jokes, stuff like that."

"I've heard." Kimball heaved a deep sigh. "I wish to hell I knew what to do."

"Let's see what the lab comes up with." Tuttle drained his cup. "Unless there's probable cause, we usually wait twenty-four hours before putting out an APB on a missing person. Once the form is filled out, it goes nationwide, and there's no stopping it. Meanwhile I'll notify state police in Skowhegan and the sheriff's office in Dover. That way we can keep a tab on Mr. Briggs's Continental."

"How'd you know what he's driving?"

"He came through town last night like a bat out of hell."

"You recognized him?"

"Every state officer from here to Kittery knows that BRIGGS license tag of his." He got up and Kimball followed him out. "He gave you no idea of where he was going?"

"He told me nothing except that the kidnaper—the alleged kidnaper—threatened to kill David if Sydney went to the police."

"That sure as hell is probable cause enough."

"I think we should call in the FBI."

"That's the only way of handling it now, Judge."

"I hope to God we're doing the right thing."

They walked up the road to Tuttle's forest-green cruiser. Kimball leaned through the open door after Tuttle got in. "The hell of it is, in an hour they could have stowed the boy anywhere. He could be two cottages away from here or two hundred miles. With all the hunters in cars and boats, in campers and pickups, with all the private planes and out-of-state charter jobs, it's the proverbial needle in the haystack. Where do you begin?"

"At the beginning, Judge. I'll clue you. It's never easy. Sometimes there's a break, sometimes there isn't. But we sure as hell are going to bird-dog it all the way. What was Davey wearing?"

"A red wool shirt, blue denim jeans, a brand-new pair of L. L. Bean boots."

"Come by later and fill out the APB form. I'll make the rounds locally on my own. Everybody knows Davey Briggs. Even with the influx of strangers, Judge, there's ways to check. The motel operators keep tabs on each other. The Mobil and Exxon guys are always in touch. The bush pilots, the Fish and Game wardens—" He started up the car motor. "Didn't hear any planes take off close-by last night, did you?"

"All I heard was Sydney Briggs bawling the hell out of David." He sighed and slammed the car door shut. "And that one time David yelled."

"We'll check it all out, Judge," Tuttle said. "Now take care and don't fret." His eyes avoided Kimball's. "How's Martha?"

"Doing fine. We had plans to bring her home about now, but with this messy business—well, we'll see."

"When you see her, say hi for me."

He backed up and drove off. Kimball had forgotten Junior's schoolboy crush for Martha, a dozen years ago. In those days, all of Greenville had a crush one time or another on the judge's friendly teen-age daughter. Greenville's year-round summer girl, they called her. She took their children on nature walks and camping trips and island picnics. Moosehead country had been wild and challenging then, before the mobile trailers and campers discovered it. It was still challenging and wild, but in a sinister way that gave the judge small comfort. He walked back to the cottage, a tired, lonely old man kicking cold pebbles.

CHAPTER SEVENTEEN

Sydney Briggs drove at high speed to the new airport at Bangor and locked his conspicuous Mark IV in the thick of cars in the parking lot. He arranged for the rental car, a dark green Impala, in the airport building and drove to his office in downtown Bangor. It was almost eleven-thirty. He marched past two clerks in the outer office into his secretary's cubicle and past her without a word of greeting, into his private office, shutting the door. He sat heavily, considered a drink and decided against it. He would need his wits more than booze for the next twenty-four hours.

He picked up the phone and told his secretary to hold all incoming calls. He wanted no interruptions. He hung up without waiting for her acknowledgment, unlocked the lower right hand drawer of his massive circular teak desk, and picked up his private phone. He called the managers of his vending machine branch offices in Augusta, Auburn/Lewiston, and Portland. He demanded to know from each of them how much cash they could get together and deliver to him by four o'clock that afternoon.

The Augusta manager estimated $3,000, but why the rush? The regular delivery of the receipts to Bangor was always made between eight-thirty and nine each evening. "Can't wait," Briggs said. "Change all coin to paper, twenties and fifties. Nothing over fifties, and have it here by four sharp."

The Auburn/Lewiston manager had been laid up with the flu and had the cash in the office safe since the weekend. He'd be able to bring up $8,500. "If you can hold out until next weekend, Mr. Briggs, I can make it close to fifteen . . ."

"Four o'clock," Briggs snapped and hung up and dialed Portland. The Portland man could deliver $13,000 by four o'clock. Briggs hung up and leaned back. Twenty-four five. Peanuts. He dialed the local office across the bridge in Brewer. The manager was a college drop-out, too bright, too smart-alecky for

Briggs's taste. He'd been wanting to fire him for a year now. Brewer could raise $4,000, the manager said. "Why four o'clock, Mr. Briggs? That means making the hotel-motel run before the dinner and drinking crowd."

"Just get it here by four, Alvin."

"You onto something hot? A horse, maybe?"

"Just get it here."

"C'mon, Mr. B., what's up?"

"Your job, you little jerk, if you don't shut up and do as you're told."

Twenty-eight five. He knew he could count on it. They were paid well and were extremely respectful of Sydney Briggs. Leaving a hundred seventy-one five. In a normal business week under normal circumstances, chicken feed. But by five o'clock at the Bangor House . . . ?

He knew where to lay his hands on the balance. It was dirty money, yet to be laundered, and here was the chance to get rid of it. Tempting but risky. Exposure of his past misdeeds could ruin him. He decided against it.

Andy Haskell was the answer. Vice-president and senior loan officer. A trip to the bank and a few words with Andy and a sixty-day note would do the trick. Andy Haskell was a hard-headed uptight Yankee, lately somewhat coolish. But Andy Haskell owed Sydney Briggs a few favors. This was the time to collect.

He locked away his private phone and went to a closet and blew the dust off a heavy leather sample case. He had used it in the past to carry architect renderings of his proposed shopping centers.

He stepped out to his secretary's office. Janice Hutchins stopped typing and waited for whatever would fall. Something always did when Mr. Briggs was around. He fascinated her and she was terrified of him. He was rude and abrupt and his business affairs seemed full of dark secrets. She had worked for Briggs longer than any other secretary he had had since he opened his office in Bangor. Janice would never quit the job. She was plain and shy and men had passed her by. She was thirty-three, unmarried, and worried about her future security. She was able, for the first time in her life, to put aside a large part of her salary. No firm in Bangor paid as well as Briggs Corporation. No employer had so many secretarial applications or such a heavy turnover. No boss was more difficult. Janice was never sure when her time would come. She often dreamed it had.

"I'm going to the bank, Miss Hutchins, then lunch. I'll be back about three."

"There are these phone messages, Mr. Briggs."

"Later."

"Judge Kimball called twice."

"What'd you tell him?"

"That I thought you were with him at the Moosehead cottage. Where you told me you'd be, yesterday."

"If he calls again, don't tell him I'm here."

"I hate to do that, Mr. Briggs."

"Don't hate it. Just do it."

She seemed on the verge of tears. "I don't lie very well."

"I know, Janice." He kissed her damp forehead, surprised at himself. He had never done anything like that before, except in his fantasies. She was efficient and he relied heavily on her. He almost liked her. She began to sniffle. "I have this feeling something's terribly wrong."

He stared at her with respect and wonder. "Nothing at all's wrong, Miss Hutchins. Now, the Yankee Trader branch managers will be here before you leave today, around four o'clock. If I'm not back, pour them some coffee and have them wait in my office."

She nodded and wiped her eyes with a Kleenex. "Hadn't you better freshen up, sir? Your suit's wrinkled. If you're going to the bank, I mean. And your face—"

"It's a face I'm stuck with." He managed a grin. "Hold the fort now."

"You're sure you'll be back by three?"

He paused at the door. "The bank, then lunch, then to Dakin's for a knapsack—" It slipped out. He had not meant it to.

She brightened. "Good," she said. "You can use some recreation."

Andrew Haskell was out. Not only was he out, he was off for a week of hunting in Allagash country. Briggs prodded his secretary. "Get him on the phone."

"I couldn't do that, Mr. Briggs."

"Why not, Mary?"

"Strict orders."

"Suppose the bank's robbed or blown up?"

"Mr. Richardson would get in touch with him, of course."

"Okay. Richardson'll do."

"I'll see if he's in, Mr. Briggs."

Briggs sat down, and swore under his breath. Son of a bitch better be in. Roger Richardson was a horse's ass, ten times tighter with credit than Andy Haskell. There was no love lost between Briggs and Richardson, who sat on the city school board. He had come to the Briggs home as a friend and neighbor one evening to suggest that something be done about David. One more disciplinary violation and the school principal had assured the board the boy would be expelled. Sydney Briggs believed Richardson but threw him out anyway. No one could talk about his boy like that in front of ailing Martha. And the Richardson kid, a classmate of David's, was a fawning, two-faced lap dog of a snitcher, headed like an arrow for valedictorian and Harvard. It was more than Briggs could stomach.

And here was funereal, pasty-faced Richardson himself, smirking like a deacon.

"Well, Sydney, what can we do for you?"

"Just for openers, Rog, you can call Andy Haskell."

"Not a chance, Sydney."

"It's a matter of life and death."

Richardson's smirk faded. "You're not serious, of course."

"We're wasting precious time, Rog. Where's he hunting?"

"Now see here, Sydney—"

"Life and death, Rog. You want the responsibility?"

"He's at Coburn Gore. It's a private preserve. He's the guest of our Chase Manhattan trustee—"

"I know the damned place. Bunch of out-of-state millionaire snobs. What's the number?"

They went into Richardson's private office. "There's no phone at the club, but they can get a message to him." Richardson gave him the number and Briggs placed the call. After considerable delay and a poor connection, the call went through. Haskell was two lakes away, camped out in the woods with his guide. He could not be reached and get back to the phone for at least twenty-four hours.

"That's that," Briggs said. "Sit down, Rog."

"I've a luncheon appointment. I'm already late. . . ." Richardson sat reluctantly.

"I need cash," Briggs went on.

"I'm sure it can be arranged," said Richardson, rising. "How much?"

"A hundred seventy-five thousand for sixty days. I want it now. Before you go to lunch."

Richardson sat heavily.

"You have collateral, of course?"

"My personal signature."

Richardson's lips tightened. He realized Briggs meant it. "A hundred seventy-five thousand, you say? No security. Right now."

"In twenties and fifties."

Richardson touched a buzzer. "Bring the Sydney Briggs portfolio, please." He glanced at Briggs. "Yankee Trader Vending, isn't it? And Briggs Corporation?"

"And Sydmar Land Development, Dirigo Dispensers, and just plain Sydney Briggs. Andy has 'em all."

The secretary returned in a few minutes with an armful of folders. Richardson sighed. "Cancel my noon appointment, Mary. I'll be tied up." He sat at his desk and adjusted his rimless glasses, all business now. He opened the first folder. Briggs crossed his legs and sat quite still, the only movement a nervous fluttering of his left shoe. He knew what Richardson would find. It didn't matter. All that mattered was time.

Richardson studied the contents of the last folder, removed his glasses, and rubbed his eyes. He leaned back in his big leather chair.

"I had no idea," he said.

"What's that supposed to mean?"

"The extent to which you've borrowed, Sydney. These loans alone add up to almost a quarter of a million."

"So another hundred seventy-five thousand won't hurt, right?"

"Wrong. You're seriously overextended."

"Bullshit. I'm meeting the interest payments on time. I've

never failed to meet a demand note on due date. You can check the records. And every single loan is backed by better than a hundred per cent collateral." His voice rose. "I'll pay a premium interest."

"No need of that," Richardson smiled archly. "We're not a blood bank, you know. But I don't see how Andy Haskell let you get yourself this far out on a limb."

"You're wasting precious time, Roger. I want the one seventy-five and I want it now."

"What, may I ask, is the money to be used for?"

"A personal transaction."

"Come, now, Sydney. You can do better than that."

Briggs rose and gripped the edge of the desk. He thrust his flushed face inches from Richardson's. "Roger, I told you this is a matter of life and death. Yet you've got the colossal gall to sit there and play games with me—"

"Games, Sydney?" Richardson was on his feet, as angry as Briggs. "I'm doing what any other right-minded bank officer would do. Protecting our depositors' funds. Who the hell do you think you are, walking in off the street and demanding a major loan when every resource of yours is committed for a quarter of a million dollars?" He paused and went on in a more controlled voice. "Personalities aside—I know you think I'm dirt, and my opinion of you is best left unsaid—I'm perfectly willing to take up the matter of this most unusual request with the loan committee."

"When?"

"It meets ten in the morning."

"Can you get them here after lunch today for an emergency session?"

"Hardly," Richardson said. "This is a bank, not a bridge club. We have rules, you know."

"Rules!" David's face, eyeless, flashed through Briggs's mind. "I know the rules," he said softly. He picked up the sample case and turned away. When he was at the door, Richardson said, "Shall I schedule you for the ten o'clock meeting?"

"I don't give a shit what you do," Briggs said and went out.

He needed that drink now, come what may. He walked to Main Street and turned south to a bar he rarely visited. He drank a double scotch with a beer chaser and then another. He sought desperately for an alternative. There was none. At one o'clock he stabbed out his cigarette. He walked back to the bank, past Richardson's empty office, directly to the safe-deposit department and signed in. A few minutes later he sat alone in a private cubicle with two open boxes before him.

All right, he muttered to the neatly stacked illegal dollars crammed in the boxes. After ten years, this is your day.

He withdrew all of it—twenty-five packages of a hundred twenties and twenty-five packages of a hundred fifties. He packed them into the sample case, signed out, and left the bank. At Dakin's he chose a roomy waterproof knapsack, paid for it, and put it in the trunk of the parked Impala alongside the sample case. He returned to his office at precisely three o'clock.

His secretary greeted him with the mail, the accumulated phone messages, and an uneasy smile. He closed the door to his office. During the next hour he refused a phone call from Kimball and feverishly attended to the day's routine until his first office manager arrived. The procedure was the same for all four. Briggs took the cash, signed a receipt for it, talked impatiently about unimportant business matters, and sent them home.

The total receipts came to a few dollars over $29,000. Briggs counted out $25,000, packed it in a briefcase, and locked the balance in his office safe. In the parking garage he transferred the ransom money from the two cases to the knapsack and stowed the knapsack in the trunk of the rental car. At five minutes to five he was at one of the two pay phones in the drafty vestibule outside the Bangor House lobby, sipping a scotch and soda and trying to remember if he had had lunch or not.

He could watch the Impala, not more than ten yards from where he stood drink in hand waiting for God knows what. Outside, the evening traffic was heavy and impatient. He could hear the bar TV blaring scare commercials from the other wing of the hotel.

The call came exactly at five. Briggs grabbed the phone. Just answer yes, the voice said. Yes, said Sydney Briggs. Yes, he had the full amount of the ransom; yes, in small bills, mostly fifties and twenties. Yes, it was in the knapsack. Yes, he knew the Silent Woman Restaurant, and yes, he could be there at six-thirty on the bench near the downstairs phone booth with the knapsack plainly visible on his lap, pencil and paper ready—

Click.

The Silent Woman is at the northbound exit of the Maine Turnpike, fifty-seven miles southwest of Bangor. Briggs held to the speed limit and arrived at the restaurant at six-fifteen. The phone booth was a level below the dining room, and some distance from the bar. Briggs bought a double scotch and soda and took it with him to the bench near the downstairs rest rooms.

Two stout ladies in last year's hats and lumpy tweeds sat on the bench and talked about the election. Briggs felt extremely nervous. It was the busy dinner hour. People came and went up and down the stairs. Briggs's chest hurt. He leaned against the wall alongside the bench and wondered if the kidnaper was watching him. The two ladies? Harmless refugees from a grange hall supper. But isn't that the way it's done? Alfred Hitchcock always pulled surprises like that.

He wondered what mischief Kimball had done since Briggs had left him in Greenville that morning. It seemed ages ago. Christ, he was hungry! The smell of roasting meat teased him. Outside, a police car drove by, siren wailing. My God, he thought. He held the knapsack close to his chest with both arms, balancing the drink in trembling fingers. He wished to hell the phone would ring. He wished the ladies would go. He resented the way they stared at him, their overt disapproval of the drink he held. He drained the glass of whiskey and soda, put it aside, and was reaching for his pencil when the phone rang. He went for it, clumsy because of the knapsack. One of the ladies on the bench beat him to it.

"I'm expecting that call," he said.

"So'm I, young man." And she picked up the phone. "Hello, Beulah?" she said in a positive tone. A moment later she snapped, "I'm certainly not," and hung up.

"Damn it," Briggs shouted. "What'd you hang up for?"

"It wasn't my call, mister." She triumphantly rejoined her friend on the bench. Briggs stood in front of the phone until it rang again. The woman shook a finger at him. "Now don't be all day about it."

Briggs found his voice. "Hello."

"Briggs?"

"Right." He had pad and pencil ready and his foot on the knapsack.

"Who was that answered?"

"A party waiting for a call."

"Listen carefully. Eat your dinner where you are. At eight-thirty drive to Skowhegan. Write this down: Follow the rotary to Route 201 north. Go 1.3 miles to a fork in the road. You'll see an Exxon station in the middle. Take the right fork toward East Madison. Go 8.1 miles to a stop sign. That is Route 43. Cross it. The road is mixed gravel and blacktop. Go 1.5 miles. The South Solon Meetinghouse will be on your left. Got that?"

"Got it." Scribbling madly, heart thumping.

"Time your arrival for nine o'clock. Place the knapsack behind the stone fence at the left corner of the entrance. Leave at once. Drive back to the Bangor House on Route 2. A room's reserved in your name. Wait for a phone call. If instructions are followed, you'll have your boy back by midnight tomorrow. If not—if the police are in on it, David dies."

"I'm trusting *you*, damn it—"

"You have no choice, Briggs." The phone went dead.

Briggs, swearing, picked up the knapsack and brushed past the two staring mountains of tweed. Eat, the man had said. He went upstairs bent and weary, his legs like lead.

The huge bill of fare was embellished with pen-and-ink period portraits of three British queens who had lost their heads. Ancient quotations, poetic and otherwise, surrounded their drapery in italicized tribute to prepackaged gastronomy. The surloynes? The salats? The pyes? It seemed too much for Briggs, beset by guilt feelings and a deep fear for his son's life. Wary of more drink, he ate a bloody rare slab of roast beef and buried it under an obscene wedge of Uncle Lenny's cheesecake. The heaviness amidships gave him a false but welcome sense of security. He watched the clock and wondered what David had eaten for his supper that night. The idea startled him. He had never in all his life given a thought to what the boy ate.

Passing waitresses and diners stared curiously at the puffy-faced, harassed-looking man in the dark expensive topcoat, sitting alone and mumbling, with a brand-new bulging knapsack between his legs.

CHAPTER EIGHTEEN

Tatum stepped out of the phone booth and walked briskly for a few minutes to calm himself. He checked his watch against the digital clock at the savings bank. *Two hours to kill.* Catchy title for a murder movie, he thought. Clever, clever, Tatum, though it's probably been done before.

Everything's been done before. Unsolved kidnapings. He smiled sweetly and bowed to his reflection in a bookstore window. Not that things done well before could not be done better. *The Ransom of David Briggs,* he thought. Flawless. The perfect crime. They will marvel at it, talk and write about it for generations to come.

He did a nimble jig step, quick and fancy as he walked, not missing a beat, very pleased with himself. Sit up and take notice, world. Gary Tatum's in the groove.

A good thing Briggs had come to his senses. No more of that obnoxious business tycoon arrogance. No more blustery threats. Who'd he think he was? Howard Hughes or somebody? Well, he knows better now. Attentive. Co-operative. Eager to please. *Humble.* Like he's been through obedience school. Eating out of my hand. And he better well had if he hopes to see that son of his again.

He got into his car and cruised the downtown Skowhegan rotary. He felt relaxed and supremely confident. Two stocky girls promenading in miniskirts smiled as he passed. Tatum smiled in return and they watched him over their shoulders and slowed. Tatum did not.

He crossed the bridge and followed the winding river road away from town. The lights of small factories and shops and the picture windows in a few modest cottages shimmered in the dark waters of the Kennebec. A few miles out he found a white clapboarded inn set behind a row of stately elms. He sat alone in the fine high-ceilinged dining room. Two faded murals of logging days flanked a huge fieldstone fireplace where pine and gray birch crackled behind a warped iron screen. Tatum ordered the most expensive dinner on the menu, rejected the hopeless wine list, and looked around.

A noisy party of hunters occupied a long table at the gable end of the room. They complained good-naturedly because no hard liquor was served on the premises. Their rough talk and barnyard manners offended Tatum. His occasional glares went unnoticed and he was barely able to finish his meal. He left as soon as he could, despising their lack of good manners. He over-tipped the waitress, a plump local girl whose astonishment and fervent expression of gratitude managed to restore his good humor.

He drove to a service station about to close and prevailed upon the reluctant attendant to fill his tank and check the oil. Tatum went to the phone booth and placed a long-distance collect call to his mother. He waited while the call went through, rubbing the thin dime between his fingers. He heard his mother's voice.

"From where? I never heard of such a place. Yes, yes. I'll accept. Put him on."

Her tone, familiar and ominous, spelled trouble. Tatum was tempted to hang up at once. Her words impaled him. "Gary? Are you there?"

"Here, Mums."

"And in trouble, no doubt. What is it now?"

"No trouble at all. Just missed you and thought I'd say hello to my Mums."

"How bloody good of you to remember your old mother."

"Forty-nine's not old—"

"Forty-seven, Gare—"

"And you're still the Pasadena prom queen."

That seemed to please her for the moment and Tatum pressed his luck. "I'm calling—" he began.

"—collect," she snapped. "What's become of that marvelous job you had lined up? Scenic tours, was it? Those fine friends of yours with the flying service? Haven't they a business phone? Why call me collect?"

"If I'd known you'd be upset, I'd never have bothered."

"You're damned right I'm upset." She lowered her voice. "Here I am with a houseful of simpering clubwomen planning a bloody barbecue for some ghastly charity and you know how I dote on simpering clubwomen. So get to the point, Gare. What is it this time?"

Whore-mother-cunt! "Just this, Mums. I used your telephone credit card for a few more calls here in Maine and I wanted you to know about it so you wouldn't be upset when the toll charges showed up. But you're already upset and I was only trying to make things easier for you."

"Gare, darling—"

"So I'll just hang up. Sorry to be such a bother, Mums."

"Don't you dare hang up now! I *am* upset and it's not only the damned clubwomen, believe me. There was a call this morning. A Mr. Grogan, long distance from Boston, for you, Gare, *collect*, and of course I was not about to accept any such nonsense, and you can understand now, can't you, why I'm so uptight just now about collect calls? *Well!* Mr. Grogan told the operator in a very nice voice, I thought, he'd pay for the call and talk to me. So of course, there I was, and he did seem rather *concerned*. It seems, according to this Mr. Grogan, that you were considering buying a car from him—"

"I don't recall anyone by the name of Grogan."

"He recalls you, dear boy. And described you to a T. Would the name 'Madman Mike' Grogan ring a bell?"

"Oh, *him?* Not Boston, Mums. Out on Mass Avenue in Cambridge. You threw me off, there. Yes, of course. I recall looking over a few clinkers he had on the line."

"He specifically mentioned a 1971 green Chevelle. He described it as—let me see now—an éclair?"

"A cream puff."

"Of course. How quaint. Mr. Grogan claims you wanted to try it out. For your mother, who was visiting in Salem. And he let you have it overnight. That was three days ago."

"How'd he get *your* number?"

"Dear boy, you gave him your hotel and the hotel obliged with your home address. Then you do have his—cream puff?"

"Actually—well, you see, Mums, when this opportunity showed up—"

"Do you or don't you?"

"Do I or don't I what, Mums?"

"Have the man's goddamned green Chevelle?"

"I do. Yes. But as I was explaining when you threw me off again, yes, but this opportunity, the scenic flying project—"

"What's become of the Jaguar, Gare? The rodeo grand prize."

"Oh, it's there."

"Where is there?"

"Why, in Boston, of course. You see, Mums"—he glanced desperately at the service station attendant who had honked the horn of the Chevelle and was now signaling that he had to close up—"the Jag's in the shop for a tune-up and I needed transportation when this scenic flying opportunity came along—"

"I can't understand a bloody word you're saying, Gare."

"Okay. *Okay.* Things do indeed seem a bit fouled up, but in a very short time, within twenty-four hours, I'm positive, everything will be just dandy."

"Mr. 'Madman Mike' didn't seem to think so. In fact, he mentioned notifying the police—"

"That's absolutely ridiculous!"

"—but he said you seemed so sincere and well mannered and that was why he called here first." She paused. "What's he like, Gare?"

"Like? Oh. You know the type. Cheap and loud. Padded shoulders and two-tone shoes."

"He sounds rather attractive."

"If he calls again, tell him he'll have his Chevelle by the weekend."

"*You* call him, darling. *You* tell him. Tell him I have no Aunt Agatha in Salem. I've never been to Salem, thank God! And you had better come up with a better story than the one about the Jag having a tune-up. The rodeo bunch out here aren't about to buy that Yankee twaddle. They want the Jaguar you promised them."

"They'll have it."

"And the postal money order went off this morning, air mail." She spoke sweetly off-phone to someone. Tatum nodded and gestured to the station attendant. His mother's voice floated back.

"Got to run, Gare. Watercress sandwiches. Sorry I snarled." She made kissing sounds. "Do take care."

"See you soon, Mums." His voice cracked as he spoke. *Sooner than you think,* he muttered as he hung up. *O gentle son, Upon the heat and flame of thy distemper, Sprinkle cool patience. . . .*

"That'll be four dollars, seventy cents," the attendant said. "The oil was okay."

He picked up the East Madison road skirting the east side of Lake Wesserunsett and followed the dirt road to within a hundred yards of the South Solon Meetinghouse. He backed the car well out of sight in a secluded woods road and cut the lights and motor. He sat for several minutes, listening intently. Nothing stirred. His body relaxed. He glanced at his watch. It was twenty-five minutes before nine.

Tatum had chosen this site carefully. He had visited here the summer before, while scouting the countryside. Once a closely knit farming community, South Solon, like so many rural communities, languished. Its population suffered a steady decline as the large lumber companies pushed northward and the young sought employment in the woolen mills and shipyards of other communities. As Maine grew, its highways bypassed South Solon. It had no post office. No corner store or gas station. The schoolhouse shut down and what few children remained were bussed to the Solon district school.

Summer visitors came to admire the unusual frescoes that adorned the interior walls of the meetinghouse. By Labor Day most of the summer residents had returned to their permanent homes and the meetinghouse was secured for the winter. Little else happened during the long hibernation to disturb the solitude of this near-forgotten country crossroads.

Tatum had learned about this from an amiable artist in residence at the nearby art school, who had worked on one of the frescoes that summer. The meetinghouse struck him as the ideal spot for the ransom drop.

He made his way cautiously through the woods to the stone fence bordering the broad lawns of the meetinghouse. The night air was crisp and the sky strewn with stars. Tatum stopped dead.

A huge silhouette loomed alongside the south wall of the white clapboarded structure. Its yellow paint gleamed like dark gold. Tatum sank to the ground. The thought of entrapment filled him with panic and an urge to run. He dared not move. He studied the contours of the monstrous, silent object for several minutes. It was a back hoe with a bucket rig. A large brown tarpaulin was loosely draped over the operator's seat. Inching closer, Tatum was able to separate its bulk from a sizable pyramid of earth scooped from the large opening in the ground nearby. The breath eased out of him.

A septic tank, Tatum guessed, being installed. It made sense. The time of year. The ground still soft. The absence of summer visitors. But could it not just as easily be an ambush? Police or federal agents staked out under the tarp or in that hole, lying in wait until he picked up the knapsack after Briggs deposited it?

Badly shaken, he crawled away, taking great pains to make as little sound as possible. When he had gone about fifteen yards, he paused. His breathing seemed close to sobs. *They're waiting for me,* he told himself. *Keep moving, Gary. Get clear.* . . . After a few more yards, he stopped and studied the face of his watch. In seven minutes, he reassured himself, Sydney Briggs will drive up with his car lights dimmed. He will get out and deliver the knapsack as directed and drive away. Time elapsed: thirty-one seconds.

How do I know? Because I timed the performance three times last summer. I timed and checked and double-checked each and every move to be made. Nothing has gone wrong so far. Nothing *can* go wrong. Because I meticulously planned it so that nothing can go wrong.

Pull yourself together, Tatum. . . .

He worked his way back to the edge of the woods, his confidence somewhat restored. He searched the perimeter of the meetinghouse, looking for movement. He had an affection for this place above and beyond the fact that it was about to make him rich. He had spent several hours inside the meetinghouse during his summer visits. He had chosen the same pew each time (number 43, the amiable fresco artist had informed him, originally belonging to the Nathan Jewett, Jr., family), located in the center aisle just inside the vestry door. The biblical impact of the frescoes—some rendered in refreshing contemporary techniques —affected him strangely, as though the presence of God in this house of worship sanctioned his scheme. Right now he would have welcomed a few moments of meditation in that sanctuary.

A minute before nine he observed the dimmed lights of an approaching car. Briggs? Or—? He flattened behind the stone fence and listened to the soft drum of tires on the hard gravel road, the engine's throb. The car passed his hiding place slowly and stopped at the entrance to the meetinghouse. Seconds later it started to move again and turned at the crossroads full circle, stopping once again at the entrance between the fieldstone walls.

It was Briggs, all right. Tatum had studied that head shape in the newspaper clipping enough times to recognize it at once.

Briggs doused the car lights and leaned over and opened the door on the passenger side and slid out. The motor was still running. He sidled like a shadow across the intervening space, hugging the knapsack in both arms close to his chest.

Tatum watched, transfixed. The scene filled him with a sense of *déjà vu,* eerily clairvoyant. He had witnessed it in its exactitude many times in his mind, reviewing it over and over again, checking for flaws, for oversights, for the insignificant slip that could mean ruin to his careful plotting. He had already envisioned Briggs crossing from car to stone fence, bending, propping the knapsack, glancing quickly about, as he now was doing.

It was happening before his eyes and it filled Tatum with an exhilarating sense of power tempered by an almost dreamlike disbelief that this performance could be an act of his own making. It took an effort for him to restrain an outcry of absolute ecstasy.

Briggs returned to the car and drove off. Tatum's eyes followed its course. The twin red taillights blinked on, headlights flared up. A hundred yards distant, the tires spun gravel and dust in a sudden burst of speed. *No need for that, Mr. Briggs!* Tatum thought, annoyed. But it was simple and swift and impeccably done and he could scarcely believe it had happened.

Now, Tatum!

He did not move. This, he told himself, is the precise moment the amateur, the bungler, makes his wrong move. He sees the coast clear and he is beside himself with greed. He rushes out.

He gathers in the ransom package, briefcase, bundle, whatever. He starts off. In seconds he is ringed in the blinding glare of headlights and the pleasant, cultured baritone voice of Efrem Zimbalist, Jr., somewhat distorted by the bullhorn, calls out, "This is the FBI. You are surrounded. Drop the money and raise your hands."

Tatum felt cold sweat trickle down his spine. A dog bayed, too far off to concern him, yet something in its mournful cry spelled danger. Was it a real dog or a signal to the others, waiting to pounce on him the moment he touched the knapsack?

He wiped his damp face with a sleeve, tasting twigs and dry bits of leaves and grass. He craned his neck to catch a view of the septic tank hole and once more searched the corners of the meetinghouse. *Are they there, or aren't they?*

He drew in a long, slow breath and stifled the urge to climb the low wall of stone and dash across the open lawn, snatch up the knapsack, and race to the car. Or walk slowly, casually. *A late fall visitor troubled with insomnia, revisiting an art treasure I've long admired . . . have you seen the frescoes, gentlemen?* They'd believe him, the sincere young man. . . .

He began to crawl on hands and knees in a wide circle, trying to maintain a fifty-yard radius from the spot where Briggs had left the knapsack. He stopped every few yards and listened. His progress was slow and painful. He realized, by the number of twigs snapped and the involuntary grunt of pain as a knee or finger struck stone, that if anyone was within fifty yards, his presence was already known. It took him an agonizing twenty minutes to skulk and crawl across three paths and the gravel road down which Briggs had just departed.

He was aware that what he was doing had thrown his meticulous schedule to the four winds. The palms of his hands were badly scratched and his clothing snagged and torn. Always, his eyes returned to the massive silhouette of the back hoe. My Trojan horse, he told himself, and could have wept.

Nothing stirred. His watch dial read nine twenty-seven. Soon, Eddie Michaud would be cursing him, wondering what the delay was, suspecting he had picked up the money and had run.

He wriggled along the perimeter of the lawn, close to the stone fence and out of sight of the back hoe until he reached the spot where the knapsack, like a small tired child, rested in the shadows. Tatum, prone, stretched fingers to touch it. Slowly, he pulled it toward him. He pressed the rough fabric to his cheek and closed his eyes. The silence remained unbroken. Moments later he slipped the leather buckle of the cover flap and reached in. The neatly wrapped packages of bills were a magic healing to the touch of his bruised fingers.

He closed the flap and buckled it and crawled back along the stone fence to the edge of the woods. He rose and ran the few remaining yards, gasping his relief with each step, and fell across the seat of the car, murmuring nonsense.

He drove with the knapsack at his side as comforting to stroke as a puppy. Somewhere along the road between Mayfield and Abbot Village, he swung off on a long straightaway, lost his dinner, and relieved himself. Back in the car, he flicked on his flashlight and took his time imspecting the contents of the knapsack.

Briggs had not welshed. Tatum thought fleetingly of his own father, long gone from his life. It was a blurred, unsatisfying image. He closed the knapsack and drove on, racing now to make up for lost time.

Sydney Briggs must think the world of that boy of his, coming up with all that cash and no back talk. Probably loves him. One of those real TV fathers, wise and tender. The kind who plays catch and takes his kid to ball games. The thought irritated Tatum, souring his astonishing success. He felt that Briggs had somehow cheated him, though for the life of him, he could not understand why.

CHAPTER NINETEEN

Michaud in the cabin at Depot Lake prepared for his midnight rendezvous with Tatum. He welcomed the moment of departure with near-hysterical relief. The damned kid was driving him nuts. He could not understand how anyone trussed, taped, and gagged like that could raise the kind of hell the kid did.

The morning hours had passed uneventfully. David slept fitfully under the zipped-open sleeping bag in the lower bunk. Michaud tended the fire, ate, cat-napped, and daydreamed of the first clean gulp of whiskey he would drink to celebrate his half of the ransom money. He searched through Tatum's valise for the porno magazines Tatum read but they were gone. *Son of bitch*, Michaud thought, *takes 'em with him wherever he goes.*

At noontime and once again in late afternoon, he removed the mouth tape so David could eat. Both times the boy resisted, spitting out the food Michaud fed him. David's threats and curses bedeviled Michaud. The second time, when the boy in a sudden burst of rage heaved out of his chair and overturned the table and everything on it, Michaud in frustration slapped and shook him through a spell of whimpering to sullen silence. He propped the boy roughly against the unpeeled cedar bedpost nearest the stove and tied him there, cleaned up the mess, and went out to sulk and check the plane's readiness for the night flight.

He refueled the plane from several five-gallon gasoline tanks stored on the open porch and checked out prop, lights, and controls. The performance of these chores took some of the tension out of him and he began to feel better. He stood at the lake's edge for several minutes smoking a cigarette, watching the sun disappear over the bank of deep woods behind the cabin, feeling the wind die, seeing the faint mist rise from the lake in the early twilight chill.

Damn kid, he thought. He wished sorely he could speak with the boy, to reassure him he would not be harmed in any way and would soon be free. But Tatum as usual was dead right and Michaud dared not risk the sound of his voice on David's ears.

This imposed silence in a curious way filled Michaud with feelings of guilt, as though David were a friend he had betrayed and Tatum the common enemy.

He carefully ground the cigarette underfoot until the last tiny spark was extinguished. The stillness calmed him. He searched the fading light of dusk for the evening star. When he was a kid here . . .

He breathed deeply of the crisp air. *Christ, what a way to finish out the years, the biggest back yard in the world to hunt and fish in. Doreen to cook and screw, Doreen or anyone,* he promised himself.

He went inside and covered the two small windows as Tatum had directed. He lighted the kerosene lamp and hung it from a nail in the central rafter. David was dozing where he had left him, chin on chest, long tangle of hair awry. Michaud felt a sudden affection for the boy. *My Christ, I've known the little bugger most all of his life. . . .* He rumpled the boy's hair and David jerked awake.

Michaud put a fresh strip across the boy's mouth and pressed it firmly to his cheeks. The strip covering David's eyes, which had not been touched since his capture, had worked loose where the ends were plastered to the boy's long hair. Michaud tore a fresh strip from the roll, long enough to go completely around the boy's head, making a blindfold of double thickness, and pulled it tight. *One sure way to get his hair cut,* he reasoned.

He heated the contents of a can of yellow pea soup and finished it off. When it was time to go, Michaud filled the firebox of the wood stove and banked it for slow burning. He freed David from the bedpost and lifted him to the lower bunk, checked his ankle and wrist bindings, and covered him with the sleeping bag. He looked carefully around the cabin, blew out the kerosene lamp, and left.

Tatum slowed at Greenville. North of town he turned left at Beaver Cove and followed the shore road past the darkened Briggs cottage. All was quiet. Fifteen minutes later he turned into Mathews Cove road and parked several yards from the shadowy silhouette of the Cessna. His body ached with fatigue and relief. He lugged the bulky knapsack and heaved it aloft for Eddie Michaud to see.

"Jesus," Michaud said, "I never thought you'd get here."

"Half an hour late is all, Eddie. Not bad." He allowed Michaud to grab the knapsack from his arms and heft it. "How fares our young charge?"

"That little bugger give me a hell of a time."

"You didn't talk to him or anything—?"

"Never opened my mouth, so help me God." He hugged the knapsack. "We dividing this up right here and now?"

Tatum restrained him. "That depends, Eddie." He tried to keep his voice casual.

"On what?" He surrendered the knapsack to Tatum, who set it down.

"We can divide it here and now," Tatum said, "if we don't go back for the boy."

"You mean, just leave him?"

Tatum nodded. "Easiest way out, Eddie."

"Up there at the lake, trussed like a pig for market?" Michaud shook his head and laughed, not believing. "He'd sure as hell freeze solid." The significance of Tatum's proposal began to take hold. "And if we left him there and he froze to death and they found him—" He stared into Tatum's eyes. "That'd be my ass, Gary. You got to be kidding."

"By the time they find the boy, you could be in Mexico. Or anywhere else in the world you choose to be, living off the interest on your hundred thousand, Eddie. Think about it."

"It's like—murder, Gary."

"Not really. It's the clean, smart way to wind up this caper. No loose ends. I *know*, Eddie."

"We agreed there'd be no rough stuff, no killing—"

"Absolutely right, *mon ami*. That's why we're having this little talk. I could have told you right off how it would have to end."

"You should have."

"I was afraid I'd lose you, Eddie."

"You damn well would have." Michaud shook his head stubbornly. "I don't go along with no murder."

"It's *not* murder, Eddie."

"Then what the hell is it, leaving a kid to freeze to death?"

"It's just omitting one step of the plan, Eddie, that's all."

"It's murder."

"Look, Eddie. You've got your revenge on Briggs, right? And a fortune to boot. A *fortune,* Eddie. I'd think you'd be grateful."

"Sydney Briggs can rot in hell for all I care. But I can't let a kid freeze to death, Gary. Not while I can do something about it. Jesus! I'd cut my arm off first."

Tatum was quiet for several moments. The wind sent small waves lapping against the plane's pontoons. Michaud shivered. "We better get going before that kid really freezes to death."

"There's an alternative," Tatum said.

"What's that?"

"Divide the money here, as you suggested. As soon as we're both in the clear, we can phone and tell them where to pick up the boy."

"At Depot Lake?"

"Of course."

"And once they know he's there, that's Eddie Michaud's funeral. Right?"

"Not necessarily. Anybody could have broken in and used the cabin."

"Look, Gary. You're a genius and a fast talker and maybe you could get away with it. Me? I'm just a plain dumb Canuck. They'd have the truth out of me in ten seconds. We got to go back there and get that kid out."

Tatum thought about it. When he spoke, his voice had the friendliest air and he was smiling.

"All right, Eddie. We'll do it your way. Divide the money here and you go back and bring the boy out and drop him off someplace."

"And what about you?"

"My job's done." Tatum reached for the knapsack.

"Hold it," Michaud said.

"What's the problem, Eddie? You want the boy saved? Go save him."

"Not alone, I don't. We made a deal, Gary. Fifty-fifty all the way. And we're not all the way. Not yet."

Tatum laughed. It was an unpleasant sound in the still night. "Funny, Eddie. You're a very funny fellow."

"I don't aim to be funny, Gary. I got nothing but respect for you. It was your brains got us this far and it's your brains'll get us through all the way. So why risk murder? All we got left to do now is pick up the kid, knock him out again, and drop him off someplace where they can find him."

"You can handle all that on your own, Eddie."

"What about the knockout shot? I wouldn't know the first damn thing—"

"Bring him back without giving him the shot."

"Too risky, me flying the plane and that crazy kid loose—he can really raise hell."

"He'll still be bound and gagged."

"Even so." An edge of pleading touched Michaud's voice. "C'mon, Gary. It's just this last run and we're home free. What d'you say?"

Tatum moved about, mulling it over. Michaud followed, still pleading. "I need your help there, Gary. Refueling, handling the lines, giving the kid the last shot. I swear to God."

"Okay," Tatum said, not liking it. "Okay, Eddie."

Michaud hugged him. Tatum pried himself loose. "We'll go back, Eddie. If that's the way you want it."

Michaud looked up quickly, sensing something ominous in the words. Tatum's smile was as friendly as ever. He patted Michaud's shoulder, went to the Chevelle, and locked it. He picked up the knapsack. Michaud wiped his hands on his slacks.

"We splitting the money now?"

"Later," Tatum said and started for the plane.

"Why not now?"

"You don't want the poor boy to freeze to death, do you, Eddie? Now get going."

CHAPTER TWENTY

David heard the man go, heard the plane start up, taxi away, and take off. Its motor roar throbbed and faded and with it went the last shred of hope in David's heart. He could not believe his father had gone this far. He truly believed he had been abandoned. He swore. No sound came. He wept tears that could not run. And soon he fell to helpless laughter, an inane gurgling of the mind. He thought of his father somewhere enjoying the telling of this. He pictured his mother, sad and alone in her funny-farm room. He thought of himself expelled, unwanted, unloved, adrift in time and space.

Heavy. Heavy.

He wriggled himself free of the sleeping bag and kicked it to the floor. He swung his bound body around and bumped his taped head hard against the solid corner post of the bunk. He lay still, panting, fighting panic and pain and the sure knowledge that if he did not get himself out of here, he would die.

The heat on his face told him where the wood stove stood. If he could roll himself to it and somehow burn the straps that bound his feet and wrists . . . And how long does it take fire to burn through thick leather? Through hair, skin, and flesh? Crazy, he decided, without eyes to see.

Eyes to see. First things first. He could feel the extra pressure of the double blindfold tape, pulled so tightly it was molded to the contour of his cheeks and across the bridge of his nose.

To see. At any cost.

He recalled something his mother had told him one morning that spring. About pain. She was off on a vacation trip, he thought. He did not know then she was leaving for the funny farm, that she was trying to ease the pain of parting.

When there is something painful to be done, she told him, you have a choice. You can walk away to avoid the pain and not face up to what must be done. Or you can move into the pain and endure it and move through it to whatever it is that must be done.

David asked her if that was what she was doing, running away to avoid the pain of living with his screwball crazy father. Only he did not call it "running." Or speak of his father as "screwball" and "crazy." She smiled and shook her head and said it was just the opposite. The deepest pain was where she was going, but it was best that way. It was most important for all of them that she go. And she kissed him and walked with him to the school bus.

It was a grown-up pain, he decided then. Not like a split lip or what a trapped animal endures in steel jaws. Funny he should think of it now.

To see. With no fingers free to tear at his blindness, he must find another way. A hook. A spike. A nail. Something sharp against which he could bring the blindfold and tear it free. *Somethin' just as good as somethin' better,* was the way old Mert Emery would put it.

He worked his way to the corner post and, using it for support, inched upward to his feet. His strapped muscles failed him. He crumpled to the floor, narrowly missing the wood stove. He tried again. With great effort he wriggled upward and was able to lean against the post. He rested his cheek against the rough cedar bark, sweaty, near exhaustion. He could feel the stove warmth on his back and he prayed he would not fall again. He did not believe he would have the strength enough to rise another time.

After several minutes, he worked his way in short tedious hops along the length of the bunk until his body met the wall. He rested again. It was the front wall of the cabin facing the lake. He knew because it was from this direction the sounds of the plane had come. A natural place to hang things, he reasoned. Just inside the door.

With his body close to and supported by the wall, he inched along. It was a slow and painful task. *Please, God, a nail,* he prayed. *One lousy, stinking nail, God, and I'll never use a swear word again as long as I live.* He reached the door and leaned against it, breathing hard. The wind slipped through the crack, thin and sharp as a knife blade. When he had rested, he started along the next wall, his leg muscles, his arms, his bruised head, racked with pain.

Please, God. One fucking nail.

CHAPTER TWENTY-ONE

When Junior Tuttle left, Judge Kimball straightened up the living room, emptied ashtrays, and dumped empty bottles and beer cans in the recycling box he kept in the shed. He made his bed and went into his daughter's room, where Briggs had spent the night. It looked as though a tornado had swept through it. Kimball gingerly gathered up the soiled clothing and stripped the bed. He carried the bundle into the mud room and stuffed it into the washing machine, sprinkled the load with soap powder, and started the cycle.

He went back to the bedroom and began stuffing the odds and ends of Briggs's belongings into his overnight bag. It was then he saw the pill bottle and read the label.

Nitroglycerin 0.4 mg. 1/50 gr. U.S.P.

Frowning, he checked the prescribing physician's name. Harvey Swann, M.D. Good. He went into the living room and placed a person-to-person call to the doctor in Bangor. After some difficulties getting past the barrier of secretaries, he reached the doctor.

"Harvey? Alonzo Kimball here, calling from Moosehead. Know you're straight out and I'll be brief."

"Shoot."

"Sydney Briggs was here last night and he took off in one hell of a hurry this morning and—"

"Sounds like Sydney."

"—putting his things together just now, I came across a prescription of yours."

"Sydney's?"

"Yes."

"What's the medication? Sydney has several."

"Nitroglycerin."

"Oh. Yes."

"Why'd you prescribe it, Harvey?"

"Really, Judge, with all due respect—"

"Knock it off, Harvey. How bad's Sydney's heart?"

"It's not good."

"How *bad*, Harvey?"

"He can go in ten minutes or live twenty years. Who knows? There are signs and there are statistics and there are exceptions and there are stubborn idiots like Sydney Briggs. My advice to him was, and is, to slow down and take it easy. You didn't know?"

"Not an inkling until I picked up that pill bottle five minutes ago."

"His blood pressure's always been elevated but we've been treating that and it's within reasonable limits. Trouble with Sydney, he avoids regular check-ups. Martha'd make the appointment and Sydney would fail to show. His cardiograms were okay so I never pushed him. Now, let's see, was it last June Martha was in and we recommended Dr. Millstein and the Acres?"

"Right."

"Sydney was with her, you remember, and I grabbed him long enough for the nurse to run an EKG on him. Frankly, Judge, it scared the hell out of me. Him, too, when I told him what it meant. But you know Sydney. Called me a few names, threatened me with a malpractice suit, tried to sell me some real estate, and stalked out. I don't need that, Judge, and I haven't the time to waste on nonpatients like Sydney Briggs. What I do I do for Martha's sake."

"Thanks, Harvey. I've taken a lot of your time—"

"I'm not finished, Judge. Two weeks after Martha went to the Acres, I got a call from Sydney's secretary downtown. First week in July, I remember, because I was going on vacation that weekend. Poor girl was almost hysterical. Janice. Janice Hutchins. He was in his office, she said, having a heart attack and what should she do."

"My God."

"Well, we got him to the Medical Center. It was mild but it sure got to Sydney this time. Or so I thought."

"Why the hell weren't we informed?"

"Martha was at the Acres, and Millstein and I agreed since the seizure wasn't too serious, it was best not to upset her with such a report."

"You could've notified me—"

"Sydney swore he'd throw out every pill I'd ever prescribed if I so much as mentioned a word about what had happened."

"What's the prognosis?"

"You know anything about stress, Judge?"

"Not clinically."

"It's the leading occupational hazard of high-pressure executive types like Sydney. Interesting word, stress. Do you have the time—?"

"You're the busy man, Harvey, not me."

"Engineers use the word to designate a force which, if exerted beyond a certain point, will deform the structure to which it's applied. So many pounds per square inch—more than that: disaster. Psychologically, the same with humans. Your oddball idol, Thoreau, said most men lead lives of quiet desperation. Well, he should see them today. Frustrations round the clock. At the office, at home, in traffic, in business deals, in sex, a hundred different ways. They stream through my office with words like 'uptight,' 'strung-out,' 'downers,' 'uppers,' the new language of the seventies. I haven't the time to go into the long list of complaints, Judge, the damage done, the pain inflicted, the variety of agonies endured on their way to the psychiatrist. And the family suffers—"

"Martha never had a bad day until she met Sydney Briggs."

"Let's leave the psychiatry to Millstein. I had a good talk with Sydney at the hospital. He admitted to business pressures, to a few bad deals, and some domestic problems. Said he'd been feeling tense and anxious but 'What the hell, Harvey,' he says, 'I've always been like that.' So I got tough. What about the palpitations and poor sleep and agitated nightmares? I asked him. The temper tantrums and the splitting headaches? Well! He swore I'd been bugging his bedroom. Hit the ceiling. I ended up making a deal with him. I'd say nothing to you or Martha if he'd promise to take the medication I prescribed and report regularly for a check-up."

"Did he?"

"He's kept his word. He's on a diuretic, Dyazide, for his blood pressure, and the nitroglycerin. He shouldn't be without that one."

"I'll try to reach him and see that he gets it."

"You've been in touch with Martha, of course."

"She calls often. Sounds fine."

"Millstein's delighted with her progress. Says she'll be ready to go home in a matter of a week or two."

"We're grateful for everything you've done, Harvey."

"For my first real high school crush? No need, Judge." He paused. "How's Davey doing at the Academy?"

"Fine." It was an effort. "Apologize to your switchboard for my bad manners."

"No strain. They're used to being hassled. See that your idiot son-in-law takes his pills."

Kimball switched the washed clothes to the dryer and placed another call to Briggs's office. Janice Hutchins reported no word from him. He spent the rest of the day in waiting. That night he slept poorly. Next morning, the phone rang. It was Junior Tuttle. One of his deputies had explored the road beyond the Briggs place and had discovered a green Chevelle with Massachusetts plates parked in the woods at Mathews Cove.

The car was locked. The deputy assumed it belonged to an out-of-state hunter, but routinely reported it. A check with registration records in Massachusetts traced the ownership to Grogan Motor Sales, Incorporated, in Cambridge. The president, one Michael Grogan, claimed he had loaned the car to a prospective customer for an overnight trial. The customer, whose name was Tatum, had failed to return the car at the time promised. Grogan had phoned Tatum's Boston hotel but Tatum had checked out. Junior Tuttle then obtained Grogan's permission to take possession of the car and force open the trunk. Which he did.

"Find anything?" Kimball tried to sound casual.

"Not much."

Kimball breathed easier. "You found something, though."

"A pair of fancy cowboy boots, size 9. With dogging heels."

"Okay, Sherlock. Anything else?"

"Some books. Kind of odd."

"Odd?"

"Two paperbacks and two magazines."

"Junior, for God's sake—" Like pulling teeth, he thought.

"One book was Shakespeare's *Hamlet* and the other, Dante's *Divine Comedy*."

"What about the magazines?"

"The November *Playboy* and *Penthouse*."

Kimball laughed. "Somebody's got problems."

"You better believe it," Tuttle said. "The center spread of those magazines were stuck together. Like somebody came all over them."

CHAPTER TWENTY-TWO

By late afternoon Kimball's fears were almost too much to bear. There had been no word from Sydney Briggs all day. Tuttle called again to report that the FBI had been contacted. They would get in touch with Kimball soon. And the Bangor police had located the Mark IV Continental in the airport parking lot. There was no record of Briggs having flown from Bangor on any of the airlines.

"What about the car rental people?"

"Why would he do that?" Tuttle asked, surprised.

"To avoid being followed in his car."

Tuttle groaned. The only request he had made of the Bangor police was to look for the Continental with the BRIGGS plate. He apologized to Kimball and said he would get on the Bangor wire at once and have them check it out.

Kimball sighed and hung up. It was after four o'clock. The faltering light and shadows in the gray November sky held the promise of a chilling dusk. He thought of the unusual run of mild weather his corner of the country had enjoyed so far. He hoped it would hold. For David's sake. Wherever he was. Until they found him, unharmed.

Unharmed. That was the phrase the media used in their newspapers and newscasts of abductions. A loaded word, full of implications Kimball did not care to dwell on. David was going to be all right. He was a seasoned kid who could meet pain and live with it. Kimball remembered the time when David, not yet ten, caught wasps in his fist and brought them to him, live and stinging. Didn't hurt, Gramp, he said, just tickled. Given half a break, the boy would handle himself well in almost any emergency.

Emergency. Another catch phrase. Kimball's mind instantly conjured the image of Tuttle's deputy opening the trunk of the green Chevelle. *The Inferno* and *Playboy?* Alighieri Dante and Hugh Hefner? What kind of a sick mind are we dealing with here? He could not shake the impact of those magazine centerfolds stuck together.

He put an oak knot on the dying fire, brought the phone close to the old sofa, and stretched out, dog-tired. Too much had happened too fast. Now this damnable waiting . . .

Where the hell was Sydney? What about his heart? And did he raise the ransom money? If Junior Tuttle and the Bangor police had been on the ball, they'd know where Sydney was.

He felt old and worn and badly used. Why should these problems be the concern of a retired old gentleman farmer who wants nothing more than peace and quiet and a chuckle or two in his few remaining years?

He had not eaten since yesterday's breakfast with Briggs, yet felt no hunger. He thought of past hungers on rivers and mountain trails and in the deep woods. The memories were tender but stirred no juices. He dreamily conjured images of past breakfasts, of woods camp flapjacks with fresh maple syrup, baked beans, and steamy brown bread. Nothing stirred inside him. He came face to face with his all-time favorite, thin venison steaks in sizzling butter with fried eggs over in a black iron skillet. . . .

Ah, Kimball, he mourned, drifting into sleep, you're a dried-out, used-up old fart. The creeping cannibalism of old age is on you, devouring your flesh and the earthy appetites of a lusty youth. How long since your good teeth sank into roasted meat? Or rinsed themselves in nut-brown Yankee rum? How long, you old rascal, since you came in ecstasy inside a fine loving woman? Ten years? Twenty?

Oh yes, ten and even twenty. But never between the slick pages of a porno picture book.

He came awake violently and fumbled for the phone. It had been ringing, he thought, in his deep troubled dream. It was Briggs.

"You had better get over here, Alonzo." The voice was small, beaten. Kimball could barely hear him.

"Speak up, Sydney. Where the hell are you?"

"The Bangor House. They—" He was unable to speak for several moments. "They still have Davey."

Kimball struggled to erase the vestiges of his ruined dream. "What time is it?"

"Three. A little after. I waited—"

"You left your pills here—"

"Fuck my pills! Will you listen to me? They still have Davey—! Do you hear? Midnight, they said, if I did everything they told me to. I did, Alonzo. I swear to God."

"You paid them?"

"Two hundred thousand. Last night. In cash. The cheating bastards. They said they'd let me know by midnight where to pick up the boy. I've been waiting here all day and night." His voice broke. "I can't take this. You had better get here. Fast."

Kimball envisioned the ninety-odd miles of deserted winding roads and highways from Moosehead to Bangor. "Get some rest, Sydney," he said as cheerfully as he could. "I'm on my way."

Fatigue and torn sleep racked his body. He splashed his face with icy water, dressed, tossed Briggs's overnight bag into his pickup, and headed for Bangor. He drank two cups of hot black coffee at the Golden Nugget in Guilford. An hour later in the first glint of dawn he eased down the last hill into the silent gloom of the city and parked under the marquee of the Bangor House.

He found Briggs in his room in rumpled street clothes, unshaven and foul-smelling. He was sprawled across the bed, his skin chalky, a dark purplish puffiness under his eyes. His stubbled cheeks were tear-stained, Kimball observed. Tears seemed unreal on Sydney Briggs.

Kimball unzipped the overnight bag and handed the pill bottle to Briggs, who looked rebellious for a moment and turned away.

"Harvey Swann said *now*." Kimball filled a plastic tumbler with water. Briggs shook out a pill and put it under his tongue. He clutched the tumbler until the pill dissolved, and drank some of the water. He stretched out on the bed and closed his bruised-looking eyes. Kimball was relieved to see that he was cold sober.

"Have you notified the police?"

"Except to call you I've done nothing but wait for the damned phone to ring."

"I'm going ahead with the necessary procedures," Kimball said.

"Be my guest. I'm licked."

"Two things," Kimball went on, "have highest priority." He reached for the phone.

"Like what?"

"The FBI."

Briggs watched him with a hopeless expression. "Why bother?"

"They've already been contacted. I want to bring them up-to-date."

"What the hell are you going to prove? Those bastards took the money and ran. They never meant to let Davey go." He sat up, whimpering. "Davey's dead, Alonzo. I feel it in my bones. Davey's at the bottom of Moosehead with a rock around his neck—"

Kimball grabbed him by the shoulders and shook him. Tears splashed from Briggs's cheeks. Kimball shoved him away, astonished at his own quick rage. "Pull yourself together. You smell like a polecat. Get out of those stinking clothes and into that bathroom and under a hot shower."

"Davey's dead—"

Kimball yanked the toilet kit from Briggs's bag and tossed it to him. He guided him not gently to the bathroom, sat him on the toilet seat, and began to undress him. Briggs pushed him aside. "All right, all right." He wiped his eyes. "Warm up my bottle, Da-Da. Fetch me my Doctor Dentons." His smile was piteous.

"That's better." Kimball stood in the doorway while Briggs finished undressing. "We'll find him, Sydney," he promised. "We'll get our boy back." He picked up the phone and began to dial.

Briggs had to have the last word. "Dead or alive?" he wanted to know.

They managed a few hours of sleep before the meeting later that morning with the field agent of the FBI in the federal building. They answered numerous questions and filled out several forms. Briggs made a recorded statement of his activities from the moment of the first phone call to the delivery of the ransom money at the South Solon Meetinghouse. Arrangements were made by phone with Junior Tuttle to meet the federal men in

Greenville and take them out to the Briggs cottage. Kimball and Briggs would follow later.

It was after eleven. They walked into the cold sunshine of downtown Bangor in low spirits, strangely ill-at-ease now that the matter was in official hands. Briggs in particular seemed disconsolate and sullen. Kimball reassured him that things were not as bad as they seemed. A matter of poor communications, he said, trying to believe it himself. He took Briggs's arm in a gesture of concern and affection that surprised both of them.

"A drink is what we need," Kimball said, "and a good lunch."

Briggs's double martini seemed to help his spirits. Kimball drank a bloody mary and said no to Briggs's suggestion of another round. They ordered a late breakfast of scrambled eggs, bacon, toast, and coffee. Briggs wolfed his food.

"You said there were *two* priorities, Alonzo."

"We can talk about it on the way out to the airport."

Briggs checked out of the hotel and drove with Kimball to the airport. Kimball seemed reluctant to discuss priority two. Briggs recovered his car and Kimball followed the Mark IV back to the Briggs home on upper High Street.

It was a fine old brick home, with granite lintels and sills, a fan doorway, and four tall chimneys, built in the lush days of the lumber barons. Now, with his daughter and grandson away, the sight of it filled Kimball with sadness.

A sleepy-looking houseman greeted them. Briggs dismissed him and led Kimball to the library and turned up the thermostat. "The other priority, Alonzo." His crisp business manner had returned.

"Martha."

"What about her?" The hostility was already there.

"We'll have to tell Martha about David."

"I was wondering when you'd get around to that."

"What do you think?"

Briggs did not look up.

"Sydney?"

"Sure. I think you should tell her."

"Not me, Sydney. You."

"Uh-uh."

"Why not?"

"I can't face Martha. Not the way things are." His voice rose. "You're her father. You're the one she listens to, the one she runs to—"

"You're *David's* father, Sydney, and it's David who's in trouble."

Briggs was up and had poured himself a shot of whiskey before Kimball realized what he was doing.

"Sydney—"

"Get off my back, for Chri'sake." He threw back the drink and wiped his mouth. "I'm not going down there."

"You're too upset. We'd better talk about it later."

"It won't change my mind. I know Martha. You think she's all sweetness and light? Let me tell you, old man, she's not. You want to see the real Martha? Okay. Trip on down to that fancy nut house and tell her her precious little boy's been kidnaped and maybe dead. Go on. You're the big fucking diplomat. You'll know how to handle her."

He's actually enjoying it, Kimball thought. "You're going, Sydney," he said very quietly. "Today."

"Bull *shit*," Briggs said.

That does it, Kimball thought. "Because if you don't go," he went on evenly, "I'll let the federal boys know where the ransom money came from."

Briggs went over to the bottle, changed his mind, and sat down. "How the hell do you know anything about where my money comes from?"

"I've known about those contractor kickbacks for years."

Briggs hurled his shot glass against the fireplace tiles, shattering it. "Some fine fucking father-in-law you turned out to be!"

"So you're going to see Martha," Kimball said wearily, "and you're going to tell her about David."

"How the hell do you expect me to go to Martha now? She's refused to let me visit her. Every time I've tried, she's turned me down."

"It's got to be you, Sydney. No one else." He saw Briggs's defenses crumbling. His voice softened. "If you don't go to her now when you need each other, she'll be lost to you forever." He paused. "Or is that what you want, Sydney?"

"You know damned well it isn't what I want."

"Then it's a cop-out if you don't go."

"She hates me, I swear it."

"It's all in your mind. Martha's still in love with you."

"The hell she is."

"She is, Sydney. Believe me."

"Will her shrink allow it?"

"That's what we'll find out now." He went to the phone. Briggs paced about for a few moments, then sank on the sofa. Kimball listened to the sad litany of long distance. He felt dirty. He had not wanted to tell Briggs he knew about the kickbacks but there was no other way. He watched Briggs now, sagging deeper into the down of the sofa, more pathetic than Kimball ever remembered. Whipped. The fight out of him.

CHAPTER TWENTY-THREE

Tatum was first through the cabin door, leaving Michaud to secure the plane. He carried the bulky knapsack close to his chest and set it down on the table. He swung the beam of his electric torch until it encountered David, slumped against the cedar bedpost where they had left him. His taped head was sunk down and he breathed noisily. Alarmed, Tatum went to him and lifted his chin. What he saw gave him a nasty shock. Blood oozed from the boy's raw, lacerated cheeks, but that was not what Tatum saw. Through shreds and tatters of bloody tape and flesh, David's blue eyes stared back at him.

Tatum in panic switched off the light and ran for the door as Michaud, whistling off-key, came in. Tatum shoved him back through the door and slammed it shut.

"Now what the hell—?" Michaud began.

Tatum clamped his hand across Michaud's mouth. He strove desperately to gather his wits. He pulled Michaud, now bewildered and angry, to the end of the porch. "A word, Eddie. We better, ah, have a little talk. If you don't mind."

Tatum's voice was so loaded with panic Michaud could almost smell it. "All I did was whistle—" he whispered.

"Not that, Eddie."

"The kid? Is he okay?"

"You blew it, Eddie." Tatum's mouth worked to hold his smile steady. "You really blew it."

"The hell I did. When I left here—"

"He saw my face. You hear that, you stupid fool?"

"He couldn't have. I swear, Gary—"

Tatum spit directly into Michaud's eyes. Michaud swung at him instantly. The roundhouse punch caught Tatum's ear and drove him from the porch where he struck the gas tanks and fell clumsily to the ground. Michaud wiped his eyes on his sleeve. "What the hell's got into you, man?" He pulled Tatum to his feet. "You want to take a swing at me, okay. But nobody spits on Eddie Michaud."

Tatum brushed the pine needles and dry leaves from his clothes. He looked badly frightened. "He saw me and we're as good as dead."

"How the hell could he?"

"*You* tell *me*. You were here last."

"He never saw you, Gary. You had the light in his eyes—" He frowned. "How the hell'd he get the blindfold loose?"

"It's torn to shreds. His face is a bloody mess."

"On a nail, the little bugger."

"Yes, maybe a nail."

"I better have a look."

"That'll make two of us he'll recognize."

"He won't see me. Don't worry."

"Tape his eyes again before you use the light. I'll stay here and figure something out."

"The knapsack—?"

"On the table. Hands off it, Eddie."

Michaud went inside and groped his way to David and fingered the remnants of the blindfold. David lay quietly while Michaud stretched a fresh length of tape tightly across the boy's eyes and around his head. He struck a match and lighted the kerosene lamp and adjusted the wick. He hung the lamp from a spike in the center rafter and followed the wall until he found the rusty nail, sticky with David's blood.

He soaked a cloth in water and dabbed gently at the torn flesh and wiped away the loose shreds of skin. The blood had coagulated over most of the abrasions. Several reddish welts could mean the beginnings of infection. Michaud swabbed David's neck and throat. He would have poured some water between the boy's lips, but knowing Tatum, he dared not remove the tape over his mouth. He saw that David was close to exhaustion. It took guts to do what the kid had done. He patted David's head and went out to Tatum, ignoring the knapsack, beginning to hate what it stood for.

Tatum barely glanced at him. "He see you?"

"'Tain't likely." Michaud settled on one of the gas cans. "We better get him to a doctor."

"You out of your mind?"

"The little bugger's tore hell out of his face."

"We have our own skins to worry about."

"Then let's divvy up and get going. We'll drop the kid where he can get some help."

"Oh no," Tatum said, quite recovered, his old confident self again.

"The kid's tore himself up on a rusty nail, Gary. That sure as hell means blood poison or lockjaw or Christ knows what."

"It was his own doing."

"We're not leaving him here, Gary."

"Now look, Eddie." Tatum put an arm around Michaud's shoulder. "Let's take a minute to talk it over, eh?" He walked Michaud away from the cabin as he spoke. "We've been through a lot together in just a few days, right? And it's kind of got to us, Eddie, now that we're on the homestretch. Nerves on edge, that sort of thing. Like what I just did to you. Disgusting, and I'm really and truly sorry and terribly ashamed of myself. You were perfectly justified in striking back, believe me. And I forgive you and I hope you'll forgive me." He waited for Michaud to say something. "You do forgive me, don't you, Eddie?"

"Go on," Michaud said.

"Okay, okay." The words spilled like bubbles now from Tatum's lips. "Back at the rendezvous we agreed to take the boy with us. Okay. Your suggestion, Eddie. Not a wise one, but a humane gesture at the time, Eddie, and I was proud of you. *At the time.* Us sitting there with almost a quarter million dollars and free to go—well, that's water over the dam. But now, here we are and it's a different ball game. The boy has seen my face. He knows me. He can put the finger on me no matter where I go. And if he does, Eddie, like I said, we're both of us goners. Now—"

Michaud stopped dead in his tracks. He did not like the way Tatum held his arm and was leading him. He no longer trusted Tatum. He did not know what scheme was on Tatum's mind. He was confused. He only knew one thing for sure and he said so. "Tatum, you talk slick as shit. If shit was electricity, you'd be a power plant." He shook free of Tatum's grip. "The kid goes back with us or I swear to God you walk home alone."

"Okay, *okay!* That's how the cookie crumbles. Now, Eddie, now then"—gesturing, shaken, groping for his lost confidence—"we've got this small fortune and we're not about to throw it away, right?"

"*I* sure don't aim to."

"And we don't want to hurt the boy, right?"

"*I* sure don't, Gary."

"Exactly. Now here's the plan, Eddie boy. Okay, we divide the money here. Like you wanted. We fly the boy back to Lily Bay. You drop me and the boy off at the car and you take your plane back to the hangar. At that moment, Eddie, you're home free. Paid in full. I'll take care of the boy from then on."

"How do you mean—take care?"

"Never fear." Tatum laughed lightly. "No harm will come to him. He'll still be drugged. I'll drop him off in one of those rest areas where he's sure to be picked up. A truck driver, someone like that, with one of those big trailer rigs equipped with CB, they're always stopping in those rest areas. Gentlemen of the road, they're called—"

"What happens to you?"

"I disappear in thin air." He laughed. "Nobody's catching up with Gary Tatum, worry not."

Michaud's taut face relaxed. "Begins to make sense now."

"Considering the change in circumstance, it's our best bet, Eddie."

"The kid won't be hurt or anything?"

"Not a hair. Except what he's already done to himself."

"Now it's you taking the big risk. If anything goes wrong, Gary, it'll be your ass."

"Worry not. Nobody's going to connect Gary Tatum with this caper." He watched Michaud anxiously. "And you'll be off the hook, Eddie, a rich man. A hundred thousand dollars rich."

Michaud's face broke into a grin. "Now you're talking."

Tatum punched his shoulder lightly. "Now fetch a bag from the plane. Something you can put your share of the money in. I'll give David his shot."

He watched Michaud trot down to the landing. Alone, he sank his teeth into his knuckles to keep from screaming. He pressed his forehead against the corner post and dug his fingernails into the flaky bark. *Whatever for?* he asked himself. *Why me?*

He was in the cabin calmly dividing the packets of money when Michaud returned with a canvas tote bag. He held a finger to his lips to warn Michaud that David still had ears. When the money was divided, Michaud held the canvas bag to the edge of the table and scooped the packets into it. He covered them with several layers from the pile of old newspapers near the stove. He watched Tatum give David the Nembutal hypodermic. While Tatum stuffed his share of the ransom back into the knapsack, Michaud gathered the rest of their belongings, checked carefully for loose ends, then carried two armloads out to the plane. He returned to help Tatum with the dead weight of David, locked the cabin, and prepared for take-off.

It did not go well. A whining northeast wind had come up as Michaud taxied into the narrow channel. The plane bounced over a six-inch chop, buffeted by the crosswind as it gathered speed in a torrent of flying spray. Moments before lift-off, a sudden gust caught the plane broadside. She veered to the left. Already compensating for propeller torque, Michaud held the yoke hard over. The plane rocked crazily as she raced toward the skeletal stumps that rose like ghostly antlers from the shallow bottom of the lake.

Before Michaud could regain full control, the port pontoon caught the splayed tips of the nearest stumps. They raked the thin metal like steel blades. The staccato drumming mingled with Michaud's French curses. The plane tore free. Michaud recovered his heading down the channel. The plane climbed, yawing to the left. Tatum found his voice.

"We—all right?"

"We're flying, ain't we?"

"What happened there?"

"Not a goddamn thing." He snarled his relief. "For Chri'sake, let me do the worrying."

"Sounded like we smashed something."

"Scraped a fender is all. So forget it."

He knew it could be worse than that. If the pontoon was punctured, a water landing could be dangerous and possibly fatal. There was no way to know until he landed and then it might be too late. Having a drugged and kidnaped passenger and $200,000 didn't help matters. Not if any one of a dozen patrol or rescue planes showed up to assist them.

He concentrated on the controls and instruments, correcting for trim, alert to any erractic behavior of the plane. He found smooth air at a thousand feet and a sky filled with stars. The pounding of the engine filled the blackness surrounding them. The tension eased out of Michaud's body. *What the hell*, he thought. *Another routine charter flight. With top pay. A money load.*

The plane was flying normally now and he felt much better. He felt marvelous. He leaned over so that Tatum could hear him.

"How you figure to spend your share, Gary?"

Tatum looked startled. His mind had been elsewhere. "Eh?"

"The loot." He pointed to the knapsack between Tatum's feet. "Broads? A new Jag? How you going to spread it?"

"Oh." Tatum thought for a few moments. "Travel, maybe. Europe, the Orient. Haven't given it much thought, really."

"It's Las Vegas for Doreen and me. A lifelong dream."

"Lots of luck, Eddie. From the bottom of my heart."

"You plan to keep the kid in the trunk of the Chevelle going south?"

"Who said I was going south?"

"I meant south from Moosehead. You know, Augusta and Portland."

"In the trunk. Yes."

"It's a long way. He'll be able to breathe, won't he?"

"He'll breathe all right."

"You might want to remove the mouth tape when you dump him," Eddie said. "So he can yell for help."

"Okay, Eddie. *Okay.*"

Michaud lapsed into silence. It troubled him that Tatum seemed to have no definite plan worked out. It wasn't like him to leave a single detail to chance. He seemed a million miles away. Michaud contented himself with the thought that, within a few hours, he would be free of this mess. He would make his approach to Lily Bay as close to shore as possible. If the pontoon *was* punctured and the plane began to sink, they would not be too far from shore.

He flew the plane as he had done so often on this run, in a state of near-reverie, accustomed to the familiar instrument

panel and its many dials and readings, responding automatically
to course and speed variations, lulled by the engine's rhythmic
throb.

He checked his watch. It would be forty minutes before he
would pick up the faint glow of Greenville to bear on. He had
chosen a slower air speed because of the damaged pontoon. It
was just a matter now of sweating it out until they landed.

He caught a movement in the corner of his eye. Tatum had
unsnapped his seat belt.

"Something wrong?"

"Thought I'd check on the boy," Tatum said.

Moments later, Tatum was on his knees on the seat with his
back to Michaud. He unlatched the door and was pushing David
feet first through it. The wind keened viciously through the aper-
ture.

"What the hell're you *doing?*"

"Just fly the plane, Eddie."

With each tug of Tatum's arms, the boy's limp body inched
out. Michaud's right fist grabbed Tatum's shirt collar and yanked
hard. Tatum was thrown against the cowling. The rush of wind
slammed the door against David's boots and, inches open, held
him there. Tatum struggled against Michaud's strong grip.

"Let go," he grated.

"Like hell, you crazy bastard—"

"He's got to go, Eddie!" His fingers tore at Michaud's face. His
teeth found Michaud's hand and bit deep into soft flesh. Michaud cursed and let go. He kept his grip on the yoke with his
left hand and tried to fend off Tatum's attack. Tatum drove an
elbow into Michaud's face, sending a spurt of blood from his
nose. Stunned and half-blinded, Michaud lost him. Tatum's
quick hands were over the back of the seat again, shoving
David's feet through the door.

Michaud in grievous pain pulled back on the yoke. The plane
nosed up and the stall warning indicator beeped. Michaud, gasping, pushed the yoke forward and opened the throttle wide. The
cabin shuddered as the plane recovered air speed. Michaud
released the yoke and wrestled Tatum back into his seat. The
wind slammed the door shut.

Tatum fought him with insane strength, whimpering and

clawing in the cramped space. Michaud, still strapped in, tried to control the plane's flight, fighting now for his own life as well as David's.

It was too late, throttle and yoke at the mercy of their writhing limbs. The plane lost air speed, stalled again, and dropped off on the port wing. The cabin shuddered. Seconds later, with Tatum in terror clutching and clinging to him, with David supine in dreamless drugged sleep, Michaud knew it was over.

The plane plunged in a violent spin. Tatum wailed. Michaud's prayers were choked in blood and lost in the screaming rush of wind. Loose gear flew about. The plane swept downward in a steep glide until the forest broke its fall.

The starboard wing was first to go, ripping through treetops that had known only sun, snow and rain and the nests of eagles. The flailing prop splintered and chopped small branches and boughs to a coarse spinach. The starboard pontoon went next, like a bobsled on glare ice. The port wing wrinkled and tore like tinfoil. Bough upon bough cushioned the crash. The fuselage settled gently, its wings awry like a gunned bird. In the last good act of his sorry life, Eddie Michaud turned off the fuel control and master switch.

The forest embraced them all.

PART THREE

CHAPTER TWENTY-FOUR

Morning light filtered wanly through the dense overgrowth in diffused silvery shafts to the forest floor. The moist air smelled of accident. Nothing moved. The early morning crash an hour past had frightened off what wildlife occupied this remote and forsaken place, now a tangled clearing of splintered tree trunks and boughs, the smashed plane with its tail aloft, and the three people. The ruptured woods lay in stunned silence in the presence of this alien violence.

David had dropped like a stone a few yards from the wreckage. Michaud, still strapped to his seat, half-buried in loose gear, hung over the yoke with his head awry, dead of a broken neck. Tatum, shivering in the chill dawn, sat propped against the trunk of a giant fir some distance away, the knapsack cradled in his arms.

He had been thrown clear when the first wing disintegrated. Cut and bruised, he lay in a comatose state until dawn. When his mind cleared, his first impulse was to grab up the money and run.

Run where? he asked himself, rising. It was then he learned that his right leg would not support him. The air stunk of gasoline. In panic now, he dragged himself to the torn fuselage, whimpering in fear, expecting the plane at any moment to burst into flames and explode. He retrieved Michaud's canvas tote bag and dumped its contents into his knapsack. He took a quick look at Michaud's dead face and shuddered. Crawling back, dragging the knapsack, he passed David inert and barely breathing. For all he knew, the boy was dying. Tatum did not have the stomach to find out. He regained the protection of the fir's broad trunk and collapsed, sobbing his relief.

He dabbed at his bloody face, fought off nausea, and tried to reason, forcing his mind to dwell on what must next be done. With Michaud dead, the money, all of it, was his. He had to get out of here. He knew the logical escape route lay to the west, to Canada. But where was west? And how far to the border?

Michaud would know, but Michaud was dead. The boy might know. Michaud had said the boy knew the woods like the palm of his hand. Alone, Tatum realized he would never find his way out of this godforsaken wilderness. His one chance for survival lay with the boy.

Tatum held the knapsack close while his mind worked feverishly. For another hour he lay in pain, scheming. He heard the boy groan. Muttering a prayer, he crawled to David's side.

David opened his eyes. The tape pulled and tore at his skin. He winced as it ripped hair from roots. Dazzling light and color blinded him. He brought an arm up to shield his face and felt the tenderness of his cheeks, newly cut, crusty with scabs and dried blood. The tape peeled back from his swollen lips and he opened his mouth to scream. His paralyzed jaw muscles drove needles of pain to his skull. He screamed with all his strength. What came forth was a dry, broken cackle. His slender body, so long cramped, was racked with pain as he tried to sit up. He fell back and squeezed his eyes shut. The jumbled sequence of the past few days (weeks? minutes?)—a TV screen out of sync—flashed through his mind. His father. The A-frame. The woods cabin. A plane . . . ?

He sat up, still groggy. It was there, what was left of it. And fingers had touched him, freeing the tapes and straps that blinded and bound him. Staring up, he saw green-gray boughs of cedar and impenetrable black growth. He smelled fresh pine resin and breathed the clean, familiar Maine air. A blurred face appeared mistily through his crusted eyes. Shaky fingers worked awkwardly at his ankles where the straps had chafed and blistered the skin.

He tested his fingers. They moved stiffly. He wiggled them. He massaged his wrists and rubbed away the dried matter in the corners of his eyes. Pain stabbed every move.

The blurred face came into focus. Nice-looking, bloodied—had he seen this face before? Neat smile, thought David, and a liar's eyes.

He tried to speak. The words would not come. He tried again and managed a croak.

"What happened?"

Tatum removed the last of the tapes, strands of David's hair still clinging. He coiled the straps and tossed them aside. He dragged himself to the plane and leaned against the fuselage with his hands clasped behind him so the boy would not see their trembling.

"The plane went out of control and"—he gestured—"here we are."

"Where?"

"It's a long story, David—"

"You know me?"

"You might say I saved your life."

David looked at the wreckage. "We were in *that* plane?"

"We're lucky to be alive."

"I don't remember—me in a plane—?"

"It belonged to a bush pilot named Michaud."

"Eddie Michaud? That's Eddie's plane?"

"It was."

"Where's Eddie?"

"In it." He avoided David's gaze. "Dead."

David got to his feet with some effort and moved about shakily. He had seen dead wild creatures. He had never seen a dead person. He did not care to see what Eddie Michaud looked like, dead. "Is there any water?"

"Water?" Tatum turned, favoring his injured leg. He rummaged through the plane cabin. "Doesn't seem to be any—no canteen, nothing."

David wiped his dry mouth. "There's water enough in the woods." He felt better now. He was beginning to remember things. "Who are you?"

"Name's Gary." Tatum winced. "I think my ankle's broken. Help me sit down, would you, please?"

David eased him down on the buckled pontoon. He gathered his courage and looked inside the plane. It was Eddie Michaud, all right, his face bloodied. Dead open eyes stared into David's face. David turned away. He squatted at Tatum's feet, untied the right sneaker lace, and rolled back the leg of Tatum's slacks. The ankle was badly swollen. David moved it slightly from side to side. Tatum yelled in pain.

"It's a sprain," David said, "but I don't think it's broken."

"You're no doctor—"

"I know a broken ankle when I see one. Yours ain't."

His cocksure demeanor frightened Tatum. The boy's too cool, he thought. I must keep the upper hand.

". . . and your face is cut up pretty bad," David was saying. "How's mine?"

"Not bad," Tatum said. "The tapes helped."

David crawled into the back of the plane, avoiding Michaud's body. He returned moments later with a first-aid kit. He cleaned and dressed the cuts on Tatum's face. He wrapped the damaged ankle tightly with a roll of four-inch elastic bandage, applying it at half-stretch across the instep, under the arch, and then upward around the ankle. Tatum's eyes never left the boy's deft fingers.

David fell back. "I'm pooped, man."

Tatum thanked him in a quiet, carefully controlled voice. "That makes us even, David."

He began in his easy and confident manner to tell David exactly what had happened. He had met Eddie Michaud, he said, last spring on a fishing expedition and found him to be pleasant and easygoing and an excellent guide. Eddie knew the best places to fish and they caught their daily limit of salmon. Tatum was delighted. A week ago he made arrangements by phone from Boston to hire Michaud as his deer hunting guide. Michaud chose the woods near Depot Lake where he had a camp. Tatum arrived at Michaud's hangar that Sunday. Michaud flew him to the camp at Depot Lake. Tatum noticed then that Michaud seemed preoccupied, but thought nothing of it. They passed an easy day in the woods, with Michaud scouting around for signs of deer. On Monday, they hunted during the early morning with no luck. In the afternoon, they jumped a large doe. Michaud fired twice and missed. Tatum again observed that Michaud's mind was not on his work and said so. Michaud finally admitted that he had an urgent private matter that was plaguing him. He had to attend to it at once. He told Tatum he must fly back to

Greenville. Also, the .30/40 ammunition he was using in his Krag rifle was old and he wanted to bring back a fresh box or two. It seemed strange to Tatum that an experienced guide would be that careless. But he believed Michaud and trusted him. Michaud took off after supper.

David, listening, watched Tatum's face and said nothing.

Alone in the wilderness cabin, Tatum went on, he passed the uneasy night hours reading, tending the wood stove, and dozing. He was awakened by the plane's return at midnight. He went to the landing, relieved that Michaud was back. Michaud met him on the dock. His manner had changed completely. He had been drinking. He carried a .38 pistol in his belt. He ordered Tatum to help unload his cargo.

"That was you," Tatum said. "Eddie Michaud kidnaped you and drugged you and flew you back to Depot Lake."

"I kind of remember that now," David said. "Getting slugged."

"That was Monday night. I tried to talk him out of it all day yesterday. He would not listen to me. He just got drunker and uglier, David. Believe me, it was scary."

"Why'd you put up with it?"

"He had that thirty-eight on him and the loose way he handled it, drunk and nasty and all, I didn't dare try anything."

"Where was his Krag?"

"In the plane, I suppose. I never saw it."

"We always figured Eddie as, you know, happy-go-lucky—"

"We?"

"My grandfather, mostly. Golly. Just that day, Sunday, Eddie helped him load some groceries."

"He had a grudge against your father, he said."

"Who doesn't?"

"He claimed your father cheated him out of some farm land. That's what was bugging him. Then you showed up. Kidnaping you was his revenge."

"What good'd that do him?"

"The ransom—"

"*Ransom?*"

"That was Eddie's mad scheme. And it worked. He grabbed you, phoned your father, demanded the money, and got it. All in one night."

"Eddie Michaud? I can't believe it."

"He did, and he got away with it."

"Ransom," David said. The word seemed to excite him. "Where is it?"

"I'm getting to that part." Tatum cleared his throat. "He said he'd fly me back, but if I leaked a word, he'd kill me. What could I do? Then he drugged you again—"

"It was you who stuck that needle in my arm."

"How d'you know that?"

"Eddie had rough hands. I know. I bit him."

"He had that revolver pointed at my head, David. I had to do what he said."

"Tell me about the ransom."

"Well. We took off. You were on the back seat, knocked out. About twenty minutes later I noticed Eddie pushing open the door on his side. 'What're you doing, Eddie?' I asked him. 'Getting rid of the kid,' he said. Just like that. A chill went through me. I'd gone along with his mad scheme that far. I had no choice. But this was murder. The cold-blooded murder of an innocent boy. I wasn't about to take that, believe you me. I begged Eddie to come to his senses. I swore I'd never breathe a word. David, I even offered my life for yours. It was no use. He began shoving you through the door. We struggled. In a matter of seconds, the plane was out of control." Tatum spread his hands. "And here we are by the grace of God."

"How could he open the door when the plane's flying?"

"Apparently he could. And believe you me he did. He had you halfway out before I grabbed hold of you and held on." The tempo of his words increased. "He was so drunk at take-off, he smashed into some tree trunks sticking up out of the water—"

David nodded. "Depot's full of them."

"—and maybe punctured the left pontoon. He said something then about flying at a slower air speed, so there wouldn't be so much strain. Of course that reduced the wind pressure considerably, and we were, we couldn't have been going at much above, say, sixty-five miles an hour, when he, when this—" Tatum heard the shrill sound of his rushing words and stopped. He grinned nicely. "I'm kind of charged up. It's been a hectic few days." He watched David for some sign of approval.

David seemed thoughtful. "Thanks for—saving my life."

"So we've shared a rather harrowing experience, David. The two of us together. A narrow escape we'll long remember, don't you think so?"

David was gently massaging his ankles where the straps had bound them. Tatum could not see his eyes.

"Don't you think so, David?"

"I think it's a pack of fucking lies," David said.

Tatum was badly shaken. "Why do you say that?"

"It's too crazy. A dumb guy like Eddie? No matter how much he hated my father, he'd never have the brains to cook up a one-night kidnap and ransom job like that. Somebody a lot smarter than Eddie put him up to it." He looked at Tatum. "How much was the ransom?"

"Eddie said two hundred thousand dollars."

"See?" David grinned. "A pack of lies. Eddie Michaud knows —knew goddamn well my dad'd never come up with two hundred thousand dollars. Not even for his own kid. Especially after —" He took a trembling breath. "You want to know something? My old man hates me. He hates me so much, he'd pay two hundred thousand just to get *rid* of me."

Tatum saw the possibilities. Ideas tumbled about in his mind. "You must remember, David, I was as much a prisoner of Eddie Michaud as you were. Eddie needed money badly. Told me so. Who knows what really went on in Eddie's sick mind? Sick, *sick.*" The word seemed to please him.

"You think he was lying? You think maybe my father could've paid Eddie to—do this?"

"You just said so yourself."

Tears welled in David's eyes. "It sure figures. Him putting Eddie up to it. Eddie sneaking in and grabbing me. Because Eddie couldn't have known—I mean about my being there. Someone had to tell him. That's why Eddie checked Grampa Kimball's pickup at the A&P. To make sure I was there."

"How come you weren't in school?"

"I got kicked out—that Sunday. And I guess that's when my father got his idea to have Eddie Michaud kidnap me."

"Would your grandfather have known about it?"

"God no!" He wiped his eyes. "Let's just skip it, okay?" He looked around. "Where's all that ransom money? You said—"

"In the knapsack." Tatum pointed to it. David went over and looked inside. "Golly!" He reached in. "He really did it!"

"It's all yours," Tatum said and watched David closely.

"Mine?"

"It's your father's money."

"I don't want my father's fucking money." He shoved the knapsack aside and stared at the wreckage. "Any idea where we are?"

"Somewhere between Depot Lake and Moosehead Lake, I'd say."

"You planning to take me back to my father?"

"I don't know, David. Right now, we're lost."

"If we got out of here, would you take me back to my father?"

"It would be the right thing to do."

"I'm not going back. Never."

"They're probably out looking for you right now."

"They'll never find me."

"You can't spend the rest of your life in the woods."

"Don't bet on it. Suppose *your* father had *you* kidnaped and—and wanted you dead."

"We don't know for sure it was your father who put Eddie up to it."

"He did, damn it! It couldn't've been Eddie. Eddie Michaud never had an idea of his own worth a piss in a snow bank."

"I can't believe a father'd play such a nasty trick on his son."

"You never met Sydney Briggs." He turned away from Tatum. "We better get out of here." He poked his head inside the plane, hesitated at the sight of Michaud's inert form, then climbed in. He emerged a few minutes later with a folded chart, a light woods ax, and Michaud's lined foul-weather parka.

"The nights get cold," he said. "We might need a fire. Do you have any warm gear?"

"Just what's on my back."

David covered Tatum's shoulders with the parka and spread the chart on the ground. It was a small-scale aeronautical information map of the northeast area. "Not much help," David said, "but let's see. You said you were flying for about twenty minutes at sixty-five miles an hour?"

"It's just a guesstimate."

"Well, that'd put us"—he brushed the ragged ends of his long hair from his eyes—"right smack in the middle of nowhere."

"I'm afraid I can't be of much help," Tatum said. "I just came for the hunting. But I have Eddie's Maine road map. The one he used for the ransom run. I was saving it—for evidence." He withdrew his map from an inside breast pocket.

David studied it for several moments. "I'd say we're somewhere between Baker Lake and Ross Lake." He grinned. "That's a pretty big stretch so it's a pretty safe guess. If we head east from here, we'll hit some good logging roads and get out, no matter where we are."

"How can you be so sure?"

"We'd run into the Allagash chain—here, see for yourself. Chamberlain Lake, Churchill Lake—"

"Sounds so veddy, veddy British," Tatum giggled.

"—then Eagle Lake. Hell, we can't miss, if Eddie flew straight for Moosehead."

"He was on course. I was watching him. Then everything happened so fast. . . ." Tatum was studying the map. "How far from here are those lakes?"

"Maybe twelve, fifteen miles, depending on where's 'here.' Anyway, there's all kinds of ponds and streams we can follow."

"I'll never make it on this leg. Suppose we headed west?"

"For Canada? That's a little closer. Boy! I'd head for Canada in a minute. If your leg was okay." He looked at Tatum, who was smiling strangely. "Did I say something wrong?"

"If my leg had a chance to rest, I might like Canada myself. Frankly, David, I'm going to have a hard time explaining how I got mixed up in a kidnaping."

"Heck, I'll vouch for you. You saved my life. But Canada—far out!"

"First things first, David. How do we get to a place—to rest up?"

"The first thing is find out where we really are." David went back to the plane cabin and, trying not to touch Michaud, gingerly removed the small compass from the windshield over the instrument panel. He set it on the map. "This far north in Maine, the needle's got to point four degrees west of the North Pole, to be accurate."

"Why's that?"

"The Magnetic Pole isn't the true North Pole and this needle is magnetic. A lot of people don't know things like that."

"I'm glad you do, David."

"Declination, it's called. Okay." He pointed. "There's north." He looked to the right. "We're kind of on a ridge. It's pretty high. If I got to the top of it, maybe I'd get some idea where we are."

"Go to it, David, but not too far, eh? Don't—desert me."

David started up the ridge carrying the compass and woods ax. Tatum watched him anxiously, not quite sure things were going the way he had planned. So far, so good. But could he trust the boy? Was David playing a shrewder game?

David was back sooner than Tatum expected. He was grinning widely. "You're not going to believe this, Gary. I think I know where we are!" He sat alongside Tatum, breathing hard from his climb. He jabbed at a small blue oval on the road map. "That's Desolation Pond, right? And the tiny one above it is Corner Pond. I saw two ponds from the top of the ridge, after I climbed a tree. Looks just like them. If it is, then we're over here, west of Desolation. The plane must've hit the west side of the ridge about halfway."

"Are you sure?"

"Pretty sure." David was excited. "If it *is* Desolation Pond it's maybe one mile east of here. I've *been* there. It's a nothing little place, kind of hard to get to by road. And there are trout in the pond and a game warden's cabin—"

"Game warden?" Tatum stiffened. "If you're serious about running away, David, why go to a game warden?"

"The cabin's abandoned. Nobody uses it. Heck, I was there with Grampa Kimball last spring. Not a soul showed up. It's a neat hide-out. A good stove and plenty of firewood. There's even a wall map of the area." Tatum's cool indifference dismayed him. "What I mean, Gary, it would give your leg a chance to get better."

"You said there's a road?"

"An old paper company private road. A jeep trail is all. They haven't logged there in years. Even with the jeep it was rough going in."

"Where does the road go?"

"Down to Caucomgomoc Lake. Maybe ten miles. There's a gatekeeper there. Then south to Seboomook and Northeast Carry at the top end of Moosehead."

Tatum checked the map carefully. Everything was as David said—Desolation Pond, the paper company private road, the gate, the ponds and streams.

"It seems to make sense to head for your Desolation Pond," Tatum said and shuddered slightly. "What a gloomy name for a pond!"

David grinned. "Ross Lake's real name is Chemquassabamticook, and there's Misery Gore and Slaughter Pond—" There was so much he could tell this nice young man who had saved his life.

"You're sure the cabin's abandoned?"

"We can scout around it when we get there."

"You really believe we'll make it?"

"We'll make it."

"You're an unusual young man, David Briggs." Tatum threw him a salute.

"I'm glad somebody thinks so." David clambered into the plane again and brought out more of Michaud's equipment—a crushed packet of tea bags, several small tins of beans and sardines, a pocketknife, a sleeping bag, a flashlight, Michaud's rusty tackle box, a coil of nylon line. "What about Eddie's snowshoes?"

"Forget it. We've too much to carry as it is."

David held out Michaud's rusty old Krag. "Do we want this?"

"Of course," Tatum said. "And I'll have that jackknife."

David checked the magazine. It was full. The chamber was empty. He made sure the safety was on and passed the Krag down to Tatum and tossed him the knife. "I don't see your rifle anywhere, Gary." He searched through the cabin again. "Can't find any of Eddie's new ammunition, either. Didn't you say—?"

"My rifle, David, yes. A practically brand-new .30-06 Winchester. When Eddie was trying to dump you out of the plane, I saw the rifle go out the open door. Several things slid out. My Tony Lama boots, some loose gear. Could be Eddie's box of ammo—but Eddie only *said* it was the ammo he went back for. He was lying, remember?" He waited anxiously. "You do remember, don't you?"

"That's what you said. Tough luck, losing a brand-new rifle." He saw that Tatum was fooling around with the Krag. "You want to be careful, Gary. It's loaded."

"Loaded?"

"Safety's on with five shells in the magazine." He chuckled. "All we got against an Indian attack." He was back in the plane again. "Don't see Eddie's thirty-eight either."

"Probably lost with the other stuff," Tatum said.

David rejoined Tatum and made a tight roll of the sleeping bag and stuffed the gear he had recovered from the plane into Michaud's tote bag. His exuberance had abated somewhat. After some hesitation, he held out the compass to Tatum.

"You better take it. You're older."

"You're the guide," Tatum said, "you keep it."

David, pleased, slipped the compass into a pocket. "We'd better get going," he said. "The sun's up."

Tatum started for his knapsack, limping.

"I can cut you a crutch," David said. "Won't take but a minute."

"I'll manage," Tatum said.

"I'll carry the knapsack, then," David said. "It's pretty heavy."

"I can handle it," Tatum said.

David helped him adjust the knapsack straps. He took a long look around the scene of the crash. "We should do something about Eddie," he said.

"We'll report it, once we're out of here," Tatum lied.

"I mean," David said, "if we leave him like that, the animals'll get to him."

"Eddie won't know the difference."

"I will." David put down the tote bag and climbed back inside the plane. He covered Michaud's body as well as he could, using the loose gear left in the plane. He closed both doors and wedged sticks of wood against them. "Fisher cats are the worst," he said. "They kill just for the hell of it."

He picked up the tote bag and went over to Tatum at the edge of the clearing. "You can lean on me if you want."

"I'll be okay," Tatum said.

David moved out in front and started through the woods. He glanced back once and saw that it was not going to be easy for

Tatum. "I'll take it real slow." he said. "If you can't keep up with me, just holler." He was staring at the muzzle of the rifle, pointed at him.

"I'll manage," Tatum said.

"Would you keep the rifle muzzle pointed down?"

"It's on safe, isn't it?" Tatum's voice was edgy. He lowered the rifle ever so slowly.

"Just to be sure, okay?" David checked the compass heading and pushed on. "Try to keep me in sight. I don't want to lose you."

"Thank you," Tatum said. "You're most kind."

Tatum was greatly relieved when he first spied the sliver of water glinting in the sun. For two hours they had crossed no stream and had seen no pond. A mile was much longer than he had thought, and his discontent and suspicion had grown. David seemed determined to hack their way through the roughest portion of the dense woods. Following David's slow, twisting progress in the dim light was cheerless work for Tatum, worsened by the throbbing pains that shot from his ankle upward to his groin. He stumbled several times on the uneven terrain. He called often for resting periods during which he sat in silence, the Krag closeby, regarding David with a fixed smile to mask his conviction that the boy was up to no good.

David used the light ax to clear boughs and the sinewy puckerbrush that blocked their way. He carefully circled blowdowns and the jungle of old cutting sites to make the going easier for Tatum. He never once doubted they were headed right smack for Desolation Pond.

He was wrong. The body of water Tatum had sighted turned out to be Corner Pond, just above Desolation. David's course had taken them slightly to the north. Now he led Tatum with confidence through a narrow path bounded by thickets. He pointed out a cached canoe hidden in an overhead rack, and in passing poked his finger through its ancient rotted hull. Minutes later they came into the clearing that was Desolation Pond.

It was almost a mile in length and about five hundred yards across at its middle. Its circular wooded shore revealed an even crop line overhead where deer had fed on the tender tips of cedar boughs, high as their necks could arch. A doe and two fawns were knee-deep in a reedy place at the distant end, perhaps two hundred yards from the point where Tatum and David emerged. The doe broke for the shore in lovely arcs, white tail aloft, the fawns splashing at her flying hooves. A brief snapping of brush followed, then silence.

"I could have had a shot," Tatum whispered, "if I'd known they were there."

"No need for it," David said. He pointed to four small wild ducks paddling in panic for cover. "We'll dine on roast duck tonight."

The sun at noon lay well to the south by the time they arrived at the abandoned cabin. It was much like Michaud's camp on Depot Lake, set back a few yards from the pond, built of stout cedar logs with a narrow porch fronting a warped, sagging dock. David used the ax to pry open one of its small windows and crawled inside. He slid back the wooden bolt and opened the door. Dirty-faced and bruised, beaming, he greeted Tatum with a low, sweeping bow.

"Welcome to Kidnap Cabin, sir," he said.

CHAPTER TWENTY-FIVE

Dusk.

They sat on the edge of the narrow porch facing the pond. Tatum's back rested against a cedar post, his injured leg straight out along the floor boards. David's roasted wild ducks had been gamy and tough, but Tatum knew this was no time for complaints. The swelling in his ankle under David's tight taping had subsided. He was able to hobble about without support, feeling little pain. Another twenty-four hours, he told himself, and we'll be on our way.

He had rested that afternoon while David swept the cabin and outhouse clear of mouse nests and droppings and evicted an indignant red squirrel. At four, David served up a high tea bolstered by sardines and some stale biscuit found in a covered tin. David's stalk and capture of two wild ducks, and their plucking and roasting, brought effusive praise from Tatum, though he had refused to witness the neck-wringing.

The boy's capabilities and his enthusiasm were a source of wonder and envy to Tatum, who did little to help. He enjoyed being waited on as much as David seemed to enjoy doing it. It stirred in Tatum delicious memories of childhood indulgences and services.

David's eagerness to serve also reminded Tatum of his own good intentions as a child. He too had loved to please. *That angel boy, Gary,* the neighbors would say, lauding his golden deed for the day. His mother would simper and trill silly nothings, fluttering her eyelashes and swearing softly as she carted him away. Once out of hearing, her comments were scathing. Gary must cease at once his silly courtesies to people beneath them. The neighbors were cheap common trash. Tatum obeyed. He no longer remembered how often or why. It was too many years ago when, having no father, loving one's mother was all that mattered. What mattered most now was David.

If he meant what he said about hating his father and running off to Canada, it fitted Tatum's plan to a T. But he must not take chances. He had come this far. He would go all the way, his triumph sweeter without Michaud to share it or David Briggs to remember it.

Canada, yes. He had studied the large-scale wall map. He would cross the Baker Branch of the St. John, reach the border at night, and follow the back roads to St.-Camile-de-Bellechasse. And David Briggs would take him there.

David had covered himself with Michaud's parka against the evening chill. It was November. The black flies and no-see-ums were long gone. The wind had died. The still pond mirrored the last faint flush of light. He had a reverence for small wilderness trout ponds. They bring a man as close to God, Grampa Kimball once said, as he will ever get. He had spent many evenings like this, more times in his fourteen years than most men spend in a lifetime.

The hike through the woods from the scene of the crash had exercised his cramped body muscles and restored circulation. His face and body itched where scabs had formed. He welcomed this quick healing and tried not to scratch. He was in a happy frame of mind, caught up in the excitement of an unexpected adventure. His only fear was that Gary might decide not to take him along, wherever he was going.

He stole a sidelong glance at Tatum, who was drumming his fingers on his raised knee.

"Where you from, Gary?"

"Out west."

"Going back there?"

"Someday."

"You married?"

"No."

"Engaged or anything like that?"

"Why all the questions?"

"Just wondering. Like if you had a family or something, you might have to go back there."

"I'm my own man. I go where I please."

"I saw the way you were studying that map on the wall. If you wanted to go, you know, to Quebec, I'd guide you. Then we could head west, huh?"

Tatum smiled, relaxed now. There was no believing the boy. "What do you charge for guiding?"

"For rich sports, fifty bucks a day. For my buddies, it's free."

"Are you a registered Maine Guide?"

"I could be if I wasn't underage."

"Are you a Junior Guide?"

"That's for faggots."

"Where do you pick up all these nasty words, David?"

"The kids at that academy I got kicked out of. It stunk."

"It's supposed to be an excellent prep school."

"A disaster area. Especially for a new kid."

"Don't tell *me* about being the new kid," Tatum said. "I went to three private schools. I even went to a public school. In New York City. But not for long. My father was what you'd call a self-made man. He made plenty but he hated to spend it. He was gung-ho for what my mother calls 'the simple life—for simpletons.' We moved east for a spell. My father's interests, import-export, took him everywhere. Right now he's somewhere, God knows, in the Orient or the Middle East. . . ."

"Like my old man. Always off somewhere."

"Anyway, we got to New York and my mother had me enrolled in a private school. When my father got home and found out, he hit the ceiling. Public school had been good enough for him; it was good enough for his son. She was spoiling me, et cetera, et cetera. Sure enough next Monday I was enrolled in P.S. Number I-forget-what in the fifth grade. A crummy joint. First day, first recess, in a concrete play yard surrounded by high iron gates, they played a game called Red Rover, Red Rover—"

"Sure, we even played Red Rover in Bangor."

"Well, I never heard of it, not out in California, anyway. But you know, the kids line up and one kid's It, and he stands in the middle and he calls out another kid's name—Red Rover, Red Rover, let Billy come over. Or Linda. Or whoever's name was called. I remember there were a lot of Lindas. If your name was called, you tried to get past whoever was It. If you made it, okay. But if he or she touched you, then you joined up and tried to catch whoever was called next."

"I never was caught," David said.

"Just listen, will you? I hated the game. But there was this one kid, Nate something. He kind of felt sorry for me being the new kid, and he insisted I join in the fun. And I did. I hated the idea of anyone grabbing at me. I don't like being touched, especially by girls, so I thought fast and I figured out how to beat the game. You remember, the last one left after everyone's caught, wins the game? So after a few kids were caught, my name was called. I played dumb. I refused to cross over. I figured they would figure I was shy, being the new boy, and they'd call on someone else. And they did and sure enough I was the last one left. There they were, all lined up and Nate called my name. 'Oh no,' I said. 'I'm the last one left. Nobody caught me. I win the game.' They kept yelling my name, 'Red Rover, Red Rover, let Gary come over,' and I wouldn't budge. I was dead right. I'd outsmarted them and they were being poor sports about it. And I didn't want a bunch of girls grabbing at me. Or boys, either."

"It was only a game, Gary."

"I like to win, whatever it is. Anyway. This one boy, the class bully, a nasty fat brute in ugly green corduroys ten sizes too small for him, yells out at me, something like 'Look, wise guy, you come across or we're coming there to get you.' Only his language was filthier than anything I'd ever heard before. It really scared me. I wasn't about to risk life and limb with that bunch of tough, foul-mouthed idiots lined up waiting to tear me to pieces just because I was cleverer than they were and had outsmarted them at their own game. So I just turned on my heel and walked away. They grabbed me just as the bell rang. But that didn't stop them. They bloodied my nose, tore my shirt, until one of the teachers broke it up. I managed to sneak off and got to a phone booth and called my mother. She was in the principal's office in ten minutes. Well—you should see my mother in action. Furious. She wanted that fat boy arrested. She was going to sue the principal, the school, the boy's family, the city of New York, the mayor—" He broke off in a shrill convulsive laughter that startled David. "Well, I never saw the inside of that school again. Or any public school. We were back in California a month later."

"What about your father?"

"Mother left his attorneys a note. Couldn't reach him by phone."

"How old were you then?"

"Ten. A bad time to be a new kid. But I showed them, didn't I?"

"You sure did, Gary."

"Those vicious girls screaming my name, waiting to sink their claws into me. That fat idiot in his green corduroys—" He shrilled again. "My mother giving that bewildered principal a piece of her mind . . . you should hear *her* tell the story. You'd split your sides laughing."

"Where'd you go after that?"

"I told you. California—"

"I mean school."

"More private schools, then a military school."

"That must've been gross."

"It was stupid and cruel. Then there were tutors, sort of, who lived in. My mother's very clever about education. She has brilliant ideas, some of them ahead of their time. And would you believe it, she never finished college herself?"

It was dark now, and David was glad of it. He did not care to see Tatum's face. Shrill laughter still rang in his ears. He shivered. "We better get inside before we freeze to death," he said.

Tatum would not allow him to use the flashlight. David freshened the fire and they sat in the darkness. He was bone-weary and wanted to sleep, but Tatum insisted on knowing more about the Academy.

"Were you suspended or expelled?"

"Both. It doesn't matter. I was ready to split, anyway."

"Tell me what happened."

"First they wanted to suspend me."

"Why?"

"I punched this kid in the nose. It was just a week or so after school began. They talked it over and they decided to give me a break so they put me on probation."

"Why'd you punch him?"

"Something he said."

"Like what?"

"It was personal."

"You can tell me."

"No way."

"I'm a student of human behavior, David. I'm deeply concerned with the interrelationships of people, children to adults, vice versa. You can tell me."

"I couldn't even tell my own grandfather. How'd you expect me to tell you?"

"For the very reason that I'm *not* your grandfather. Related to you in no way. I can be completely objective in discussing your problems."

"Bullshit."

"Let's get one thing straight, David. Right now. I detest obscenity and vulgarity of any kind. Please don't use that word again. Or anything like it."

David searched the soft firelit darkness for some expression on Tatum's face. He decided Tatum meant what he said. "This kid, Corey Latimer, said a really terrible thing, Gary. So I punched him. I'd do it again."

"What was it he said?"

"I'll have to use a couple of dirty words."

Tatum did not speak for several moments. "All right. What was it he said?"

"He told me every time you screwed a girl, you were shitting in your mother's face."

Another long silence. "How'd you happen to be discussing something like that?"

"That's all those kids ever talk about. Sex. Girls. Dope. After Lights Out, they rap in whispers half the night. They smoke pot, sniff glue, shoot horse, guzzle booze—"

"Do you do those things?"

"I tried pot once—"

"A mistake, David." He spoke sharply. "Marijuana is a dangerous drug. It leads to all kinds of bad trips."

"Come off it, Gary! That's like saying booze stunts the growth and if you play with yourself, you'll go blind! Those Academy kids know all about that. They'd try anything for kicks. Weird things with girls. Half the time I didn't even know what they were talking about."

"Did you ever—have a girl?"

"You mean like Latimer said? Hell—heck no."

"Why not?"

"You just don't know Bangor. Anyway, I'm only fourteen."

"Do you agree with what he said?"

"I punched him, didn't I? That's not agreeing."

"Your friend Latimer sounds a bit depraved." Tatum giggled in the dark. Its shrillness startled David. "And why were you expelled?"

"For having pot in our dorm room."

"You were smoking pot? You said—"

"Not me. I hate the smell of it. It stinks. My two roommates. Corey and that weirdo, Stanley Lutz from Darien, Connecticut. They were kicked out, too. Lutz brought the stuff with him. He bragged about swiping it from his father. 'Boss grass,' he called it. A package of fifty joints rolled and ready to go. He said his father'd never know the difference, there was so much of that kind of shit around their house. So the three of us were kicked out."

"You could've told the truth—"

"Nobody asked me and I wasn't about to rat on them. It didn't matter. I hated the damn place. And those weirdos! Like Lutz. Lutz was kicked out of two other prep schools. One in Switzerland. Latimer was arrested last year for stealing a car and wrecking it. His mother's Mercedes. He got off with a lousy reprimand. What a pair! They didn't dig having a square like me living with them. They were always making fun of me—the way I talked and the things I'd do—"

"What things?"

"Like I'd cut classes and split for the woods. One thing, the Academy sure has beautiful woods, a real mountain to climb, a neat trout stream except it was almost dried up when I was there in October. The first time I cut class, Latimer and Lutz went with me. But all they wanted to do was sit around and smoke pot and tell dirty stories. They said I was crazy, wanting to climb the mountain. I climbed it anyway. They never went with me again."

"What kind of dirty stories?"

"You know. The way kids talk."

"How do kids talk?"

"You were a kid once. You know how kids talk."

"I wasn't that kind of a kid."

"What kind were you?"

"Like you."

"Heck, I talk dirty. You know that."

"I mean in other ways. Decent. Did they do anything funny?"

"What do you mean?"

"In the woods. Fool around with each other—?"

"They were always fooling around."

"I mean expose themselves? That sort of thing?"

"Not with me around. They cracked wise a lot at night and horsed around. They talked about girls and what they did to girls back home and stuff like that. Latimer swore he once screwed a girl going through an automatic car wash. Two minutes flat, zip to drip." The drift of Tatum's questions began to embarrass him. "You picking my brains or something?"

"I'm interested in you, David. You remind me—my doctor said talking things out was the best way to learn about yourself—"

"Were you sick?"

"Oh no."

"Then why a doctor?"

"I had some problems."

"You mean a shrink. I know about them because that's what happened to my mother."

"What happened to your mother?"

"She couldn't take the kind of shit—sorry—my father was dishing out. So she's getting her brains unscrambled. If I go anyplace from here, that's where I'll go. The funny farm where my mother is."

"You love your mother, don't you?"

"I sure miss her. Every kid should have a mother like I have."

"Your mother ever beat you?"

"My father takes good care of that."

"So you blame him for your mother's—condition?"

"Who else? He always treats her like dirt." He was quiet for a while. The silence in the woods around them broke occasionally with the stealthy night sounds of some wild creature. On a distant pond a loon's chilling cry was answered. David stirred uneasily. "Weather's going to change," he said. Then: "You know something? Sometimes I blame myself. I tell myself it's my fault Mom and my dad don't get along."

"Why?"

"The biggest fights they have are over me. Like why I hate

school. Why I get in trouble. Why I'm not like other kids who dress up and cut their hair and stuff like that. Mom's like me. She loves the woods. So she takes my side and it drives my dad out of his skull. A kid's supposed to love his parents, one as much as the other. How can I love him? I get kicked out of school for no good reason and, without even asking why, he slaps me around." His voice broke. "And tries to get rid of me—"

He could barely stem the emotion that welled up. Tatum thought to comfort him with a friendly arm, a shoulder to lean on. He dared not. A long day, he thought tiredly.

"David." He touched the boy's shoulder gently. David jerked away.

"I'm okay," he muttered. "You make me talk too damn much."

"Take it easy," Tatum said in a strange voice. "I'll do the talking.

David wiped his eyes. "Sorry about that," he said.

"I'm twice your age, David," Tatum began, then hesitated. "I have occasional crying jags myself—"

"I didn't cry," David said quickly.

"It's nothing to be ashamed of. What I'm trying to say, David, is, there's a small boy inside all of us, who never grows up. My mother still treats me like a child. I'm all she's got, really. Sometimes I see myself as the boy I was at fourteen, comforting her. Some of the things you say and do remind me of the kind of boy I was. So I understand your feelings."

"What about *your* father?"

"I haven't seen him since my tenth birthday. That bad scene in New York."

"What happened?"

"He came to my birthday party. Brought me a present, a fantastic magic set from Dunhill. Then he just—dropped out of our lives."

"Is he dead?"

"I guess not. He's very rich. So rich he can't be reached. He just doesn't want any part of us. Which I can understand. My mother's kind of hard to take."

"In what way?"

"A spoiled army brat. Vicious and very beautiful. A general's daughter. All that stuff. Point is, I missed having a father all those years—"

"I got one you can have cheap."

"It bothers me, hearing you talk like that, David—"

"After what he's done to me?"

"We still don't know the truth of it."

"When your leg's better, I'm going with you, Gary. Please."

"Have I a choice? Without you, I'm a babe in the woods."

"I mean, wherever you're heading—where's your mother?"

"I'd rather not say."

"Why not? I spilled my guts to you."

"I'm in a bind, David. After we separate, who knows? Your father could say I was involved with Eddie Michaud. His word against mine. If you know my real name and where I'm from, they'd trace me. I'd be an innocent victim of circumstances."

"You don't have to tell me your name or anything. Just let me travel with you. Can't you do that?"

"Let me sleep on it."

"You won't be sorry, Gary, I swear. I'll do anything you say. Just take me with you."

"We'll see in the morning."

"I don't want any of that money. And I'll work hard. I'll earn my keep—"

"Money's the least of our worries," Tatum said. "Now let's get some sleep." He put wood in the stove and banked it for the night.

David climbed to the upper bunk. The cabin was silent for a time in the glow of the wood stove.

"Desolation Pond," Tatum muttered.

"What about it?"

"The name depresses me."

David half asleep thought of what it must be like to be twenty-eight and rich and free to travel wherever one pleased. He was beginning to like Gary even though he was an awful bullshitter and straight as a church deacon. The man had saved him from violent death. And hadn't he come right out and said how he admired David's knowledge of the woods and admitted his own helplessness? Praise made David feel good all over. The prospect of traveling anywhere in the world excited David. The Canadian Rockies, the Himalayas, the Amazon, the Matterhorn. Bright-colored images from his schoolbooks and sports magazines flashed through his mind. Gary had spoken of tutors. He could probably tutor David as they traveled and David could teach survival and wilderness techniques to Gary. The money was there and Gary had said he was his own man. . . .

He'd write his mother, of course, long letters from exotic corners of the world, describing the life and customs of the people. He'd write Grampa Kimball of the wildlife and the local woods lore in those out-of-way places. He'd keep a journal and make sketches. And he'd take a million pictures and bring them back and write a book. . . .

He'd come back sun-tanned and strapping strong and greet his father coolly and forgive him. He'd do these marvelous things with Gary, who had come into his life at a time, it seemed most clear to David, when each needed the other—Gary to survive and David to get away. It was the luckiest of chance meetings and David swore to himself he would do nothing to spoil it. He'd get used to Gary's eyes.

Tatum below soon slept, waking once when, turning, pain shot through his ankle. He lay awake, reviewing the latest course of events, the crash, the smooth lies that had won David's confidence. In his cunningness he had known that David, in his mind betrayed by those he loved, was ripe for hero worship.

It had been a close call, his yielding to sentimentality and nostalgia. The boy stirred poignant memories. No more of that, Gary. Boyhood's gone. Manhood's what will take you where you must go.

He was startled to hear David stirring above. The boy clambered down. Tatum tensed and gripped the rifle at his side. What was the little rascal up to?

David pattered to the stove and added two chunks of firewood and climbed back to his bunk while Tatum feigned sleep. In the silence that followed, Tatum's thoughts were disturbingly mixed. To the border, yes, as soon as the ankle could take it. But he was no longer sure of how to dispose of David. In spite of himself, he felt a kinship for the boy. The time would come soon when he no longer needed him. Killing him, he reflected, is destroying a piece of myself.

It was a troublesome thought, a torment, and he grappled with it until he slept again.

CHAPTER TWENTY-SIX

Sydney Briggs sat in the moss-green colonial reception room of the Acres, waiting to see his wife. Dr. Millstein, after a few remarks, had gone to fetch her. It was a large, pleasant room designed to relax visitors. Briggs was an exception. He had eaten hurriedly at the airport and was uncomfortable. Mostly, he dreaded the next few minutes of confrontation. He nervously paced about when he could no longer sit and stare across the autumn lawn to the slate-gray expanse of mountains and lakes.

He had come down to Portland on an afternoon flight and drove a rental car to the country place. The Acres occupied a former private estate on a hilltop overlooking three lakes about thirty-five miles northwest of Portland. A dense wooded tract surrounded carefully tended lawns with an impressive view of the Presidential Range in New Hampshire. Briggs had been here once before—that spring morning when he had driven down from Bangor with Martha wan and dejected between him and her father.

The conversation during that sorrowful drive had been understandably strained, marked by Kimball's painful efforts to keep it cheerful and alive. There was little the Briggses had to say to each other at that low state of their relationship. The journey was interrupted only once when Martha, emerging quite suddenly from a reverie, announced that she wanted an ice cream cone—pistachio, please—from the Howard Johnson's on the turnpike strip near Auburn. And would they join her? It seemed an obscene indulgence to Briggs at the time, the three of them among the tourists in bright sunshine, licking away at the melting cream in awkward silence. Their farewells at the Acres were hasty and for Briggs surprisingly emotional. He had tried, but had not seen her since.

Millstein was a bony, balding man in his thirties, mustached and long-haired. He held the door for Martha Briggs. She came

directly to her husband and her lips brushed his cheek. Briggs
was surprised to see how fit she looked, her color good and her
movements lithe. Only her eyes were red-rimmed and sad. "Sydney," was all she said, and sat.

"I've told Martha about David," Millstein said without pream-
ble. "It seemed best and she's taken it quite well."

Briggs felt cheated. During the flight south, he had carefully
rehearsed the steps of breaking the news to Martha. Now this
meddling doctor had usurped that privilege. And had the nerve
to call her Martha . . .

"You must have gone through hell, Syd," she was saying.

"Just doing what had to be done. It's a stalemate now, and still
no word of David." He stared at Millstein, clearly hostile. "Do
you suppose I can speak with my wife alone?"

Millstein looked at Martha for confirmation. She nodded. Millstein shrugged and rose. "I'll be in my study if you need me," he
said to Martha, but he looked at Briggs when he said it.

"Who the hell does he think he is?" Briggs snapped when they
were alone. "Who needs *him*?"

Martha sat with her hands clasped in her lap. "Everything
was going so well," she murmured, "Davey, poor darling—"

He'll be okay." Briggs spoke with a brisk confidence he did
not feel. "Alonzo's got the police and the FBI on it now. It's a
matter of time. You've been crying."

"It was quite a shock. But not a setback, Syd. Dr. Millstein
was careful, oh very careful, telling me about it." Her eyes
dimmed. "You've had no rest, Syd. You look terrible. You must
take care of yourself."

"Don't worry about me."

"But I do."

"Look," Briggs said, "when can you get out of this place?"

"Dr. Millstein thought, well, if I felt really good about it, in a
week. Maybe less. That was before—David."

"I want you with me. It's a lousy time for both of us. We
should be together." He hesitated, in trouble with the words.
"We need each other, Martha."

"I wanted you to say that, Syd. Thank you."

"I never felt any other way about us, Martha."

"How could I know? We never talked. You were always racing

off—well, never mind that. Those last few months, Syd, when I never got out of bed, just let each day run into the next? I was ready to kill myself. I thought about it many times."

"Over and done with now."

"Coming here—this place—whoever thought I'd need it? I was strong. You know, the tough Kimball fiber that licked the wilderness—?"

"Martha, for Chri'sake!" He glanced at his watch.

"Let me talk, Syd," she begged. "Please?"

"Sorry."

"Sometimes even the strongest of us needs help. You can't do everything alone. And so you reach out. I was scared. Terribly scared, Syd. I felt you didn't love me. I felt David didn't need me. I had nothing to look forward to, no one to do things for, to live for. I didn't like myself, the kind of person I had become. I hated to face each day. Hated to get up. And soon didn't. Well. That's done with. Since I've been here and helped, I've been able to look back at all that and understand it."

He went to her and put an arm around her. "Everything's going to be all right." He tried clumsily to kiss her. She stiffened and he moved away. "Now what the hell's the matter with that?" He sat heavily.

"Please, Sydney. Nothing's the matter with it. I want you to kiss me. And all that. But not yet. Not for a while." She went to him, touched his hair, his cheek. "Now for God's sake, don't feel so rejected. I want to be with you. I've missed you terribly. It's just—we must go slowly."

"I shouldn't have come," he said. "Another of your old man's ideas." And added brusquely, "Okay? I've done my duty. You've heard the news about David. I'm going where I'm needed. Let the good doctor take care of you—"

"Stop it, Syd—"

"—and when he tells us you're ready to go home, we'll come and get you. Or maybe you'd rather stay here where it's nice and cozy."

He was struggling into his topcoat, tense and angry, his cheeks mottled. For a moment it seemed she would turn on her heel and go. Instead, her voice softened. "Dr. Millstein's told me I'm ready—"

"Ready for what?"

"To leave here. I'm okay."

"Okay. So you're okay."

"Yes. And I told him I want to go back with you. Today."

He stared at her, not believing. "He bought that?"

"He said it's up to us to decide."

"And what did you say to that?"

"I told him as far as I was concerned I belonged wherever you were. It's up to you, Syd."

He stood for a while unable to speak. "You really told him that?"

"I certainly did."

"And you meant it?"

"More than anything in my life, Sydney Briggs."

He slapped her rump. "Go pack your bags."

"They're packed. They were packed this morning, ten minutes after Millstein told me about David."

It made sense, Briggs decided, to drive the rental car north to Greenville rather than fly. It was about 150 miles from the Acres. To backtrack to Portland for a flight to Bangor and still face the eighty-mile drive to Greenville would be time-consuming and uncertain. The weather forecast was ominous, with a sinking barometer and a cold front moving in from Canada. Martha balked at Briggs's suggestion of a private charter. She was not yet ready for that sort of adventure.

It was early enough in the day for them to reach Greenville before dark. They bypassed the cities. Lewiston. Augusta. Waterville. Briggs drove hard, pushing past the limit, ignoring Martha's soft protests. It was an emergency, wasn't it?

Newport. Dexter. Sangerville. The countryside sped past. White clapboard towns and pointy steeples. Trees swept bare of their autumn leaves. Bright yellow school buses, reminders of David. The sense of speed was rejuvenating to Martha, exhilarating. But it was Briggs who filled her heart with joy. He spoke incessantly, rambling, laying bare the long accumulation of his pent-up feelings, his hopes and secrets and the error of his ways. He told her of the ransom, where most of the money had come

from, and how sorely that illegal cache had troubled him
through the years.

"All that dirty money sitting all those years in the safe-deposit
boxes. A cancer on my brain," Briggs said. "It's gone now. I'm a
free man."

Those were the beginning years that followed earlier failures,
he told her. Years full of self-doubting and insecurity, full of
envy of the Kimballs and awareness of his own inadequacies.
Kickbacks gave him the confidence and power he needed then.
Not an uncommon practice, he told Martha, almost pleading. It
was the modus operandi among contractors. Why should he be
the exception?

"It's done with," she told him again and again, close to him,
loving his presence and in her heart praying for the safety of
their son. "It doesn't matter."

Though she knew it would always matter.

Through Abbot Village and the main street of Monson. The
beginning of dusk and the last stretch of road to Greenville. The
air curiously warm and clammy, with thick patches of fog drap-
ing the hollows.

On the heavily wooded downhill run past the roadside rest
area two and a half miles south of Greenville, Martha, who had
been dozing, came suddenly awake with the blasting of the car
horn. Briggs, cursing, had his foot hard against the brake pedal.
Tires screeching, the car swerved and rocked crazily from side to
side. Briggs fought to control it, to avoid the disaster that faced
them.

A bull moose, huge, ambling, fearless, had chosen this moment to cross the highway. He turned at the sound of the
onrushing car and saw a wild creature that screamed against the
wind, that moved on him more swiftly than any creature he had
ever faced.

Had it been the rutting season of September, he would instantly have charged. But this was November, a calmer time, and
the rutting drive was out of him. He braced his forefeet and
lowered his monstrous head. His half-ton body tensed and met
the screeching, wailing thing head-on. The impact drove him up
and back and to his death, but not before his massive horns

crashed through the windshield, shattering it, joining carcass, car, and contents in the gathering dusk.

Kimball in the cottage at Moosehead listened to what Earle Wyman, the regional FBI agent, had to say. A federal agent in Arizona had had a long talk with Tatum's mother in Scottsdale. The remarks she made about her son were worthy of an investigation all its own.

"Here's his report," Wyman said in a dry voice. "You're a state official. Let me read you an excerpt." He thumbed through the report. "'The subject's mother met me at the door herself. I identified myself. She showed no surprise, in fact, seemed pleased. Inquired if I had come to investigate her or her son. She offered a drink (refused) and wasted no time describing her activities against the government, local, state, and federal; letters written, wires sent, speeches made. She seemed eager to establish a malcontent image, yet I could not escape the conviction it was all tongue-in-cheek, a put-on.

"'Matter of her subject son another kettle of fish. She regards him as brilliant, misunderstood, a victim of paternal abuse and abandonment. Blames society, not subject son, for his past scrapes with the law. Claims no knowledge of his whereabouts, explaining he is deeply involved in cultural and charitable pursuits world-wide.

"'Home and furnishings in $100,000 class. Subject's mother about fifty, appears younger, physically attractive, well groomed, the hyperactive type, chain talker, chain smoker. Holds valid license for possession of small arms, self-defense purpose (information volunteered). Record of subject's mother will be kept, investigated further, and added to surveillance list for federal purposes of security.'"

"Lovely people," Kimball said. "Backbone of America."

What Wyman had come to tell Kimball related to information another agent had gathered from Tatum's psychiatrist in California.

Gary Tatum, he learned, had a history of behavioral disturbance since childhood. Aside from fights and thefts, he was caught at age thirteen examining and manipulating the genital area of a girl classmate in the private school he attended. Other more serious offenses followed as he grew up. In each case, his mother's charm, money, and influence, and the boy's remorse and sincere promise to straighten out, got him off.

At nineteen, he was apprehended for beating a fifteen-year-old girl almost to death at Malibu Beach. She had fallen in love with him, boldly followed him about, and had written numerous love letters. She had come to his beach house uninvited, he claimed, had made sexual advances, and refused to leave. His defense had been aided considerably by his earnest and self-effacing demeanor, some unfavorable evidence of the girl's past sexual behavior, and the services of a notorious and expensive attorney. The cases provided a field day for West Coast reporters and photographers during an otherwise dry and listless summer. The headlines called him "Mr. Clean." In spite of that, Tatum received a suspended sentence and was placed on probation.

An APB was out for him. He was wanted in California for fraud and in Arizona for a long list of traffic violations. What mattered, Wyman said in summing up, was the psychiatrist's opinion of Tatum's present condition.

"He advises us," he told Kimball, "that Gary Tatum must be regarded as extremely dangerous. He is chronically subject to severe psychotic episodes that are unpredictable and increasingly violent. There's no telling what will touch one off, or when."

"And there's no doubt in your mind that it's this Tatum who kidnaped David?"

"None whatever." Wyman rose to go. "One other development. A Fish and Game pilot, name of Toothaker, thinks he saw a crash site through the treetops—"

"Where was this?"

"North of Baker Lake. He was returning from a routine fire patrol and spotted what looked like a tail assembly sticking up out of the woods. It was getting dark and he was low on fuel, but he knows the area and wants to go back with the chopper for another look."

"Any planes reported missing?"

"We don't know of any."

"Can the chopper get in?"

"Too dense. But he plans to hover and possibly put a man down by ladder." Wyman sighed. "The way the weather's blowing up, chances are slim."

"I know that piece of woods," Kimball said. "Once they locate the exact spot, the game warden could come in from Daaquam Gate at the border and check it out."

"That's all wilderness, isn't it?"

"Our game wardens could get in. They use heavy four-wheel-drive equipment."

"That's probably what it'll have to be. There's no telling with this switch in the weather what's going to happen."

"Get hold of the chief game warden at regional headquarters in Greenville. I've got a hunch this is it."

The phone rang. Wyman glanced warningly at Kimball and they picked up their phones together. When Kimball hung up he looked ten years older. "It doesn't rain, it pours," he said. "I better get over to the hospital in Greenville."

"Use one of the police cars," Wyman said. "You'll never get through the crowd outside without it. The line of thrill seekers stretches halfway back to town."

Chief Tuttle had been checking around as he promised Kimball he would do. Half a dozen local bush pilots flew out of the Moosehead area. Tuttle touched base with all of them. None had anything unusual to report. He swung into the packed gravel driveway of Michaud's Flying Service and drove down to the metal Quonset hangar at the lake's edge. Neither Michaud nor his Cessna 180 were in sight. He found Doreen in the cramped office. She had just slammed the phone down and reached for a cigarette. Doreen and Junior Tuttle were old friends from high school days.

"Damn that Eddie," she said.

"What's up?"

"That was a charter, Junior. Some sport calling long-distance from New Jersey. I had to turn the guy down. Second one in two days."

"Eddie drinking again?"

"Not this time. He's been good about that lately. It's just he promised to radio in from Depot so I could know his schedule and he hasn't and it makes me goddamn mad. Each time I turn down a charter it's two hundred fifty bucks a day down the drain."

"Where is he?"

"Depot Lake. Flew this sport up Monday morning. Not a word from him since."

"Maybe they haven't got their deer yet."

"'Tain't likely. Hell, Eddie could get him his deer in ten minutes. He knows every stick of those woods around Depot Lake since the day he was born."

"I could try to raise him on the police band," Tuttle said.

"I've tried. He doesn't answer his call letters."

"I'll try him. I'd like to talk to him, Doreen."

"To Eddie? Why? Something wrong?"

"Not really. It's the Briggs kid. You know, Martha's boy—?"

"Davey? Sure. What's he done now?"

"Took off somewhere. The judge brought him up to the lake, let's see, Sunday—"

"Last me and Eddie heard, he was off to some fancy prep school."

"He was, and I get the idea he fouled up again. Anyway, he's been missing since Tuesday morning. We've been making a routine check—"

"He sure hasn't been here, Junior. He used to hang around Eddie quite a bit, asking all kinds of questions. Poor little bugger never has anyone around to keep an eye on him."

"You haven't seen him?"

"No, and he's not with Eddie." She opened the worn logbook. "Eddie's got him one of those rich sports, a smart-ass he guided last summer, couldn't even take a fish off of a hook."

"When'll Eddie be back?"

"All he told me was maybe five days or until this Texas cowboy gets himself a deer."

"Cowboy?"

"You better believe it. The whole package. The hundred-dollar deerskin jacket and the fancy high-heel cowboy boots—"

Tuttle grabbed the logbook and was reading the entries. "Tatum?"

"That's the dude."

"Gary Tatum. Copley Plaza, Boston." He tossed the book on the desk. "May I use your phone, Doreen?"

"Is he bad news, Junior?"

"Could be."

She struck the table with the flat of her hand. "Leave it to my Eddie to pick the winners."

CHAPTER TWENTY-SEVEN

The next day at Desolation began in dappled sunlight. Grimy and scratched and dead to the cold night air, they slept in the bloodstained clothing they had worn in the arduous trek from the crashed plane to the game warden's cabin in the dense forest.

Tatum in the bottom bunk had pulled the rotting mattress behind his head and used the bulky knapsack for his pillow. He had slept fitfully, his mind racked with outrageous dreams. A nocturnal man, like most late sleepers he awakened slowly in the sourest of moods. This time it was to the grating sound of off-key singing. His eyes on opening met the sight of David's bruised wrist and hand, hanging over the side of the bunk inches away. He thought of twisting it suddenly to stop the awful singing. The boy's been through a lot, he told himself, and more to come. Let him be.

He lay back with his hands clasped under his head and his eyes half open. The dreams, he thought. The dangerous thoughts, the outrageous dreams. The barrel of the Krag nestled snugly between his body and his arm. *A quick swing out, aim*—David's singing in a cracked alto overhead excited him now. It was one of the popular country/rock ballads that was sweeping the country and soon would be forgotten. It surprised him that David knew the lyrics.—*fire! Deadeye Tatum.*

David Briggs. Who would believe a kidnaped boy who refused to go home? Tatum recalled O. Henry's Johnny Dorset in *The Ransom of Red Chief*, but that had been a cave in Alabama, and fiction, and the kidnapers had happily paid the boy's father $250 to take him back.

Fat chance of that.

Turning, Tatum put his arms round the ransom knapsack and closed his eyes. David's cracked voice rose shrilly. Tatum sat up. Who would *believe* it? He wished the boy dead. As he had dreamed it, planned it. As it soon would be. Right now, alive, he was worth his weight in gold. Tatum pounded his fist against the upper bunk.

"Stop that ungodly screeching!"

David's head appeared, upside down. "Aha! You're up. Boy, do you snore!"

"Your voice would wake the dead."

"How's the ankle?"

Tatum ran his fingers gingerly across his leg. "Stiff," he said.

David slid down to the floor boards, poked the fire, added a chunk of wood. He wore his socks and jockey shorts and his wool shirt. Tatum stared at him. "Aren't you freezing?"

"Heck, no." He sat on the edge of Tatum's bunk. "Did you decide about Canada? Are we going?"

"Don't rush me." Tatum stroked his tender ankle. "It calls for careful planning."

"We've got the map and a compass—" He peered outside. "The weather's changing. The earlier we go, the better."

"How do you know it's changing?"

"The loons last night. When they cry like that, it means they're heading for shelter in a protected cove." He went to the door and opened it, bent against the sharp wind. He leaned against a post and began to pee.

"That's filthy," Tatum shouted. "Cut it out."

"In midstream?" David cackled.

Tatum heaved out of the bunk and hobbled over to David and shook him roughly. "You think people like to walk around in your filth? Now stop that."

"Bug off," David warned, "or I'll squirt you."

Tatum backed off. "You're stupid and filthy, David. I'm surprised at you."

"All I'm dong is taking a leak, Gary. Golly—"

"Next time use the outhouse. That's what it's for."

David dressed and went out to the warped dock and stretched out on the narrow boards and splashed his face with icy water. What a prissy type, he thought. Bitching about a guy taking a morning leak. A million miles from nowhere. Jesse James wouldn't have batted an eye. Or Dillinger. Or Clyde or even Bonnie.

He shook the water from his hair and watched the surface of

the pond until it was still again, mirroring trees and billowy white cumulus brilliant against the honest Maine sky. His eye followed the shore of the pond where the deer had evenly cropped the tender tips of the cedar boughs. Below the browse line, not fifty yards from where he lay on the wood dock, a large trout broke the surface. He watched the widening ripples. Below him, close to the mossy piling, a yellow perch circled lazily, its olive stripes hard-edged as prison bars in sunlight.

He remembered the last time here with Grampa Kimball. They had come to ease the distress of his mother's departure. Her going was a shock to him. She had kissed him as usual when he left for school that morning. That was the time she had talked to him about pain. She was gone when the school bus brought him home that afternoon. It was the houseman's day off. Only Grampa Kimball was on hand to meet him, appointed to bear the burden of the telling. Which he did as gently as he could.

David resented the way most adults kept tragedy and hard truths from kids. In a family like theirs, it was more than a wrenching rupture. It was a betrayal.

"I'm treated like a baby around here," he had said to his grandfather.

Later they drove into Desolation on the paper company's private road. Kimball had tried with little success to cheer the boy. "We decided this way would be easiest all around. Especially for your mother."

"She could have told me. I can take it."

"She didn't want you to know she was sick, David."

"She didn't look sick to me."

"Minds become ill, just like bodies," Kimball said.

David watched the roadside for partridge signs. "Is she going to die?"

"Of course not."

"Will she be away a long time?"

"A month perhaps. We'll know more after she checks in."

"Checks in where?"

"The sanatorium."

"What's a sanatorium?"

"A place of healing."

"You told me she was okay. Everybody lies, damn it." He

wiped angrily at his tears. "Sanatorium—that's the funny farm, isn't it?"

"You might call it that." He could not repress a smile. "Where'd you hear that phrase?"

"The kids at school—they know things like that."

"It's called the Acres. She'll be fine there, David."

"Can I visit her?"

"Of course."

"When?"

"Soon."

"I just don't like being treated like a damned baby."

"You're no baby, David. We're proud of you."

"Dad isn't."

"He may not show it, but he's proud of you."

"That'll be the day." He looked ahead where a spruce partridge stood for a moment, then scurried into the brush. "I knew something was wrong."

"How did you know?"

"The way she kissed me good-by. What she said."

That time last spring at Desolation, David's mood continued sad. He worked strenuously to hide it, not wanting to spoil the holiday for his grandfather. He gathered dry brush for kindling and split wood for the cookstove. He swept and cleaned and cooked some of the meals.

Kimball had brought along the fly rods. At sundown they drifted in the light canoe over patches of water where the trout lay in the shadows, dimpling the surface in their classic rise to the evening hatch. During that twilight hour the "red spots," as Kimball called them, seemed to lose all caution in their swirling attack on the artificial flies with which Kimball and the boy matched the hatch. At dusk the action died as mysteriously as it had begun.

It would be different now, David reflected. Early morning. No rod, no flies. No hatch this late season of the year. Yet the trout were out there and he was not about to settle for yellow perch. Worms were the answer, or a few fat slugs if he could find them.

He returned to the cabin. Tatum lay on the bunk flipping the blued chamber of Michaud's Krag. Five shells lay on the mattress beside him. David went to Michaud's sorry little tackle box and fumbled about until he located a hand line, rigged with a hook and sinker. The hook was rusty but small enough for trout. David rubbed it on the stove top until the barb was needle-sharp. He started to leave. Tatum swung up to a sitting position in a single movement and aimed the rifle directly at David. "Stop right there."

David glanced at the mattress. The cartridges were gone. *Not funny.* "C'mon, Gary. That thing loaded?"

"It's loaded all right."

"You don't fool around with a loaded gun, Gary. Point it some-where else, will you?"

"Don't tell me what to do, you juvenile delinquent."

David watched him, puzzled, trying to understand what was bothering Tatum. He did not like the look he saw in Tatum's eyes. "Honest, Gary," he said, "I'm just going out there to catch us a trout or two."

"Why were you out there so long?"

"All I did was wash my face and see what was around." He felt more confident, though the muzzle had not wavered from his chest. "You got to trust me, Gary. I got you here, didn't I? I'm not running off. I'll get you to Canada. If you'll take me. Just point that thing the other way, huh?"

"Say please."

"Please."

Tatum clicked on the safety. His smile was benign. "I had a bead on you the moment you stepped outside. One false move and I'd have riddled you."

"Don't worry. I'll stay in sight. I'll dig a few worms and I'll be close to the dock and I swear to God I won't try to get away."

"No tricks," Tatum warned and lowered the Krag. He grinned slowly. "Had you scared, didn't I?"

David admitted that he had indeed been scared.

"You should have seen the big doe Eddie missed," Tatum went on. "I'd have dropped her in her tracks."

"Why didn't you?"

"It was Eddie's deer. He spotted her first, the bungler."

"I'll be close-by," David said, trying to sound casual.

"You better had be," Tatum said.

David probed the rocks close to the shore for worms and slugs.

Tatum's swift-changing moods troubled him. What had happened? Was he one of those trigger-happy freaks? He played around with the old Krag like a kid with a new toy. David began to think it would have been wiser had he left it in the plane where he found it.

It was slow going. He looked up once, startled, thinking he had heard the distant sound of a motor. He listened and did not hear it again. After twenty minutes of searching, he had gathered a meager handful of bait. He walked back to the dock, baited the hook generously, and tossed the lightly weighted hand line as far as he could. Luck was with him. In less than an hour he had caught four small red spots, quarter-pounders. He lined them up on a grassy bed on the bank.

Brook trout on a hand line with worms for bait, he thought. Grampa Kimball will never forgive me. But he'd understand.

Tatum limped down from the cabin unarmed and stood over David with a contemptuous smile.

"Kind of small, aren't they?"

"For sharks, sure. But these are brookies and just right for the skillet." He held out his hand. "I'll need the knife to gut them."

"No way."

"You can't eat 'em 'til you gut 'em, Gary."

"I'll gut them."

"You ever gut fish?"

"A million times."

"Because if you don't know how, you'll ruin what meat there is."

Tatum crouched and eyed the four sleek shapes, glistening, gasping, surely dying, with some distaste. He tossed the pocket-knife to David. "You need the practice more than I do. Just be careful where you stick that blade."

"You're a weirdo, you know?" David said and Tatum shoved him so savagely and suddenly that David, off-balance, fell to the ground. He scrambled up angrily. "What the hell's wrong with you, Gary?"

"Get going on those fish." Tatum turned and limped back to the cabin. David watched him go. He opened the long filleting blade and started on the first trout and stopped. Once more he heard sounds, voices this time, too faint to be certain. He did not hear them again.

David found a hard wedge of salt pork in one of the cabin's tin canisters. The split trout fillets sizzled in a black iron skillet on the crackling wood stove. David stood over it, spatula in hand, his face shiny with sweat and pleasure.

"You know what, Gary?"

"What?"

"This is so great."

"What's so great?"

"This trip. Super. This is my kind of life."

"Goody gumdrops."

Tatum on the edge of the sagging bunk had removed his sneaker and sock. The swelling was down, the ankle looked normal. The bruised area had changed from purple to a liverish green. Tatum massaged the area with the palms of both hands, meanwhile watching David at the cookstove.

"Smells good," he said.

"It's the salt pork." David grinned at Tatum over his shoulder. "You should taste fried trout the way my grandfather fixes it. With bacon strips. He slices up onions and makes home fries with plenty of salt and pepper. And his biscuits. You should see the *size* of the biscuits he bakes. When we go camping, he does the cooking. Even my mother—"

"Shut up!" Tatum started the sock over his toes and carefully pulled it up his leg. The sneaker followed, Tatum wincing, thinking sourly: *Mothers.*

David turned to the wood box for a chunk to keep the fire hot. His eye caught a flash of movement through the open window. Too bad, he thought. It was too good to last. "Someone's coming, Gary," he said.

Tatum had got to his feet to test his weight on the injured leg. He stared at David, then hobbled to the window, his brain whirling.

Two blobs of scarlet almost invisible through the thick growth of cedar showed briefly, disappeared, appeared again, bright in the sun. A hundred yards perhaps, and heading down the trail toward the cabin. Tatum ducked from the window and grabbed up the Krag.

"It's a man and a woman," David said. "Hunters."

"How come? How'd they get here?" Tatum was angry and badly confused.

"The paper company's road ends maybe a mile from here. They must've come that way, past the gate."

"You told me no one ever comes here!" His eyes bored into David's. "Where's this gate?"

"Three or four miles, Gary. Way back. Like I said, there's this gatekeeper who lets nobody through. Unless they get the permission of the paper company."

"Now you tell me!"

Tatum pressed himself against the wall alongside the window and peered at the approaching figures. "You filthy little sneak! You swore nobody ever comes here!"

"A couple of harmless hunters, Gary—"

"Harmless?" His grip tightened on the rifle. "I'll show 'em who's harmless."

"Look," David warned. "The last thing you want to do is point a gun at them. Just be friendly, Gary. We're hunting, too. That's all you got to say. They'll go away."

Tatum stared hard at the boy. "You lied to me, didn't you?"

"No way, Gary."

"If you did—"

"Put down the gun, Gary. They're just a couple of hunters. You've got nothing to worry about." He grinned at Tatum. "You're clever. You can handle them."

Tatum's mind reeled. *Doesn't this idiot boy understand what's up?* "Shut up," he said in a choked voice. "They're coming this way."

"Ah, come on, Gary." David removed the skillet from the wood stove. "Fish is done. Chow down."

"One wrong move," Tatum said, "and I'll blow your head off."

He could hear the voices now, calling out, the woman cheerful and shrill, the man laconic, deep-throated, native. He grabbed David by the collar. "Go out there. Get rid of them." He pulled the knapsack off the mattress and shoved it under the bunk. He remained in the shadow of the doorway and shifted the Krag in his trembling fingers.

David planted himself in the path a few yards from the cabin and waved to the approaching couple. The man was middle-aged, burly, wan-cheeked. Works in a paper mill or a shoe shop, David guessed. The man's heavy paunch rolled over the top of a wide leather belt. He wore red suspenders to hold up his thick green woolen pants. Despite the cold, his sweat ran free. Coarse hairs sprouted from his nose. He carried a heavy red and black buffalo plaid hunting coat and cradled in his arms an ancient, heavy-gauge double-barreled shotgun, muzzle downward.

"Hi, sonny. You the new game warden?" He laughed in hearty, phlegm-racked gasps.

"We smelled your fish frying," the woman said.

David like her homely, large-featured face, familiar as Saturday night beans and grange suppers. She was bundled into a padded nylon parka. A cheap reflex camera hung by a black plastic strap around her collar. The man threw his coat down and leaned the shotgun against a tree trunk. Twelve-gauge, David estimated. An old LeFevre Nitro Special or a Parker. A farmer's work piece for varmints and crows. The man stuck out his hand. "Sam Sewall, Machias," he said, "and this is my wife, Evelyn."

"Pleased to know you, sir."

Mrs. Sewall was staring at him. "Whatever happened to your face, you poor boy?"

David grinned and nodded toward the cabin. "We were just sitting down to dinner."

Tatum came out smiling, limping slightly. Empty-handed, David noted with relief. "Care to join us?"

"Well," said Mrs. Sewall with a big smile, "that's right neighborly, but we had a lunch, thank you, no more'n ten minutes ago, up the trail."

"In that case," said Tatum.

"You too," she said, staring at his face. "You boys have an accident or something?"

"Fell in a ravine," David said. "And we got to go now. The fish is getting cold."

"Sam just had to see who was in here. Didn't you, Sam?"

Sewall stuck out his big paw. "Sam Sewall, Machias," he said to Tatum.

"Glad to meet you, Mr. Machias."

Sewall looked confused. "Machias is where we come from."

"Must be you're from away." Mrs. Sewall's eyes feasted on Tatum's expensive clothes.

"Matter of fact, yes."

"Where's your car?"

"We packed in," David said.

"Seen any deer?" Sewall asked. At the same moment his wife said, "Where from?"

"A big doe," David said, "and a last year's fawn."

"Get a shot off?"

"We're after a trophy rack," Tatum said, his charm smile fixed.

"A shame, the killing of deer," Mrs. Sewall said. "And of all things, a doe. Their eyes—well, I just couldn't. But Sam here—"

"It's meat for the winter," Sewall said. "Never a hunting season without I don't get me a deer."

"Well, good luck," said Tatum and turned to go.

Sewall shook his head. "Those days are over for the likes of me." He mopped his face with a large red cotton square. "Got to slow down some." And he tapped his chest. "Can't track 'em like I used to."

"It's just the weather's been so grand, and Sam's retired from the rayon mill, so we loaded up the camper and drove on over." Mrs. Sewall fumbled with her camera.

"Course should a foolish deer get in my way," Sewall said, patting his shotgun, "I'd be obliged to touch 'er off." The laugh erupted into choking coughs.

"You have to get pretty close in, sir, don't you?" David asked. "With a shotgun?"

"Fifty yards is all, give or take a few. She's loaded with double ought, both barrels." He grinned. "That'd slow a deer some."

Mrs. Sewall had the camera in her hands. "Would you boys do us a big favor? Take our picture? The light's real good."

"Well," Tatum said with a nervous smile and a warning glance at David.

"C'mon now, Evelyn," Sewall protested. "Their dinner's gettin' cold."

"Do you mind, Mr. ah?" she said to Tatum. "Just the one?"

Tatum did not move. Something about his frozen smile set David's heart pounding.

"Be glad to," David said to Mrs. Sewall and took her camera.

"And then we'll shoot one of the two of you," Mrs. Sewall said. "A souvenir, like."

The Sewalls stood together, Sam with the shotgun in one hand, the other resting on his wife's shoulder. They faced the light and David took their picture. Mrs. Sewall set a fresh exposure.

"Now you two." They exchanged places and Mrs. Sewall said, "Say cheese." David and Tatum said cheese and Mrs. Sewall snapped their picture.

"We'll be on our way now," Sam Sewall said. He reached out for Tatum's hand. "A pleasure, Mr.—?"

"Bogert." Tatum was looking at the shotgun. "Dick Bogert. And this is Tommy."

"Any relation?" Sewall asked.

"My kid brother."

"I can see the resemblance," Mrs. Sewall said.

"I mean to *the* Bogart," Sewall said. "Humphrey Bogart."

"We spell it with an *e*. E-r-t. No relation." Tatum's fingers twitched. He put his hands behind his back.

"You'd be on easy street was you kin to Bogie. All them re-runs."

"He could pass for a movie star himself. Couldn't he, Sam?" Mrs. Sewall giggled and took a pencil from a pocket in her parka. "All I need now's an address to send you boys your picture."

"How is it," Tatum asked slowly, each word very clear, "you folks came such a long way into the woods?"

"Why," said Sam Sewall, "the campground's just up the road a piece—"

"Campground?"

"—mebbe half a mile is all. Opened to the public this summer. You must've come by it when you packed in here."

"You hear that?" Tatum looked squarely at David. "A public camping ground." He turned to the Sewalls. "Any other folks in the camping area?"

"We got the all of it to ourselves," said Sewall.

Mrs. Sewall's pencil was poised. "If you'll give me the address—"

"I've been admiring that shotgun of yours," Tatum said, "ever since I laid eyes on it."

"She's an old-timer, all right," Sewall said, patting it again.

"A family heirloom, no doubt."

"Belonged to my father when he farmed, back forty years ago. And his father before him."

"A collector's item, I'd say."

"An old LeFevre is all." He shrugged. "They don't make the LeFevre no more, that's for sure."

"I collect antique guns," Tatum said. "Mind if I have a look?"

Sewall beamed. "Be handy to know if she's worth somethin'. Not that I'm about to sell, mind you." He passed the shotgun to Tatum. "Just be careful, Mr. Bogert, eh? Safety's on, but she's loaded, both barrels."

"They always are, aren't they?" And Tatum smiled together with Mrs. Sewall.

Tatum moved off a few feet to inspect the stock and breech. He peered along the barrels, aiming to the treetops, snapping the piece to his shoulder, swinging as though tracking a target on the wing. On the last swing, he thumbed the safety forward, releasing it.

"A real beauty," he murmured and turned to Sewall, who heard the quiet click of the safety. Sewall started toward him, protesting. Tatum shot him in the stomach.

The force of the blast flung both of them backward. Sewall seemed to hang in the air for a moment, his features twisted in wonder and pain. He sagged and pitched forward heavily on his face. Mrs. Sewall screamed. A torn chunk of his pink flesh and red cloth slid greasily down her cheek. Still screaming, she darted toward her fallen husband. Tatum stopped her, the muzzle of the shotgun against her throat.

"Shut up, madam," he told her calmly, "or you are next."

The scream died in her throat. "You shot Sam," she said in a whisper. "You *shot* him."

"Into the cabin," he said. "*Now.*"

The air smelled of burnt powder. The discharge had stunned

and deafened David. Tatum had acted too suddenly for David to stop him. He looked down at the bulk of Sewall's crumpled body. He had seen one dead man before. Michaud. Yesterday. Today he saw another one, murdered before his eyes.

The load of shot at close range had torn through Sewall's middle, leaving a coarse round pattern of fabric and flesh in his back. David could not tell where the coat ended and Sewall's gore began. Gagging, he ran to Mrs. Sewall's arms. Everything inside him let go.

Tatum grabbed his shirt collar and shoved him away. "Inside, big mouth." Tatum's blue eyes were glazed and milky, his smile awry. It was a face David had never seen before.

Mrs. Sewall turned and once more tried to reach her husband's side, calling his name. It was clear from the way he fell and lay there, he was stone dead. But his mind had not yet taken in the cold hard truth of it. Tatum barred her way with the smoking gun barrel. David's stomach heaved again in raucous gasps he was helpless to control.

"Get with it," Tatum snapped and pushed him toward the door. Mrs. Sewall stumbled along behind him. Tatum limped after them, clicking the safety back on.

He ordered them to opposite corners, facing the wall. The cabin smelled strongly of fried fish. Tatum yanked the straw mattress from the top bunk and pushed it with the gun barrel to the middle of the room near the stove. A surprised mouse scrambled out of the ticking and Tatum recoiled in horror. It raced insanely along the wall, reversed course several times, and disappeared between the dry strands of the wall's loose oakum.

Tatum reached for the black plastic strap around Evelyn Sewall's neck and tore the camera free and smashed it underfoot. He yanked out the roll of film and flung it into the glowing wood stove.

"Off with your parka," he told her.

She broke from shock and began to sob. "In God's name, mister—"

"Off with it."

She started to plead with him. He shoved the gun butt into her face. Blood spurted. "Do as you're told," he said, "or I'll blow your guts to God."

Evelyn Sewall in deep pain looked to David in the other corner. His face was hidden from her. Her eyes sought Tatum's. No hope there. Very slowly, she pulled the parka over her head. Her tongue licked at the blood from her swelling nose. She eased the parka to the floor. She wore a man's gray sweater, a zippered cardigan with worn elbows, loosely tucked into the top of her woolen slacks.

"Strip," Tatum said. "Everything."

She slowly unzipped the cardigan, revealing a swell of pale heavy breasts confined in a thick worn cotton bra.

Once again her eyes beseeched him.

"Everything," he said.

"Please don't kill me."

"Get going," he said.

"I don't want to die. I'll do anything." Her voice broke. "I'm a mother—"

He struck her mouth with the back of his hand. "Stop whimpering, Mother, and take off those filthy, smelly rags."

It took Evelyn Sewall several minutes. Still dazed, she fumbled with buttons, hooks, and snaps. Her fingers were clumsy, her brains like jelly. Tatum watched her without expression, missing nothing.

David in the nearby corner turned his head. He tried not to look as the woman undressed. Tatum still held Sewall's shotgun. David's eyes searched for the Krag. He wondered where Tatum had hidden it. The aroma of fried fish mingled in his nostrils with the foul smell of his vomit. That was not all. He wished he were anywhere but in the presence of so much human shame. He wished he were dead.

Evelyn Sewall stood naked with her thick arms crossed. She had folded her clothing neatly alongside her. Her woolen socks were rolled and tucked inside her boots. Her tallowy flesh was pebbled with cold and she trembled uncontrollably. Blood had trickled down between her breasts. Tatum's eyes took her in, head to foot.

"You should shave your legs," he said. "They're as hairy as a man's."

He ordered her to the mattress. She sat with her arms about her knees, head lowered. "Stretch out," he said and she did, her hands over the dark wide thatch of hair at her pelvis. Her lips moved in prayer. Tatum never took his eyes off her. His stiff smile was gone now.

"David."

The boy looked at him with open hate.

"Take your clothes off." Tatum's voice was steady and quite cheerful. David shook his head. Tatum pointed the shotgun at him. "Come on, David."

David looked at the gun and back to Tatum and did not move. Evelyn Sewall sat up. "Do what he says, sonny."

"You heard the lady," Tatum said.

"Do it, dear. He'll kill you sure." She stifled a sob.

"Quit stalling, David." Tatum slid off the safety and fingered the rear trigger.

"Please, sonny," she begged. "No more killing."

"I—can't," David said.

Tatum prodded him with the shotgun. "And why not?"

"I—dirtied myself."

"A little puke won't hurt you. Now—"

"Worse," David wailed. "*Worse!*"

Tatum stared. "You mean, David," and he backed off, "you *defecated?*"

"I shit in my pants!"

Tatum's rage erupted as sudden and chilling as the shot that killed Sam Sewall. "You filthy little fiend! Off with every stitch!"

David got out of his clothes. Evelyn Sewall turned her head away. David faced the wall again, his arms high. His black nails dug into the cedar bark. Tears started and the heart went out of him. Evelyn Sewall whimpered softly on the mattress.

Tatum prodded him again. "Get on her, David."

The boy had never touched a woman's nakedness. He had dreamed of it often with the yearning wonder of adolescence. It was too bad the first time had to be like this, in terror, with the fouling of his body, with this crushing humiliation. He could not move.

Tatum kicked him savagely and howled in pain. He had forgotten his own injury. He raised the butt of the shotgun and furiously rammed it into David's ribs. David fell gasping. He dragged himself to the edge of the mattress. He could go no further. Every decent instinct rebelled. He lowered his head and on all fours waited for the next blow. Tatum put the shotgun down. He grabbed David's long hair. In two short vicious jerks that brought a scream to David's lips, he flung the boy face down, obliquely across Evelyn Sewall's nakedness. He took hold of David's ankles and swung him round. The boy sprawled in pain and shame with his head between her soft breasts and his legs together inside her parted thighs.

She lay quite still. David could feel the mound of her crotch, warm and coarse-haired, against his. He wondered if she was dead.

Tatum stepped back. "Now, David," he said, "do it."

David gripped the edge of the mattress and shut his eyes tight. Evelyn Sewall beneath him began to breathe in short, uneven gasps. Her hand sought David's and gripped it tightly. Tatum ground the heel of his sneaker against their twined fingers until they parted.

"You're stalling, David," he said. He reached down and took the boy's fingers and pressed them against her nipples. Evelyn Sewall put her arms around David and held him to her body and moved her pelvis against his. "God save us," she whispered through bruised lips.

Life or death, he thought. He did not want to die. He shut his mind to everything except what Tatum asked of him. His thoughts tumbled about in swift distorted images of the past few days. The headmaster's stony dismissal. His father's rage. The kidnap ordeal. The plane crash. The senseless killing of Sam Sewall of Machias, Maine. And now a middle-aged woman's naked body rocked beneath him like the sea against a beached skiff. Rockabybaby . . .

Tatum's voice erupted through his reverie. In throbbing cadence. On a coarser note. "Go on, David. Fuck her. Shit in your mother's face."

Evelyn Sewall beneath him wept. Her warm tears on his cheeks filled him with more pity that he had ever in his lifetime known. He wished with all his heart to help her.

"Try, you poor thing," she said, pathetic little catches in her voice.

He squeezed his eyes shut and tried. Flesh, hair, lips, tears, and blood were cold comfort. Too much had happened. Too much was in the way. It was no good. It was no good at all. He would have given his life for this woman in her anguish and grief and suffering. He could give her nothing. All that filled his mind was his mother's sad sweet face.

He'll have to kill me, David told himself.

He rolled free of Evelyn Sewall and opened his eyes. Tatum stood above him unzipped, exposed, enthralled, masturbating.

"You crazy bastard," David croaked.

Tatum may not have heard him. On the brink of orgasm, he plunged downward and fell on Evelyn Sewall. His lips in spasmodic thrusts sucked at her mouth. She threw her head from side to side, gagging and retching. David's fists pounded uselessly on Tatum's neck and back.

The shotgun lay beyond their writhing bodies where Tatum had dropped it on the floor boards. David crawled on his belly and reached his swollen fingers toward it. Tatum spied him. They lunged and clutched as one, Tatum at the breech, David's fists tight around the double barrel. They swayed and panted as they fought for the gun. Weight and balance and strength favored Tatum. He wrenched the shotgun free and stumbled to his feet. David lunged and fell to his knees, but his fingers once more found the barrel. They faced each other for a hung moment, breathing hard. Tatum put his good foot to the boy's throat and tugged once, twice, until David, choking, let go. Tatum stepped back, gripped the barrel, and swung in a wide vicious arc. David's upflung arm deflected the blow that would have killed him. The solid hardwood stock glancingly struck the side of his head and the boy fell senseless.

Watching their struggle, Evelyn Sewall in her own deep agony of flesh and spirit saw her chance. She plucked her nylon parka from the neat pile and fled naked from the cabin before Tatum was aware of it. She would have made it, but an untimely instinct for modesty doomed her. As she ran, she slipped the parka over her head. Blinded for the moment, she tripped over her husband's body. She staggered to her feet too late. Tatum was upon her. He swung the shotgun barrel across her ankles and dropped her in her tracks. He stepped close and jammed the muzzle up-

ward between her soft bruised thighs and squeezed the trigger—
the wrong one.

Evelyn Sewall was not yet ready to die. In that stunned instant of reprieve, before Tatum realized what had gone wrong,
she grabbed the barrel and with desperate strength pulled
Tatum to the ground and wrenched the shotgun from his fingers
and flung it aside.

They fought. In her final moments Evelyn Sewall's tenacity for
life bore out the oak-hearted heritage of her Yankee forebears.
Her broken nails clawed gashes in his flesh. She tore at his eyes,
his lips, his genitals. Her teeth sank deep into male flesh and
stayed there. Tatum twisted in rage and pain. He grunted and
cursed and pounded his fists together in sledge hammer blows
into her face and breasts and pelvic mound. He kneed and
heeled her until, with a moan, her bloody teeth released him.
Her fingers went limp, and he rolled her from him.

It was not enough. Tatum crawled, whimpering obscenities, to
the shotgun and brought it down in a smashing blow across her
skull. Blood and gore clung to the splintered stock. He bludg-
eoned her repeatedly until nothing recognizable remained, not
of the gunstock, not of Evelyn Sewall.

He threw aside the shattered weapon and dragged himself
exhausted to the cabin porch. His thoughts rambled. *"Of carnal,
bloody and unnatural acts . . . All this can I truly deliver."*

His mind and body cried out for the sweet escape of deep
sleep, but there was work to be done.

PART FOUR

CHAPTER TWENTY-EIGHT

The smart Maine people knew their luck with the weather could not last and they made the most of it. In their prudent way, they worked long hours getting the last of the garden in, canning the carrots and squash, quick-freezing the berries and corn, potting the window box geraniums for inside the house. They nailed down the loose shingles and tar paper, got the storm windows up and the stovewood downcellar with the potatoes and winter apples, shook out their long johns, and listened to the weather reports from the top of Mount Washington.

"... *The Arctic cold front which for the past week has been locked over the Canadian midwest and the Great Lakes region, has blown east-southeast carrying gale winds rising to hurricane force reaching more than a hundred miles an hour. Blizzard conditions with zero visibility and drifts to ten feet have brought all movement of air and surface transportation to a standstill. Motorists are warned ...*"

The same killing weather that froze the Montana sheep into pewter statues swept down in hundred-mile flurries. It blasted Duluth and Thunder Bay and walloped the Great Lakes and the Upper Peninsula. In Lower Ontario, it buried the parked cars along the streets of Ottawa under twelve-foot drifts. In Quebec it piled the ice floes like pulp logs along the banks of Trois-Rivières.

For forty hours, nothing moved that lived. The huge airliners that ferried travelers between Montreal and New York and the overseas transports that linked Europe with the West Coast stayed grounded, lashed down and buttoned up.

In the cities and mill towns of the northeast country, winos stocked up. Shivering skid-row drifters sought cover. Along the seacoast, the doughty lobsterman turned tetchy and stayed ashore. A blow like this could wipe out half his traps, smash his hull, drown his engine, wreck his gear. It could keep him landlocked from his living and cod-poor all winter.

Folks everywhere in Maine were sorry to see the fair weather go. Like losing a good neighbor, they said. They could live with the bad. The good was a mite nicer. And dour Yankee pessimists allowed as how no matter how bad the weather got, 'twas a sight better than most folk deserved.

One old cutter who lived close-by the New Hampshire border had a visit from the town's first selectman. They had surveyed the state line, the man said, and come to find out the cutter's land was over on the New Hampshire side.

"Well, thank the Lord," the old man said. "Don't think I could've stood another Maine winter."

CHAPTER TWENTY-NINE

David came awake naked under the thin blanket on the bunk where Tatum had dumped him. The fragmented nightmare remained. Terror at point-blank range. Rankness and shame inside him. His scrambled thoughts glued fact to fancy, remembering. Pain grew large, and fear with it, two gross numbing creatures sucking bone marrow and the roots of teeth and hair. And in the shadows a vague smiling presence beneath dark crusts of dried blood.

Dream? he wondered and heard the friendly wood stove hiss, dying.

Beyond pain and the ringing in his ears, somewhere on the far side of reason, a sweet silence teased him, an elusive sanctuary out of reach. He stretched toward it and gasped in pain. Chastened, he moved his jaw to loosen his tongue, swollen and gummed with red sweetness to the thick moist flesh inside his cheek.

His eyeballs ached. The lids fluttered weakly against the light of day where Tatum like a kiddie cutout blocked in an angular space across the open doorway. David's head throbbed and he felt bilious and squeezed his eyes shut. He pulled the blanket tightly round his trembling body. Where am I again . . . where . . . ? The memory slammed against his brain, brought a sourness to his lips. He whimpered. Tatum heard.

He turned from the doorway where he leaned. He wore Michaud's lined parka. Behind him, mist rose from the pond. He stood the Krag against the doorframe alongside the knapsack and sleeping bag and limped to the wood stove where the black kettle steamed. He dampened a cloth already pink with rinsed blood, cooled it, and wiped David's puffy face. The boy moaned. Tatum stood back and snapped his fingers.

"Get up, David."

The boy raised himself, fearful, dully obedient, wincing. His bloodshot eyes shifted past Tatum's blurred features to the cabin floor still damp in patches where Tatum had mopped up. The walls, the scarred sticks of furniture, even the corners of the room, were wiped clean, his own foulness wiped clean . . . his bruised fingers probed where his head throbbed and found jagged locks of hair, crudely chopped.

"Up, David." A sharper reminder.

A length of the nylon rope had been strung across the cabin and sagged where David's shirt, jeans, and socks hung to dry above the wood stove. Who and when, the boy wondered, and why? He dared not look directly at Gary or speak. How do you thank a murderer for small favors?

He swung himself a leg at a time to the cold floor, gripped the corner of the upper bunk for a moment's support. With a sudden lurch he reached the open porch, clutched the post, and threw up. Stumbling and heaving, he made it to the pond and fell to his knees on the dock. A thinness of morning ice veneered the surface. He plunged his elbows through ice to water so cold it burned. He laved his mouth and face, spit and gargled, splashed his bruised flesh and the fuzz at his armpits and crotch, as much to remove the touch of Tatum as to cleanse himself.

He ran back shivering. The chill air against his wetness felt surprisingly good. Approaching the cabin he slowed, clinging to trees, swift memory like stab thrusts. Here was where— His eyes searched about for tell-tale signs, found nothing.

Tatum in the doorway watched him narrowly. "That was stupid, David. You could catch your death—" He covered the boy with the blanket. "Dry yourself and get dressed. Fast."

He's being so kind, David thought. God help me.

He slipped into his T-shirt and pulled his clothes from the line and dressed. The jeans were still damp. He sat on the edge of the bunk and finished dressing. Each move sent a sharp pain through his right side. His teeth chattered and he was unable to control it. He fought back nausea and tried to think clearly.

"Where are they?" His voice a cracked whisper.

"Gone."

"Gone where?"

"Away, David."

"Bullshit."

Tatum went to him, the Krag leveled. "You saw what happens when people upset me, David." His manner was earnest, almost pleading, his voice weary. "Keep those filthy words to yourself and behave like a gentleman."

"You lied. I saw what you did—"

"I don't want to talk about it again."

"You lied about Eddie and the money and you're lying about the Sewalls. Innocent people—"

"If you want to stay alive, David, shut up."

"You should've killed me, too."

"I considered it."

"You should've."

"Unfortunately I need you."

"A dirty-mouth, smart-ass kid?" David sniggered. "More bull-shit."

The muzzle was inches from his chest. He watched Tatum nervously finger the trigger. The safety was off. The hell with it, he thought, and pushed the barrel aside. Tatum shoved it hard against his chest.

David's eyes met Tatum's. He remembered how it was with Sam Sewall. He did not want to die like that. He was sure of it now for the first time. "Okay. No more dirty words."

Tatum backed away. "Just remember that."

"Why'd you butcher my hair?"

The question seemed to relax Tatum but the Krag remained steady. "Long hair upsets me."

"Mr. Sewall didn't have long hair."

"They were snooping. Took pictures—"

"So you killed them." His eyes filled. "We had a good thing going. We'd have made it. Canada, anywhere you wanted. We didn't need—" He could not speak the words. *Murder. Killing in cold blood.*

"We'll still make it. Finish dressing."

"You don't need me. Take the Sewalls' camper and go."

"I thought of that."

"If it's me you're worried about, I won't tell. I swear to God I won't tell."

"The gatekeeper'd ask questions."

"You can make it to Canada, then. You've got a map and compass and all that money—"

"And leave you here to squeal?"

"Please, Gary—?" His voice broke.

"Quit stalling." Tatum prodded him with the barrel tip. "Get those boots laced." He turned away. David heard the click of the safety catch and breathed easier. He won't kill me. He needs me. Without me, he's lost. With me, he's got a guide and a hostage and—who knows?—his next victim, just for kicks. . . .

Tatum went to the wall and took down the game warden's district map. "Show me how we go, David," he said.

David buttoned his red shirt and tucked his jeans inside his boots and laced up. He joined Tatum at the table. He pointed to Desolation Pond. "We're here. We can head northwest a few hundred yards and hit the township line—"

"You mean there's a *town?*"

"It's just a dotted line through the wilderness. What they do, they lay out the area in six-mile squares and give them township numbers. Like this one we'll be going across, see? T8R16 WEL? That means Township Eight, Range Sixteen, West of the Eastern Line of the State. Going west, we get into Range Seventeen—"

"Skip it. What's this crooked line?"

"That's the Baker Branch of the Southwest Branch of the St. John. See, it says so, here. All these streams flow north—"

"Okay, okay. How far to that stream?"

"Maybe eight miles. The scale's a mile to an inch, so we can figure it out."

"You're sure there's no town?"

"In this wilderness? No way. There could be loggers, some poachers—"

"Poachers?"

"French Canadians. They come across the border for the deer and moose."

"Suppose we run into these loggers or poachers?"

"We'd hear the loggers' chain saws first. As for the poachers, they'd split before you'd see them."

"How do we follow this township line?"

"Trees are blazed yellow both sides, east and west."

"You're sure of that, David?"

"Sure. I've seen them. All you got to do is follow the yellow blazes to the border."

"The Canadian border doesn't show on this map. How far is it from here?"

"I'm not sure. Furthest west I've been is to the Forest Service cabin on the Baker Branch. This red triangle. See? We could stay there if the weather gets bad."

Tatum unfolded his official state highway map and studied the route. "If we follow a due west course from here, it'll bring us between two check points, Ste.-Aurélie and St.-Cyprien. Think we can get across the river at night?"

"A lot of people do it. If it's a real dry summer, they say you can walk across the St. John."

"Good. We should make it tonight."

"No way."

"Why not?"

"It's at least eighteen miles through rough woods and swamp is why. This isn't the Adirondack Trail, Gary."

"It's a straight line, isn't it?"

"More or less. But tough going. Five miles a day would be very good going—if it was a good day."

"You trying to scare me, David?"

"I'm trying to tell you what's ahead."

"Eddie told me you were a real woodsman."

"I'm leveling with you, Gary. We're both in bad shape. Your leg—"

"My leg's fine."

"Now, sure. But after a few miles in those woods—if we make a mile an hour, we'll be doing good. And my side. Every time I move, it feels like a mule kicked me—"

"Sorry about that."

"—and the wind's getting worse by the minute."

"Come off it, David. The sun's shining."

"It won't be, an hour from now. See those clouds? From the northwest and black as—" He saw Tatum stiffen. "Don't be fooled by the warm spell. It gets like that before a bad storm. Honest, Gary, our best bet is to stay where we are, lay low, and keep warm and dry until it blows over."

"And get caught here? Uh-uh. We move out and we keep moving."

"And if it snows?"

"It'll cover our tracks."

"Okay. Do what you want," David said angrily.

"I intend to."

"Don't blame me if we both freeze to death."

"It's your job to see that we don't, David."

"I'm seeing that I don't." He went to the bunk bed and ripped open a corner of the mattress and began to stuff chunks of it inside his jeans. "If I were you," he said sullenly, "I'd so something about those dumb sneakers you're wearing." He reached for the blanket. "And I'm taking this along."

"Another Nanook of the North." Tatum folded the maps and tucked them inside his parka. He lashed the sleeping bag and woods ax to the knapsack. "Here. Give me a hand."

David helped him slip the wide straps over his shoulders. Tatum took down the nylon line while David packed more of the mattress stuffing between his shirts and made a tight shoulder roll of the blanket. He took half the wooden matches from the tin box near the stove, gave some to Tatum, and put the rest in his shirt pocket. He wedged an empty #10 can rigged with a wire bail into Michaud's canvas tote bag which held their food supply—several small tins of sardines and a few tea bags—and slung it across his free shoulder. He felt giddy and weak. He looked around for a head covering but could find nothing suitable. In a pinch, the blanket would do. "Okay," he said, "I'm ready."

Tatum had coiled the fifty-foot length of nylon line and stood near the door. "Come here, David." He deftly fed the nylon through the belt loops at David's waist before the boy realized what was happening.

"What's that for?"

"To keep you in sight." He doubled the line through some of the loops, knotted them, and coiled the rest of it over his arm.

"I'm no damn animal, Gary—"

Tatum allowed a few feet of line to go slack. "Let's go," he said.

"Fuck that shit!" David tore at the line with his bruised fingers. Tatum cuffed him with an elbow and sent David sprawling. "You filthy-mouthed little cretin." He stood over David, his face contorted. "So help me I'll kill you!"

David clamped his lips shut. *Crazy son of a bitch means it.* He got to his feet slowly. Tatum raised the gun and watched him through narrowed eyes. "Start walking, young man." He wiped the spittle from his chin.

David led the way, not without fear, tethered to Tatum, who followed a dozen feet behind. Tatum tucked the looped end of the line through his belt. The Krag nestled in the crook of his left arm, with the loops of extra line. His right arm swung free.

The morning air was sharp. The northwest wind snapped at their cheeks. The mist over Desolation had deepened to thick haze where it met the dark forest. The terrain rose gradually. They circled the west shore of Corner Pond and began the climb to the ridge of beech, birch, and maple.

The silence between them grew tense as they struggled through tangled undergrowth to the dense thicket. At times the line between them snarled, bringing David up short. Tatum snapped instructions while David worked to free the line. It became a curious challenge of endurance and wits, each intent on measuring the other's limits and cunning. The crunch of leaves and twigs underfoot and Tatum's heavy breathing was all that broke the stillness of the woods; that and the crack of branches as David cleared the way. They traveled thus for twenty minutes. Once, David thought he heard the whine and grinding gears of a car motor. He dared not stop or show that he heard it. The sound faded almost instantly. He did not hear it again. Moments later and quite abruptly David felt a tautening of the line and stopped dead. Had Gary, too, heard the sound? David turned and faced suspicious eyes over the leveled Krag.

"Why are you bending those branches?"

"To keep them from snapping back in your face."

"You're lying, David. You're making a trail so we can be followed."

"Why the hell would I—"

"Shut your filthy, lying mouth," Tatum said. "And don't break another branch."

David remained silent. He had not expected Tatum to observe what he had done. He would be more careful now. They reached the township line, barely noticeable in the tangled woods, an hour later. David pointed to the first yellow blaze, high as a man's head. Tatum consulted the compass and checked the blaze line on the next few tree trunks. It led unfailingly due west.

They plodded on. In spite of the misery in his side that seemed to dog each step, and the humiliation of being leashed, David's spirits began to rise. He was alive. He was into what he knew best—the deep woods. He clearly understood what lay ahead and how to cope with it. His captor did not.

He looked over his shoulder. Tatum's head was bent. The knapsack had sagged and hung crookedly. His limp was more noticeable. David turned to the trail ahead and almost smiled. Your time will come, you crumb. You weirdo asshole. You'll pay. You'll pay for all of it. So help me God.

And looked up startled. The first few flakes of snow had touched his face.

David raised his head, signaling a halt. Tatum moved up half the distance and readied the rifle. "Why are you stopping?"

David pointed to the thickly wooded rise of land south of their position. The snow flew against his face in large flakes, quickly melting. "The plane's up there. We should make for it."

"Keep moving," Tatum said.

"It's no more than a hundred yards, Gary. We can make it before the storm gets any worse."

"We can make the border if you'd knock off your stupid ideas." But Tatum seemed to welcome the break. He leaned against a tree, breathing hard.

"Even if we don't stay there, Gary, we can pick up Eddie's boots and snowshoes—"

"We don't need snowshoes and I'm not wearing a dead man's filthy boots."

"Gary, for God's sake, will you trust me? Will you just for once take my word for it? We're in for a real bad storm. A blizzard, maybe. I don't want to die, Gary. And I don't want to have to leave your frozen carcass in the woods just because you were too dumb to listen to me. How far do you think you're going to get in those stupid sneakers—"

"Those," Tatum said, "are Adidas track shoes."

"They could be God's golden slippers, but in a snow storm

they won't help much. Eddie Michaud's wearing a pair of insulated boots he doesn't need any more."

Tatum frowned and looked up the wooded slope. "How far did you say it is?"

"Maybe two hundred yards or so."

"A minute ago you said one hundred. You're lying again, David." He hefted the knapsack higher on his back and lowered the rifle. "Okay," he said, "but no staying."

"Even if the storm gets real bad?"

"I said no staying." He waved David on. "We'll pick up the snowshoes and hit the trail again."

"And the boots?"

"Okay, okay. Just quit stalling and keep moving. We're crossing the border tonight."

"Right, Gary. Thanks a million. You won't regret it."

Fifteen minutes later, they reached the wreckage of Michaud's plane. Tatum sat down to rest, breathing noisily. David pulled open the plane door. Everything was as they had left it. The snowshoes were stowed behind the pilot's seat. But the boots were gone and so was Eddie Michaud.

CHAPTER THIRTY

"Your daughter's doing well, Justice Kimball. It's her husband we're concerned about."

The attending physician at the Dean Memorial Hospital walked with Kimball down the powder-blue hall to the accident ward. "To begin with, they were lucky. Those seat belts probably saved their lives. There were the usual contusions, abrasions, and lacerations. But I'm afraid Mr. Briggs's situation is more complicated."

"In what way?"

"He's suffered a coronary. Myocardial infarction, to be precise."

"How serious?"

"Well, he's in the intensive-care unit. The next twenty-four to seventy-two hours will be critical. We've done a cardiogram and blood test. No doubt about it being an M.I. Pulse is eighty and irregular. Blood pressure low. He's on the cardiac monitor, and getting intravenous drug therapy, just in case."

"Just in case what?"

"A heart block could develop. Or fibrillation—"

"Over my head, Doctor. What's the prognosis?"

"We'll know better in the next day or two. Maybe three. Meanwhile, it means complete bed rest and no visitors."

Kimball frowned. "Tell me, do you know my son-in-law?"

"I've certainly heard of him. Around town, you know. Greenville's a small place. But I never had the pleasure of meeting the gentleman, socially."

"He's not the social type. Now that you've met him—and I regret the circumstances—let me suggest that the coronary is long overdue. He's been driving himself hard for too long. Drinks too much. Smokes. Eats like a glutton. You might check with his physician in Bangor—Harvey Swann. He can give you chapter and verse on Sydney Briggs's medical record."

"I'll do that."

"A word of warning, Doctor. The minute Sydney knows where he is, he's going to make your life miserable until he's out of here. So prepare yourself. Now where's my daughter?"

"Down the hall in Room Five."

"May I see her?"

"By all means. She'll be well enough to leave in the morning, if she wants. And don't worry about Mr. Briggs. We'll deal with things as they come."

She was sorrier-looking than he had ever seen her, cheeks as pale as the bandages that bound them, her left eye blackened, her left arm in a sling. She smiled and he went to her side. "If I didn't have the facts, child, I'd swear you and Sydney had an argument."

"Daddy," she murmured and wept for a few moments while he dabbed carefully between the sutures. "I'm dandy. Really. I've had worse on skis. But Syd . . . how is he?"

"Alive. A coronary, though, and they're doing whatever it is they're supposed to do. I have the feeling this doctor has everything under control."

"Such a mess for you."

"It's David I'm concerned about."

"Any word?"

"They've spotted a crashed plane somewhere north of Baker Lake, near Desolation. With this storm on the way, it's doubtful they'll go in until it blows over."

"My poor Davey . . ."

"An FBI agent's monitoring the phone in Sydney's room at the Bangor House. Could be the kidnapers already released Davey or are going to and something fouled up. Could be he ran away—"

"Davey wouldn't do that, Daddy."

"He was mad enough to, the last time Sydney and I saw him. Well, there are those possibilites. The FBI agents are checking everywhere. And Junior Tuttle unearthed a bit of news. Eddie Michaud's plane was chartered by the same man whose rental car was found parked near Mathews Cove—a stolen car with Massachusetts plates."

"Eddie Michaud? He's too simple to get himself involved in anything like a kidnaping."

"Doreen's in custody—questioning, mostly. Eddie's charter was to Depot Lake. He has that old camp up there used to belong to Ami. His plane's not there. Fish and Game checked."

"You know how those bush pilots are, Daddy. He could've changed his mind and flown his party to a dozen other lakes."

"Well, that's how things stand. Unfortunately this storm is lousing things up. Planes are grounded. We won't be able to do a damned thing until it's over."

The chief nurse came in. "We have an incoming call for you, Judge Kimball."

He kissed Martha's hair and followed the nurse down the hall. He returned a few minutes later. Martha was sitting up, sipping bouillon through a straw. "That was Earle Wyman, FBI. He called to say he just had word from Gray Morrison, the game warden supervisor here. They sent a warden to the crash site this morning from Ste.-Aurélie by jeep. It's Eddie Michaud's plane and Eddie's dead—" He saw her expression and hurried on. "No one else in the plane. Eddie's neck was broken. The warden picked up a foot trail. Two people. He loaded Eddie's body in the jeep and followed the trail. It led over the hardwood ridge west of Desolation. Interesting, because it was marked with bent and broken branches, chest-high, all pointing in one direction."

"The way you taught us."

"It ended at the cabin on Desolation Pond—where I took Davey fishing last spring. The warden poked around. Everything seemed okay. Scrubbed clean. The ashes in the wood stove were still warm. He decided to check out the campground at the other end of the pond. Found a new Dodge camper, food in the refrigerator, a man and woman's clothes, everything unlocked. It was registered to a Samuel F. B. Sewall of Machias."

"Please, Daddy, get to it."

"The warden went back and searched around the cabin and found the Sewalls' bodies, dumped in the bottom of the privy. A smashed shotgun, bloody rags. A horrible mess. Nothing else."

"My God . . ."

"Davey couldn't have done it. But"—he sighed—"it could be he's with someone who did." Kimball still could not speak to her of Tatum. "The warden's staying until the medical examiner gets there." He sat on the bed and took her free hand in his. "Look, child. Feel strong enough to make a decision?"

She nodded and brushed an eye.

"The doctor said you can check out of here tomorrow morning."

"Neat."

"Eddie Michaud's plane crashing up there worries me."

"Why?"

"Eddie saw us when we drove into Greenville last Sunday, and he hung around. Rather odd, now that I think of it. Perhaps we should have a look inside that plane."

"You think Davey might have been in it?"

"May as well find out and face it."

"Could we get in, with this storm and the planes grounded?"

"The Fish and Game boys'd get us in. It's their job."

"You really want me along?"

"That's the decision you must make. Davey's your son and he's in trouble. Sydney's in trouble, too. Needs you now more than ever."

She scarcely hesitated. "I'd head for my boy like a flash. The way Syd did when they—grabbed him. But you'll be there. And you'll have the best professionals in the business. The FBI and the game wardens. I want to go, God knows. But Sydney'd be alone. He'd have no one here. And he does need me. We've learned that much."

"Whatever you say, child."

"I'll stay with Syd, Daddy, and pray like mad for Davey."

He kissed her. "Sydney may get rambunctious. Keep an eye on him."

"Two eyes, black, blue, and devoted. Daddy?"

"Yes?"

"Bring Davey home."

"I'll do my best."

"You must, Daddy. We've half a ton of moose meat to eat before the spring thaw."

Outside, the snow streaked in whining gusts. Kimball drove through town. A small crowd had gathered where Briggs's smashed rental car dangled from Porter Garage's blue and white wrecker. At the Fish and Game compound, a plane crew had loaded the G-3 Bell helicopter with its sausagelike land/water Garrett floats onto a dolly, bucking wind and flying snow to get it into the hangar out of the storm. Two Cessna 185s on pontoons rode their moorings hard in the shelter of the high concrete retaining wall. Moosehead was a dirty gray sea topped by whitecaps under a leaden sky.

Inside the cluttered headquarters office, Kimball chatted with Morrison. They were going in. A four-wheel-drive pickup in the adjoining garage was being loaded for the trip. A snowmobile, cans of gasoline, a tow sled, snow suits and boots, two spare tires, two sets of chains, extra foul-weather gear, two days' rations.

Morrison told Kimball the county medical examiner was expected any moment. Morrison had cleared the search party with the commissioner in Augusta, and the judge was welcome to join them. Kimball thanked him. "How do we go in?"

"Through Rockwood to Pittston Farm on Great Northern's road, across the border to St.-Zach. We'll cross back at Ste.-Aurélie. Bill Vail, our warden inspector, is meeting us there with another pickup and snowsled. From Ste.-Aurélie we go in on International Paper's logging roads past Baker Lake into Desolation country. That used to be Bill's district. He knows every inch of it."

"I need half an hour to get my gear together."

"We should be ready to go by then." Morrison paused. "We're taking rifles and shotguns in, Judge."

"Is that usual?"

"Earle Wyman called a few minutes ago. Tatum's a criminal-at-large, armed and very dangerous. Wyman's notified the Border Patrol and the RCMP."

"Can't fly that big Bell chopper in, can you?"

"Only if it means saving a life. All we've run into so far are corpses."

"What about my grandson's life?"

Morrison could only shrug.

Driving to the cottage, Kimball reflected on matters as they now stood. Martha, battered as she was, had cheered him. She had made a swift decision, clear and wise. Whatever had transpired between Martha and Sydney in that brief aborted reunion might well be the healthiest thing that had happened to them in all the years of their marriage. It warmed his heart to see her the wise, bantering, blithe-spirited woman he had known and loved through the years. If Briggs did not pull through, it would not be because Martha had not tried, had not given the relationship every ounce of love and strength and understanding she had.

Breeding, he thought. Someday it will save the world.

He thought of Briggs's ransom run. Headstrong and foolish. And in the light of the outcome, a tragic failure—three dead, and no telling how many more to go. One thing was clear to Kimball. Right or wrong, Briggs had done it for David. Without hesitation. A selfless act. Perhaps the only selfless act of Briggs's turbulent career. No one could fault him for that. The risk he ran of exposure, should the kickback money be recovered and questions asked, made it clear to Kimball that Briggs had acted out of pure love. He would make his feelings known to Briggs when the time came.

When the time came. David's freedom? Or funeral? Dead Eddie Michaud and two dead Sewalls might be the mere beginning. Where will it end? What role did the Sewalls play in this Grand Guignol? Were they among the actors? Or had they had the bad luck to stumble on stage at the wrong moment?

Junior Tuttle waved Kimball's pickup through the line of cars that jammed the roadside bumper to bumper for several yards to the drive down to his cottage. My God, where do they all come from? A reporter plucked his sleeve, asked a question. Kimball shoved him aside. What is it about violence, he wondered, that so preoccupies the soul of man, fascinates his mind, and starts those ancient vibes pounding in the human breast?

CHAPTER THIRTY-ONE

The wilderness west of Desolation Pond is heartbreak country. From the close ranks of cedar and spruce that rim her western shore, the terrain rises in a shapeless tangle of woods and brush to the hardwood ridge of beech, birch, and maple, leafless now and prey to the smashing winds. Beyond that crest, beyond the scarred slope where the wreck of Michaud's plane embraced the land, the hills dissolve into a snarled and cunning jungle. Fallen timber, sinewy alders, and huge lichened boulders dominate the bogs and cedar swamps. And the dense black growth a hundred feet high forms a canopy over all.

A man's progress through this mean country on the raw edge of winter may not be as misery-ridden as in the summer plague of mosquitoes and flies (flies named black and moose and copperhead, and cursed by other names in many tongues), but it is miserable enough. The forest floor is a treacherous no man's land. It cannot be trusted underfoot in any season. Blowdowns and puckerbrush, cutovers and wild raspberry vines clutch, entrap, and bedevil the trespasser. A man cannot march a dozen yards anywhere in a straight line. Eye-level branches blind him. Gnarled roots and sharp-edged boulders trip and spill him, all part of nature's timeless conspiracy against him.

The township line west of Desolation divides land of the International Paper Company from that of the Oxford Paper Company to the north. Because of this dual ownership, the line is better tended than most township lines within one company's boundaries. Even so, as Tatum and David moved toward the border, it proved to be an agonizing course to follow, blocked by windfalls, half buried in new growth. Blaze marks once yellow had faded or disappeared. Where fallen trees impeded progress, they were obliged to circle. In doing so they often lost their way. The nylon line that joined them made things no easier.

By midafternoon, the storm had worsened. The canopy overhead somewhat lessened the brutality of the storm in the deepest wooded sections. Yet when they emerged into slash areas open to the sky and abandoned by the loggers, the intensity of the storm fell upon them. Snow driven by the wind stung their cheeks and obscured their way to the next stretch of woods. David stumbled often, dragging Tatum with him. Sometimes it was Tatum who held them up.

Tatum had begun acting strangely soon after they resumed their way from the wrecked plane, staring over his shoulder and searching the woods. He had added Michaud's snowshoes to his backpack, and wore the dead pilot's parka over his shoulders. He also had found and now wore Michaud's leather mittens, with thick home-knit wool liners. But he moved in a state of semi-shock, unable to fathom Michaud's disappearance. David tried several times to talk about it but each time Tatum sharply cut him off.

David had wrapped himself in the thin blanket and wore it over his head like a shawl to keep the snow and wind off his face. His hands were snug in his armpits, or alternately in his crotch, for warmth. He had wanted to stop and dig in hours ago, but chose to suffer rather than repeat the suggestion to Gary. He was beginning to understand the kind of psychology Gary responded to.

It was Tatum who called a halt. He was blue with cold. His teeth chattered. They had come through a big cedar swamp. His legs were soaked to the hips. David had gotten through with nimble log-stepping that Tatum, burdened and lame, was unable to duplicate. He moved closer to David. "How's that side of yours feeling?"

"Hurts real bad, Gary," David said, not lying.

"You should've said something."

"I figured you might want to stop soon." He pointed to Tatum's feet. "I've seen frostbite before. Your bare skin shows and I'd swear your right foot's getting frostbitten."

"I've been rubbing snow on it," Tatum said.

"That's the worst thing you can do—"

"Don't tell me! Everybody knows that's what to do for freezing."

"Well, it's stupid. How can adding one frozen thing to another do anything but make it colder? And rubbing's not a good idea. You need heat and the quicker the better. If we dig in, I'll have a fire going in a jiffy. And I'll have time to rig something to cover your feet."

Tatum was staring at David's boots.

"Too small for you," David said. "Sorry."

"Okay, okay. We'll rest here awhile."

"Right on, Gary. Thanks."

Tatum searched their surroundings carefully. They were in flat dense country surrounded by several huge boulders covered now with several inches of snow. They had wandered from the township line an hour past and settled on a simple compass course west. "How far've we come?"

"Maybe four miles." Closer to five, David thought. But he saw no reason to encourage Gary to strike on.

"Only a few minutes, you understand. Then we push on," Tatum said.

"A shelter'd help, Gary. The snow's getting real bad."

"No time for that."

"I can get one up real quick. Just a lean-to, maybe against that fallen fir there." He pointed to a tree wedged against sheer ledge that slanted upward about ten feet, creviced with moss. He considered prayer while Tatum surveyed the site.

"Over there against that big rock would be better." Tatum limped to the spot David had in mind. He slid the knapsack from his shoulders and settled heavily on the fallen fir. "Get firewood, David. On the double."

"We ought to get the lean-to up first—"

"The wood, David. I'm freezing. I'll get the fire going while you're putting up the lean-to." He uncoiled several lengths of the nylon line. "Get going. And don't try anything." He rested the rifle across his knees.

David untied Michaud's tote bag and began to gather bark for kindling. Tatum called out. "I'll need some matches."

David returned with an armful of birch bark. "I gave you matches before we left the cabin, Gary."

"They're wet." He showed David the wood matches he had taken from his Levi's. David unbuttoned his shirt pocket and deliberately counted out six matches. "That's half of what's left,

Gary." He went back for firewood several times and added each load to the stack against the ledge.

The tether kept him in sight of Tatum. David no longer minded. What mattered was to rig a shelter and get in a supply of wood for the night. There was plenty within reach under the steady fall of a light dry snow. He was mostly troubled by the sound of each match as Gary struck it and failed to light a fire.

He dropped the final armful of wood and squatted alongside Tatum. The pile of kindling Tatum had arranged held too much bark, and most of the pieces were damp. Tatum glanced at David, waiting for his comment. David remained silent. Tatum struck the fifth match. It flickered. Its flame spluttered and died. David reached into the pile. "You're wasting precious matches, Gary." He started to peel paper-thin curls from the piece of birch. Tatum slapped his hand. "Get the shelter going." He reached for the sixth match.

David's eyes met Tatum's for an instant. David shrugged and moved off. He'd seen that look before. The crazy bastard, he thought. He's ready to kill me. Just because he pissed away five matches and I told him so. He'll kill me and he's crazy enough to burn up all the matches, just for spite, and let himself freeze to death. . . .

"I'll need the ax," he said.

"No way."

"Why not?"

"You'll cut the line and split."

"You want a shelter, don't you?"

"There's wood enough around for that."

"I need green boughs—"

"We won't be here that long." He held the last match, ready to strike. David watched him. Tatum slowly passed the match to David. "It's these wet Levi's," he grumbled. "No fault of mine."

David gathered up the small pile of kindling and went closer to the ledge. He cleared a space in the snow and rebuilt the pile with thin dry slivers and an air space beneath. He struck the match and carefully fed its flame to the bark. Out of the wind and protected on all sides, the fire caught. Smoke and flame curled upward. Tatum moved close and held his trembling fingers over it. He avoided David's eyes. David rolled a storm-split length of tree trunk close to the fire. "You'd better rest that game leg, Gary, while I work on the frostbite." Tatum sat without a word.

David wasted no time. He stripped the flimsy shoe and sock from Tatum's foot. Holding the foot as close to the fire as Tatum could stand, he gently massaged the toes and ankle to restore circulation. In ten minutes he saw the color restored and turned the task over to Tatum.

"How is it your fingers aren't frostbitten?" Tatum demanded. "No gloves, nothing—?"

"I hold them against my bare flesh," David said. "Under my shirt, wherever it's warm."

Tatum turned away without a word of thanks. David knew the shelter must be ready before dark. With cover and something hot to drink and enough wood to keep the fire going through the night, he was confident Gary would stay until the storm blew itself out. Without an ax, his only hope for a roof was the fallen fir with its cluster of green boughs at the tip. Thank God it's fir, he thought, and not spruce. A man could tear his heart out trying to strip a spruce of green boughs.

He braced a foot against the fir's trunk and tugged at the brittle branches until they snapped. He dragged them painfully to the small clearing. He tried not to think of his aching muscles and the sharp pain in his side. He thought of all the times he had spent in the woods, the shelters, good and bad, he had built. He was grateful for the evergreen canopy far overhead that slowed wind and snow. He tried not to dwell on Gary's stubbornness and vanity and his strange behavior during this day. He could not remember a scarier predicament in the woods, or a danger equal to this. Nor was the excitement of the adventure completely lost on him. They won't believe me when I tell them, he thought.

He continued to gather boughs for the roof of the shelter. The wind blew in and around them in vagrant gusts. He could not remember a wind sound as ominous as this one. He glanced at Gary from time to time, to see that he tended the fire well. It blazed nicely now. Gary had set his knapsack against the ledge and opened it. David, fascinated, watched him bring out packets of money, thumb the ends like playing cards, and stow them

back in the knapsack. The rifle and ax were at his side. David
went back to the tip of the fir, and savagely tore the boughs,
swearing to himself, determined he would survive this ordeal if
only to learn the truth that lay behind those packets of bills.

He dragged the last of the boughs over. Tatum's leg rested on
the tote bag. An empty sardine tin lay near his side, its con-
gealed oil waxy in the firelight. David dropped the load. "These
boughs should do the trick."

"Told you so." Tatum glanced up lazily and smirked. "Didn't
need the ax at all, did you?"

David ignored him. The warmth reflected from the ledge
eased some of the resentment that flared in him. Gary had not
raised a finger to help. He had instead devoured a good part of
their food supply.

Just keep score, David counseled himself. The pay-off will
come.

Resting, he studied the situation now facing him. The felled fir
was the key. Supported at its high end by the top of the ledge, it
would serve as the ideal ridge pole. Its branches formed rafters.
One more pole, parallel to it, set about six feet away, would complete the skeleton of a roomy shelter. He would have to find such
a pole. Meanwhile, the work, must begin. Darkness was no
more than two hours away. And at any moment, finicky Gary
might decide to move on.

He pulled himself together and went to work. He hammered
two forked sticks into the ground with a rock—one at the foot of
the fir, the other six feet distant, both parallel to the face of
the ledge. He found a straight length of three-inch spruce that
fitted snugly between the crotches of the forked sticks. Foraging
at the end of the tether, he finally came to a dead cedar sapling,
lightning-struck and still standing. He snapped it after many
tries and dragged it back and laid it parallel to the big fir.

He spread a floor of green fir boughs, concave side down, and
began the tedious interlacing of the boughs through the
branches of the fallen fir to thatch the shelter. It was finger-
breaking, sticky work. He left a small opening for wood smoke
and a narrow crawl space for the entry at a right angle to the
northwest wind, to avoid a pile-up of snowdrifts. He fitted the
last bough in darkness and stumbled into the shelter. He held his

pitch-blackened fingers over the fire to warm them. His body was in a cold sweat. He lay there, rubbing his hands, close to tears, faint with hunger and exhaustion. It was a good shelter, warm and dry. He was safe for a while. There was no way to know for how long.

Tatum in the high corner had a brooding look. His Levi's were almost dry. His leather-trimmed sneakers were caked with swamp muck. "We'll be moving out soon," he said.

David searched the words for a clue to what Gary really wanted. He thought he had heard an edge of anxiety, almost pleading. Yet the man's unpredictable rages warned David to react with caution.

"Before we go, Gary," he ventured in a servile voice, "could we please have some hot tea?"

"If *you* need it."

David felt better now. Tatum had actually welcomed the suggestion and appeared greatly relieved. David knew he was on the right track.

He took the ✕10 can out of the tote bag and fetched some snow and set the can carefully between two flat stones over the fire. Soon they were sharing the hot strong tea, Tatum drinking from the can, David using the discarded sardine tin.

"Can I say something, Gary?"

"Course. You don't need my permission, silly."

"I'm real serious, Gary. We've come a long way together. Just in a few days, right?"

"Go on."

"Since the plane got wrecked and—all that. What I want to say is—you got us this far. You're a really bright guy—"

"Make your point, David," Tatum said and sipped his tea.

"What I'm getting at—you're really in control. You know how to run things. Like taking over after Eddie got killed and figuring out how to get us to the border. Super. Really super."

"Why this flattery all of a sudden, David?"

"Because I've had time to think about it, to watch how you operate. How you make decisions." He knew he was floundering. "And I owe you a lot, Gary. The way you rapped that first night, like—like a big brother. I told you things I never told anybody. About myself. And you listened. You didn't laugh or jump down my throat and treat me like a kid. Like most grown-ups do. And I'm grateful for that, Gary."

"Make your point," Tatum said, not displeased.

"Okay. The point is, I'm going to ask a favor and I know it means a change in your plans, in your schedule, but I'd like to ask this favor and see what you think about it."

"No harm in asking."

"It takes a lot of guts to do what you want to do, to get out there in this storm and make it to the border. Not everyone—"

"The favor," Tatum snapped.

"Stay here 'til the storm blows over."

"Can't do that." His earlier gloom seemed to settle over him.

"I need the rest, Gary, is why I'm asking this favor. My side feels worse, like maybe it's a busted rib."

"All I see is a badly confused young man behaving in a selfish way."

"It's not me alone. Think of yourself. You were limping again, worse than before. And those—track shoes of yours are shot. You'll get frostbitten again. But if we stay, I'll have time to rig some covering for them. Meanwhile we got food"—he grinned—"like this sardine tea. We're safe here, Gary."

"You also said we'd be safe in the cabin at Desolation."

"How did I know—?"

"Okay, okay." Tatum did not speak for several moments. "The favor. Don't think you're fooling me with all those kind words and flattery. I'm aware of what you've done, David. Except for that foul mouth of yours, you've been a good boy. Helpful. It won't be forgotten." His voice became a whisper. "Yes, it takes guts to push on in this storm. But if we don't, David, the both of us die right here."

"How d'you figure that?"

"He'll catch up with us."

"Who?"

"Eddie Michaud."

It was this swift and chilling unpredictability that David knew he must cope with to survive. Like the shot that killed Sam Sewall. Like God knows what else to come. He could not trust himself to speak. He glanced at Gary. Perhaps he had been kidding.

But he saw that Gary meant what he had said and David was truly frightened.

"He sure looked dead to me, Gary."

"Why wasn't he there?"

"Somebody got to him after we left."

"Who? How?"

"Poachers, maybe."

"Did you see any tracks?"

"I didn't think about tracks."

"Why not?"

"I was too scared."

"He's alive, David. A cunning, vengeful man. As your father found out. And you, and me. He's following us. We must keep moving."

My God, David thought. He added a stick of poplar to the fire. "The snow covered our trail, Gary. Nobody could track us. Not even Eddie."

"Nothing will stop him. Nothing . . ." His voice rose, tinged with hysteria, then trailed off. David stared at him. Tatum's head was nodding.

"He'd dig in someplace, Gary. He wouldn't risk his life—"

"What life?" His smile chilled David to the marrow. "Your favor is granted, young prince. We spend the night here. In your castle without a moat." He sat up. "Can I trust you, David. Truly?"

"You sure can, Gary."

"We shall see. You will bed down in that far corner. I will remain in this corner." He slid the ax and rifle into his sleeping bag and zipped it up. "I, too, am tired. I, too, need rest. You are not to leave your corner during the night. As you see, I have the weapons by my side."

"Somebody's going to have to feed the fire. And we're running low on firewood."

"Later. You said I can trust you, did you not?"

"Yes, sir."

"If I fall asleep, will you run away?"

"That'd be dumb. I'm roped to you. Anyway, I wouldn't get twenty yards in this storm."

"But you're very clever in the woods. You'd find a way."

"I swear I won't run away."

"Or take the gun or ax or otherwise try to trick me while I sleep?"

"I swear."

"Swear to God."

"I swear to God I won't do any of those things."

"Swear on your mother."

David was silent.

"I said swear on your mother."

"I can't do that."

"Sure you can. Just say—"

"I *won't* do it."

"—just say you swear on your mother that if you break your word she'll drop dead on the spot. Say that."

David covered his face with his hands. He could not erase the image of Corey Latimer's leering face back in the dorm room at the Academy. A week ago? A month ago? A hundred thousand years . . . lying atop the naked, pebble-fleshed hulk of poor Mrs. Sewall—

"David?"

The fire flickered. More wood, David thought, numb with despair.

"You love your mother, don't you?"

"I love her very much."

A long silence. "I envy you."

"That's okay."

"The way I see it," Tatum continued in a drowsy voice, "if you do escape, you'll die out there. If you try for the ax or gun, you'll die in here."

"Yes, sir."

"So we may as well turn in."

"What about the firewood?"

"Aaah?"

"We're just about out of firewood."

"Ah," Tatum mumbled. "Firewood." He sat up and loosened the coil of nylon line, allowing David most of the fifty feet. The ends remained knotted in Tatum's belt. "Ten minutes, David. I trust you."

David pulled the blanket round his body and covered his head. He got to his hands and knees. Each move sent a sharp stab of pain through his side. He had one thought. Without fire-wood they would not make it through the night. He crawled out of the shelter.

The shrieking wind grabbed him. An icy blast snatched his breath and whipped the blanket parka from his head. He gasped. The biting snow flew into his mouth, his throat, pinned his lips against his teeth. With a great effort, he dragged himself back to the entry out of the wind. He lay there almost senseless, weeping.

"David?"

"It's like a hurricane out there."

"It was your idea, David, not mine."

What the hell's the use, the boy thought. Let the fire die. I'll lie here and die with it. Just close my eyes . . . sleep . . .

"Ten minutes are almost up, David."

He struggled out of the deep, sweet reverie. "I—can't make it."

"You said we needed firewood, didn't you? Fetch it."

Fetch. David thought. *Arf-arf. Bow-wow.*

His bruised fingers reached toward the fire and closed round a short stick. A quick dive toward Gary, a quick chop, could change their world. The ax, the rifle, the sleeping bag, his. The food and the snowshoes, his. And the power to lord it over Gary for a change . . .

"Some woodsman." Tatum sneered. "Can't fetch a few sticks of wood."

David covered himself with the blanket. He took a few turns with the nylon line to secure the blanket tightly round his head. He crawled out, prepared now. He foraged through three-foot snowdrifts in the howling wind until he could stand the cold no longer.

When he crawled to his corner to sleep, the fire hissed around a hardwood log over a bed of glowing coals. With luck, the woodpile would last until morning. Tatum in the high corner snored loudly. Testing, the sly bastard, David thought. Well, the hell with him. The wood's in.

The cold wakened David. The cold and Tatum's scolding voice. He knew at once what had happened. He did not need Gary to tell him. His heart sank. Dim gray daylight filtered through the smoke hole, revealing a small mound of snow on the dead fire. Outside, the wind howled.

"I'll have those matches," Tatum said.

David struggled up on an elbow and sank back. "You need kindling."

"Don't tell me what I need, you stupid boy. The matches."

David clawed at the pocket flap of his shirt with numb fingers and handed three matches to Tatum. He could not think clearly in the grip of sleep and cold. He watched Tatum kick the snow and dead ashes of the fire and add a pile of broken sticks. "It won't work, Gary. You need dry birch bark or paper."

Tatum ignored him and used two matches without success. David in pain crawled to the meager woodpile. Nothing was there that would serve for kindling. He had gotten up once during the night to replenish the fire, which had almost died. He had realized then they would run out of firewood by morning, but had failed to waken for the next replenishing.

"You're wasting matches, Gary."

Tatum whirled on him, shook him. "It's your own stupid fault. You let the fire die."

"Sorry, Gary." He truly was.

"Okay, okay. Get out there, then. Before we freeze to death."

"Save that match." David crawled to the entry. It was blocked by a wall of snow. During the night, the wind had swept the drifts round to the lee side. "We're snowed in," he called to Tatum.

Tatum shoved him aside and in panic clawed at the solid snow wall. David grabbed him, "For God's sake, go easy. The whole thing'll cave in on us."

Tatum sank deeper as he fought to get out. David pulled him free. Together they sat inside, snow-encrusted, breathing hard. "I need air," Tatum whined. "I'll suffocate."

David began to burrow carefully, aware that at any moment the overhanging snow might collapse on him. Several minutes later, he had tunneled to a patch of daylight. The dazzling whiteness almost blinded him. The blizzard raged. After a look around, he crawled back. Tatum watched him with suspicious eyes. "What's wrong?"

"It's sure death out there."

"What about firewood?"

"No way. There's two feet of snow over everything."

Tatum picked up the gun and ax and tried clumsily to make his way through the entry. David huddled down, too chilled and miserable to care. Moments later Tatum backed into the shelter, parka awry. He turned to David, who looked without pity at Tatum's strained face. The eyes reddened by the gale were full of terror, his lips gray-blue. Ice particles clung like tears to his unshaven cheeks.

"What do we do, David?"

"You're not going to like it," David said. He nodded toward the knapsack.

It took Tatum several moments to understand what David meant. He shook his head violently. "Absolutely not."

"No other way, Gary." Through the layers of pain and chilled flesh David felt a flush of grim pleasure. This time it would be his way or not at all.

"Never." Tatum pulled the parka over his head and stalked about, muttering under his breath. David tried not to listen. It no longer mattered. Nothing mattered. He had read enough about wilderness survival to know what it was like to freeze to death. First, the numbing cold. Then a false sense of warmth followed by drowsiness and sweet sleep. Silent death.

Why not? he asked himself. What else is there for me?

Minutes passed. Hours? He could no longer measure time. He sat with his arms around his knees, teeth chattering, huddled under the blanket, waiting for the warmth of death to blot his mind to drowsiness and sweet sleep. . . .

The line round his waist jerked suddenly. "Get over here, David."

He resisted the idea, deep in a languorous spell. But some deeper instinct acted for him. David slowly crept to Tatum's corner. Tatum held out his third match. No words were spoken. David took the match in stiff fingers and waited. Tatum reached inside the knapsack, his clumsy mittens fumbling through the packets of money, his frost-hung eyes peering at the numbers on them.

He handed one to David. "Small bills first," he said.

It snowed all day and through the night. Nothing stirred in the surrounding woods. A branch fell, or a tree, or clumps of heavy snow, thudding to the ground like dead bodies. These moments, like reminders of another life, startled Tatum out of his brooding silences to a bristling wariness. Sometimes he cat-napped, muttering phrases David could not understand. Awake, he mouthed delirious threats and warnings as frightening to David as any of Tatum's previous tantrums.

It was impossible to go after firewood on the outside. They burned each stick from the woodpile with care, alternating with the crisp, dry paper money from the knapsack. Tatum presided, in a ritual as unholy to him as the burning of sacred vestments.

David occupied himself by preparing new coverings for Tatum's feet. He sat close to the small fire and tore wide strips from his blanket and wrapped and tied them securely over the ankle tapes Tatum wore. The tapes were still intact. It pleased David to know that his handiwork had survived. There was little else here to give him pleasure. The shelter, yes. It had stood the storm well. And the living fire. They would both be dead by now without it.

Tatum wept, an embarrassment David found himself helpless to escape or to deal with. His greatest fear was that at any moment, Gary's grief might erupt in some wildly violent act. He looked away each time Gary fed the green bills one by one into the licking yellow flames.

The packets dwindled through the night hours. The knapsack sagged, collapsing in wrinkles. Tatum no longer wept. David dozed. An ominous silence sat between them, broken by night sounds—a lone owl's hoot, the bark of a coyote. And the steady devouring of the money by the fire until all of it was gone.

Gross, David thought. What you can do with money, and what money can do with you.

The search-and-rescue party reached Ste.-Aurélie before dark but got no further. The blizzard's force had paralyzed all movement. Power lines were down. Ice conditions had disrupted walkie-talkie communication with the game warden at Desolation Pond. The last word from him, drowned in static, was that he would sit out the storm holed up in the murder cabin with dead Eddie for company.

Kimball fretted over the delay, though he knew the region and conditions well enough to understand nothing could be done about it. They sat in the game warden's snug trailer drinking coffee and making painfully polite conversation. The game warden's wife kept her fears for her husband to herself and did what she could to make the men comfortable. Morrison and the medical examiner talked quietly or read from a stack of *Reader's Digests*. Kimball played with the two small children, a shy towheaded pair in awe of their unexpected visitors. At bedtime, they soberly kissed him good night.

The men dozed. They knew that when the storm had blown itself out, there would be plenty of work and some hard truths to face. And danger. It was a routine they had to live with in this wilderness, a fact of life and never easy.

That is how it was at this time in Ste.-Aurélie.

CHAPTER THIRTY-TWO

Morning.

The storm had passed. The branches of the conifers were bent low, boughs buried deep in snowdrifts higher than a man could reach. The air smelled clean and frosty. The sun, a cold bronze disk, glinted through gray chinks in the somber black growth overhead.

Tatum stood outside the entry to the half-demolished shelter, the Krag ready, a watchful eye on David. The boy, still tethered, had pulled down several of the green boughs. He chose two, thawed and stripped them for frames from which to fashion a crude pair of bear-paw snowshoes for himself. With Tatum's knife he cut narrow strips of leather from his belt for webbing. The extra long ends of the rawhide laces from his boots went to harness toe and instep to each snowshoe.

He had already fitted Tatum into Michaud's snowshoes. He stuffed the odds and ends of their loose gear into the empty knapsack and loaded it on Tatum's back. Tatum's first few steps were clumsy until David showed him how to walk naturally, taking longer steps. "You're raising your shoes too high in front and taking too short steps," he explained. "That wastes energy." Tatum pocketed the knife and said nothing.

David started out. Tatum yanked the nylon line. "Before we go, I want a word with you."

David waited. What now?

Tatum seemed in no hurry now. He studied the compass and squinted into the forest ahead. It worried David. The temperature was somewhere below zero. He could feel the chill of it and had to keep moving. "Something wrong?"

"Nothing." Tatum smiled and David's heart sank. He knew that smile. It was the last thing Sam Sewall had seen. David busied himself with the remnant of the blanket, covering his arms and shoulders snugly, tucking the ragged ends into his trousers. Metal clicked. He looked up. Tatum had opened the bolt of the Krag and loaded a cartridge into the chamber and closed the bolt. David's fear grew. Tatum caught his eye. He seemed amused. Not funny, David thought, heart pounding.

"You said you wanted a word with me." He almost added "sir."

"Yes, David." He held the rifle in a casual way, not quite pointing it at David. Same as with Sam Sewall, the boy thought in panic. He dared not move. He stared down at the snow, kicked a tuft of it, felt sorry about his nice new Bean boots, hardly used. He could not run. He was lucky if he covered a mile or two walking, before the bear paws gave out.

"David?"

"Sir?"

"I'm doing this," Tatum said in a clear kind voice, "to let you know who's in charge here. I want to make that very, very clear."

"Yes, sir."

"There are occasions, in your enthusiasm to please, when you take over. I've indulged you, David, out of the goodness of my heart. No more need for that. I'm rested. My leg is fine. The weather's clear. We'll be on our way in just a moment." He smiled again. "After the surprise."

"Surprise, sir?"

"I've decided to take you all the way with me. To Quebec, Montreal, whatever."

David kept his eye on the muzzle of the Krag.

"You hear me, David? This was not in my original plan, you know. The original plan was to drop you at the border." He paused, pleased with the image the words evoked. "I've changed my mind now."

"Thanks." David barely croaked the word. He trembled with cold and fear. "Can we start off now?"

"It's what you wanted, isn't it? To go all the way to Canada with me. Remember how you begged?"

"Yes, sir." He was close to tears.

"Do you know what a hostage is, David?"

The boy nodded.

"How do you know?"

"It's in the papers all the time, and on TV."

"You're going to be my hostage, David. Know why?" He did

not wait for David's answer. "Because you're all I've got. I have no other protection. Money's gone. Burned to ashes. It could have bought me everything. Now I've got nothing."

"Sorry," David mumbled.

"Nobody's fault, David. No one's to blame. I thought it over very thoroughly. I want you to know that. There was no choice. So I've swept the matter from my mind. As though the money never existed. You, David, are my medium of exchange."

"Yes, sir."

"And I want to make this, too, very, very clear. You may recall that I spoke of Eddie Michaud. Said he was following me. You do remember my saying that, David?"

"Yes, sir."

"It was fatigue. A weariness of the mind, nothing more."

"I figured you were kidding, Gary. Just making it up to pass the time, kind of."

"Be that as it may. I never want to hear about it again. Michaud or the money. Is that clear?"

"Yes, sir."

"Then we're off." He waved David on and followed, whistling a worn-out army hiking tune, happy as a scoutmaster.

Bonkers, David thought. The weirdo's gone bonkers. He pushed ahead slowly enough to allow Tatum time to accustom himself to the snowshoes. It felt good to be on the move, to feel his flesh warming again.

I'm alive, he reminded himself, but I could be dead in twenty minutes. Or twenty seconds. Because behind me marches a madman weirdo shmuck with a loaded rifle who'd blow my head off if it tickled his fancy. Bawls half the night like a baby and next morning he's cheerful as a chipmunk. Uppers and downers around the clock. Well, maybe he can take that kind of shit day in, day out. I can't. It's driving me out of my skull and I better do something about it before it's too late.

The air grew colder as they proceeded west, and the going rougher. The snow was soft and feathery here, the woods less dense, open to the harsh wind. They forded several small brooks, ice-fringed, trickling northward. David knew they were getting close to the Baker Branch. Tatum behind him was limping again and stumbling often. He was snappish and sullen now and spoke to David only to direct his course.

They walked without rest for almost four hours, crossing fresh moose and deer trails and the tracks of small animals and birds. Twice David halted and pointed ahead to spruce partridge. "Fool's hens," he told Tatum. "An easy meal." But Tatum doggedly pushed on.

It was almost noon when they reached the Baker Branch. David was idly wondering what they would eat or if they would eat at all, when a rifle shot shattered the stillness. David stared around, bewildered. Tatum slid to his knees, terrified, got up and plunged back to the nearest tree, where he fell, snowshoes awry, dragging David with him.

"Eddie," he hissed. "Caught up with us."

You said it, you weirdo. I didn't. David searched the woods ahead. Tatum burrowed down behind the tree, pulled off a mitten with his teeth, and fumbled the Krag to his shoulder. Crouched low, whining, he peered in the direction from where the shot had come.

David's hopes leaped. Whoever had fired (and he knew it was not dead Eddie Michaud) could mean his freedom. He stayed low, his arms crossed, his hands warming in his armpits. A minute passed. Please, God, David thought. Let's not lose him. He nudged Tatum. "We can go closer," he whispered, "and have a look."

"No!"

"Don't want him to get away, do you?"

Tatum thought about it. An eerie silence surrounded them. They inched closer. Tatum's courage grew. His tongue worked spasmodically over his lips. The Krag aimed ahead, Tatum's finger inside the trigger guard. A moment later David touched his sleeve and pointed.

In a small wind-blown clearing scarcely fifty yards to the left, two men with rifles stood over a fallen buck deer. The deer's antlers, a huge ten-point rack, were all that showed above the snow where he had dropped. The men wore thick suit coats over heavy sweaters, visored caps with earlaps, dark woolen pants tucked inside the tops of green rubber pacs. One of them kneeled and drew a knife from the sheath in his belt.

Now, thought David. He sprang up and shouted at the top of his voice. The men turned, startled. David ran a few steps and

stumbled in the tangle of his disintegrating bear paws. He continued to shout, flailing through the snow until the tether brought
him up short. The two men bounded away like bears, snowshoes
flying, as fast as their thick legs could take them. They were
gone from sight moments later, swallowed up by the dark forest.

Tatum approached cautiously, the rifle raised. David gripped
the nylon line in cold wet fingers and pulled himself up, weak
from his effort and in pain. Tatum shoved him with the rifle butt.
The boy toppled in the snow. Tatum stood over him, angry and
suspicious. "What was that for?"

David clawed the snow from his face. "To get rid of them." He
could barely whisper the lying words. He lowered his head to
hide the disappointment clouding his eyes.

Tatum grabbed his chin and forced David's face up. "I don't
believe you."

"They're gone, aren't they?"

"Why'd they run like that?"

"Figured us for game wardens."

"Couldn't they see we're not?"

"Poachers never stop to look. They run."

"You tried to trick me, David—"

"I swear—"

"—yelling for help." He glared at the distant woods line where
the men had disappeared. "If those men hadn't run—"

"They're poachers," David cried. "They get caught and it's a
thousand bucks and a jail term."

"You didn't have to yell at them."

"It scared them off. It worked—"

"We were okay where we were."

"If they saw us first, Gary, I swear to God they'd kill us."

"You're lying—"

"Thanks," David said angrily. "Thanks a lot. I save your life
and this is the thanks I get." He got up slowly and brushed the
snow from his clothes. "You're in charge. Do what you want." He
turned his back and retrieved the remnants of his bear paws.
Tatum watched him narrowly, still uncertain. David worked the
leather strips and rawhide laces free and wiped off the snow. He
took a step, another, and sank to his hips. He struggled to move
on, lunging, gasping at the sharp pain. No use, he thought. I'll

never make it. He lay there, his mind a muddle of frustration and self-pity.

He looked up at Tatum. *You crummy mess. Parka cockeyed, snotty-nosed, one mitten adrift, knapsack riding on your ass . . .*

Suddenly he was fed up with Gary, with cold and hunger.

"Let's go, David. No stalling."

"I'm staying here."

"No way."

"You've got the gun, the compass, snowshoes. Cut me loose, huh? You'll make the border by dark." He saw the torment of indecision in Tatum's face. "Just take off. You'll never make it with me."

But Tatum was staring past David at the wide sweep of the Baker Branch. "That's a real river." He shaded his eyes with a hand against the snow's blinding whiteness.

This is it, David thought. He eyed the Krag loosely held, muzzle down in the crook of Gary's arm. Just out of reach, yet a tempting chance, perhaps his last. He rose to one knee and took a step toward Tatum—too late. Tatum's head came round. David's outstretched arm reached past the Krag to Tatum's mitten in the snow. He handed it to Tatum, who seemed distracted.

"How do we get across?" he demanded.

"We should do something about that deer first," David said.

"Like what?"

"Cut a chunk of hindquarter for steaks. And skin some of the hide to cover our feet."

"No time for that."

"We got to eat, Gary."

"Up, David. We're crossing into Canada tonight."

"How? You going to carry me piggyback?" He sank back into the snow.

Tatum prodded him with the gun barrel. "Last chance," he said. "Get up."

"You'll have to kill me first."

Tatum scratched at his stubbled, ice-beaded cheeks. "Okay. I can deal with that. I have a postgraduate degree in dealing with the spoiled adolescent. Magna cum laude. Thanks to my dear mother. My advice to you, young man, is to get up at once."

"Fuck off, you faggot."

Tatum's bloodshot eyes gleamed. "You're an ungrateful little cretinous wretch. I should shoot you in your filthy, lying mouth. But that's too easy. You really want me to kill you, don't you? I won't kill you, David. I will shoot you, yes. First in one leg, the right one. Then in one arm, the left one. So you won't walk or even crawl. The frost will slow up the bleeding. It will be a long time before you die. A long time in which to think about your filthy ways. And I'll cut out your filthy tongue. It would be a boon to mankind." He leaned close to David and thrust the muzzle of the Krag into his crotch. "Do you dress on the left side or the right, young man? Have you a preference?" He prodded the boy. "Answer me," he shrilled.

"Yes, sir."

"And what is that?"

"I don't want to die."

"A moment ago you wanted to die. Now you don't want to die." He withdrew the point of the gun. "Do you mean, David, that you repent?"

The boy nodded.

"He repents!" Tatum's eyes rolled skyward. "Do you hear, O Lord? The sinner repents. Arise, sinner."

David struggled to his feet and leaned against a tree. Tatum padded round him, round the tree, making a crisscross pattern in the snow with the snowshoe webbing. "Even had I shot you, David, as I described, you might have lived. With your boy scout pluck—nice word, pluck—you'd have lived to be a helpless cripple unable to hunt or fish or do anything but sit around in your cottage on Moosehead Lake and tell the tale, with appropriate obscenities, to your grandchildren."

"Please, Gary, can't we move on? If you want—"

"Yes, I want!" His voice exploded over them as startling as the poacher's rifle shot. "I want to know how to get to the other side of this stupid river! But you and your filthy mouth—"

David was pointing. "There's a beaver dam downstream. I saw it through the trees when I—ran off those poachers. We can cross over it."

"Another of your sly tricks, David?"

"I swear to God."

"How far downstream?"

"Maybe thirty, forty yards."

"Okay. We'll stop on the other side. Can you make yourself another pair of snowshoes?"

"Yes, sir." He looked across the clearing to the snow-flecked carcass of the fallen deer.

"No," said Tatum. "And keep a civil tongue in your head."

"I meant every word I said."

"So did I, David. Now move."

They stood at the edge of the woods. Tatum peered cautiously in both directions along the clearing that bordered both sides of the Baker Branch. "Think anyone's spotted us?"

"Nobody's around."

"I have a feeling we've been followed."

"We'd hear them or see tracks." He showed Tatum where a few branches atop the dam broke the evenness of the far shore. They descended the slope toward the stream. Patches of gray ice showed in the middle. David wondered how thick it might be. Along the banks the wind had swept away much of the snow and the going was easier. They trudged silently along the east bank, the wind on their backs moaning through the frozen reeds.

The stream narrowed where the beaver had built their dam. It was about twenty-five feet from shore to shore, ten feet at its base, five feet high, narrowing at the top to a small jungle of jutting alder, poplar, and birch, mud and stones. Thin ice, almost invisible, coated much of its surface. A ticklish crossing, David observed.

They approached the base of the dam. Tatum hesitated. "Why can't we cross over the ice?"

David picked up a rock and threw it. It splintered the thin surface ice at midstream and disappeared.

"I don't know," Tatum muttered. "I don't like this."

"You'll have to take your snowshoes off." David climbed up on the dam. "See? It's easy." He leaned into the wind and pointed upstream to a crude, ovenlike structure of sticks, grass, and moss woven together with mud, on the west bank. "That's where they live. They go back and forth under the ice."

Tatum did not look up. He fumbled with the stiff buckles of his snowshoe harness, kicked his bound feet free, and stuffed the webbed ends of the snowshoes into the knapsack. He checked the tether line and the safety on the Krag.

He's stalling, David thought. Afraid to cross. He waited while Tatum adjusted the pack straps and tested the loop that held the ax. Pathetic, David thought. He reached down to help Tatum onto the dam. Tatum waved him away. "I can handle it," he muttered.

He clambered to the top of the dam using his left hand to steady himself. He straightened up, shaky, rifle at the ready, panic in his eyes. For a fleeting instant David felt a tug of sympathy for Gary. I'm as psycho as he is, he thought sourly.

"All set?"

"Roger," said Tatum.

David started across. He picked his way cautiously, testing each branch and stone before setting his foot down. God bless these rubber-bottomed boots, he thought. The line tightened abruptly, almost spilling him. He turned. Tatum was squatting. His right hand clutched a thick branch, the rifle in the crook of his arm. "Slow down" he shouted.

David waited, half the distance across the dam. The tether slackened as Tatum inched along. He stopped about ten feet from David. "I don't like this," he muttered. "Too risky."

"We'll be across in no time."

"We're going back."

"We're almost there, Gary."

"Too slippery," Tatum said in a shaky voice. "I'll fall."

"You can make it. Grab the line. I'll keep it taut."

"Start back, David." Tatum half turned to watch David over his shoulder. "*Now.*"

David ignored him and pulled ahead. The line tightened around his waist, almost squeezing the breath out of him. He tugged in fierce thrusts. The line yielded slowly, dragging Tatum, who was shouting. David dared not look back. He jumped from the dam and fell gasping to the bank before Tatum could brace himself and stop the boy's headlong dive.

On firm ground and in the clear, David scrambled to his feet. "C'mon, chicken," he jeered, "you're almost there."

Tatum found a firm footing and raised the rifle. "Get back up here, David. Right now!"

David stood feet apart, head thrown back. "Red Rover, Red Rover," he taunted, "let Gary come over."

Tatum snapped off the safety and aimed. David froze. *My God, he means it!* Tatum squeezed the trigger. The hammer clicked emptily. Tatum jacked out the cartridge, slammed another into the chamber, and locked the bolt. Steady now, he took more careful aim.

David came to life. He grabbed the nylon line and yanked hard, jarring Tatum off-balance. The rifle fired skyward with an ear-splitting roar. David frantically jerked the line from right to left until Tatum slipped and with a stream of chilling curses tumbled from the dam. He crashed through snapped twigs and flying stones shattering thin ice like window glass.

Tatum's body sank from sight. Its dead weight dragged David helplessly to the edge of the stream until, heels in, he braced himself against a rock. The blast and Tatum's scream still echoed in his ears. He heaved on the line with all his strength. Tatum's head bobbed up, dripping. The ends of the snowshoes showed next. David worked the line around a tree trunk for leverage. Moments later, Tatum floundered to the bank and sprawled there, retching in spasms.

The gun and the ax were gone. Muddy water coursed through the knapsack like blood from many wounds. Tatum lay limp, sobbing. In all his life, David had not heard a more piteous human sound.

He moved in, avoiding Tatum's outflung arms, and pulled the knife from its sheath and slashed himself free of the tether. He lifted the snowshoes clear and ran.

Ran plunging, falling, crawling through the snow, choking and gasping until he could no longer hear the sound of Tatum's suffering. Breathing hard, he stuck the knife in his belt, buckled the showshoes to his boots, and weeping, crooning, pushed upstream away from the bank and alder growth to a high place where the going was easier. Somewhere ahead lay the state forester's cabin. He did not know how far. Miles no longer mattered.

He was free.

The ordeal had taken much out of him. The pain in his side forced him to favor it. He barely lifted the right snowshoe with each step. The sharp wind numbed him. The padding between his shirts had lumped in clammy packets. The gift of freedom alone kept his spirits high. He pushed on.

At times his mind grew sluggish and his thoughts confused. The need to lie down and rest, to close his half-blind eyes, swelled as his strength ebbed. He clung doggedly to the trail, one foot ahead of the other. He knew the impulse to quit now meant sure death.

He fought the drowsiness that drugged his mind, the fatigue that dragged at his limbs like sash weights. Ahead of him in the snow against the leaden sky, or framed in the alder bushes, the image of the forester's cabin, the bright red triangle on Gary's map, beckoned. It was out there. Someplace. He had seen it before. He would see it again. Perhaps round the next bend.

Upstream, he wondered, or downstream? North or south? Had he got turned around at the beaver dam? Was this the east bank or the west? Had the wind shifted and thrown him off? Was he following a stream that would dead-end in some nameless bog?

"My name is David Kimball Briggs," he yelled. "I'm going home!"

It felt good to yell and he yelled again until his throat and chest burned raw. He heard voices, carried on the wind, and he mourned their fading.

My mind is playing tricks on me, he thought in panic.

He tried to think of happier times (I'm happy now, he insisted) and punched himself and pinched his cheeks and the meager flesh of his arms. Fun things. To make me laugh, he thought. And shouted again at the top of his voice, "Fun things!" And his shout was a croak in the wind.

He conjured up the image of old Mert Emery's weather-beaten face and thought back to the time last summer when they had spent days together fitting the windows into the A-frame. Mert was always good for a laugh, looking down his nose at "ship-shod" work and chores done "half-hazardly." Mert, who called a bulldozer a "bullnozer" and blamed the troubles of the world on all them "Commonists" . . .

Fun things. He saw his mother's face in anguish and his father in drunken rage. He saw the seams and wrinkles on Grampa Kimball's cheeks and Mrs. Sewall's pleading eyes. "Try, you poor thing . . ."

O my God, he thought . . .

. . . and thought of Gary teetering, teetering, and the sound of Gary's shouted curses moments before he tumbled into the stream.

Laughter deep inside the boy's belly rose through his starved body to his throat and erupted in sounds resembling muffled war whoops, so joyous, so filled with delight and zest he was, the ecstasy flowing out of him as he remembered, as now he heard again, Gary's obscenities. "He said those filthy dirty words," he whispered, too weak to shout. "The screwball weirdo who never said a dirty word, who said he'd kill me if I cursed again."

Other words of Gary's came to mind and deeds fouler than any he had ever known. He did not laugh. Following a sharp bend in the stream, the round black chimney of the forester's cabin came in full view not twenty yards away. It was time for a quiet cry.

He squatted close to the wood stove and gently stroked his fingers and toes. His clothes were drying. His belly was full of hot bean soup and hard biscuit. Except for a small knot of loneliness and the dull ache in his side, he felt super. Drowsy and clean and safe and super.

For almost an hour he did nothing but lie there, in all ways sensing the sweetness of being alive. Too bad, he thought, I had to bust the window to get in. But it saved my life and that's what wilderness cabins are for.

A smart kid like me could hole up here all winter, he reflected. Everything on hand. Pots and pans. Canisters of dry food. Traps, tackle, and tools. A locker full of foul-weather gear. On the rafters overhead there was equipment for survival in the woods. Outside there was cut wood in the shed and a forest to cut from. The state forester would not be back until the spring thaw. By that time, David thought, I'll be gone. Canada. Wherever.

He went to the window and looked out. The cabin stood in a sea of snowdrifts, in a clearing on a bare bluff overlooking the bend of the stream. If they were searching for him, now that the storm was over, he could make the job easier with a large smudge fire on the point of that bluff. All he had to do was gather the green boughs and branches and touch her off. But who would be looking for him? Who gave a damn for Davey Briggs?

The hell with them. What he needed most was sleep. He fed the fire and lay down on the rough bunk and closed his eyes. In the shelter of this rustic sanctuary he felt at peace for the first time since he had been taken. The wind and the crackling fire and the kettle hissing on the black stove soothed his nerves. He thought of other cabins where he had spent the nightmare days. Three? Five? He could not be sure. He probed the dried sores on his cheeks and body. No nightmare. Those crazy things had really happened.

Far out.

He tried to image what it would be like when they finally found him. One way or the other, dead or alive, they would find him. Dead would serve them right. Alive, who would it be? Loggers? A game warden? The state forester? Poachers? Maybe. Or coyotes. No one would believe his story. They would feed him warm milk and wiggle a finger at the side of their heads. He would have to show them Gary, frozen stiff at the beaver dam. He would lead them through the woods to the shelter where the ashes of all that loot would open their eyes some. And if that didn't convince them, he'd take them to Desolation Pond and poke around a bit. They'd believe him then. You better the hell believe they'd believe him then.

They would start to fire questions at him. They'd want to know who he was and how they could get in touch with his family and all that bullshit. And that was where he would have them. Because he would tell them he was Bongo the Jungle Boy. That was it, period. Bongo. He had no family. Family was a bad trip. He was all the family he would ever need. F for family. The Big Eff. As in "Sesame Street," or whatever it was those stupid indoor faggots loved to look at Saturday mornings instead of getting out into the woods where a real red-blooded American boy belongs.

He would have gone to Canada with Gary. He would have gone anywhere in the world with Gary. Before Gary went bonkers. Before he did those terrible things. Jesus, the guy had so much going for him. The smooth looks and the crinkly blue eyes and the easy way he moved. That first night when they sat in the dark outside the cabin at Desolation, he had watched Gary's profile while he talked about the neat places he'd been and the things he had done, and right then and there, he had promised himself, Boy, that's how I'm going to be someday. That's how I want to live, free to travel the world, matching my wits against jungle rivers and mountain peaks.

And then the weirdo had to go and . . . *tried to kill me!* Sure, I teased him and dared him but I never dreamed he'd do it. Said he needed me. *And he did.* He really needed me. If that first shot there on the dam hadn't misfired, sure as hell I wouldn't be here thinking about it.

What had happened? Eddie's old Krag, that's what happened. Probably a worn firing pin spring. It happened to me once with an old thirty-thirty. In weather that cold it could happen to anyone. The spring'll freeze up and the pin'll barely tap the cartridge primer the first time or two. That's what it was. A worn-out, froze-up firing pin spring . . .

And there he is and here I am and the hell with him.

He sat up and wiped away angry tears. No use to lie here, Briggs. Get to work. Do something. Screw Gary No-name.

He sat there sullenly resisting the course his thoughts were taking. He squirmed, scratched his butchered hair, picked at scabs. No escape. He could not shake the last look he'd had of Gary sprawled and sobbing on the riverbank. When he realized he could not change it, he rose from the bunk, softly swearing.

He dressed warmly, helping himself from the forester's clothing locker. He climbed a chair and, ignoring his pain, brought down a long narrow moose sled from the rafters. He tested the rigging and towline and covered it with a blanket and tarpaulin. He banked the fire and carried the sled outside and put on his snowshoes.

He stood for a time, unable to make up his mind about a signal fire. If I reach Gary, he told himself, and he's still alive and I get him back, he's going to need more help than I can give him.

He left the sled and went about gathering green boughs and branches. He tore them free and dragged them to the bluff and heaved them on the growing pile. Each movement stabbed into his side. After ten minutes of it, the deepening pain surprised him. He stumbled and fell and lay there resting, breathing noisily, until the seizure seemed to pass. He had not expected such simple labor to drain him so. He had rested, hadn't he? Eaten well. Dressed snugly, warmly, what could happen to a woods-wise fourteen-year-old smart-ass that he couldn't handle?

He kept at it. When the boughs were piled twice the height of a man, he lighted kindling beneath them and tended it until the heavy blue smoke soared up, carried southward by the wind. He added enough dry wood to ensure a slow burning fire for several hours. By that time, he'd be back with Gary.

He picked up the towline with an effort. "Ought to have my head examined," he grumbled. With the moose sled behind, he plodded down the slope toward the bank of the stream until he found his old wind-blown tracks still visible in the snow. Bent low, doggedly pushing one snowshoe past the other, he headed for the beaver dam. He knew before he had gone a hundred yards, he was not going to make it. He pushed on. When he had fallen for the third time, he tried to turn back. This time he did not get up. He barely made it to the moose sled on hands and knees before the lights went out.

It was Dana Toothaker, flying the first search plane out of the Inland Fish and Game air base, who spotted the smoke. He radioed his find to Greenville and circled low and flew as close to the bluff as he could. It was not close enough to bring anyone out of the cabin. If anyone was there. He notified the duty warden he was heading back to base. He would make a return trip with the helicopter.

The word was passed along to the search party from Ste.-Aurélie. They had just cleared the north end of Baker Lake on the I.P. road and were heading for St. Francis Pond. They unloaded the snowmobiles from the trucks, warmed them up, and turned northward for the five-mile run cross-country, following the Baker Branch downstream.

Morrison broke trail, carrying the medical examiner behind him. Kimball rode with Vail on the second machine. They bucked and slammed through deep soft drifts, over stumps, and under sagging boughs loaded with snow. It was a slow and noisy journey, the men silent, the woods ominous. Kimball caught the first whiff of wood smoke half an hour later. As they approached the south edge of the clearing, he tapped Vail's shoulder. "Shouldn't we slow down? This man Tatum's supposed to be dangerous."

"Whoever's there wouldn't have made that big fire if he didn't want help."

They pulled up a short distance from the cabin. Morrison got out and slipped two shells into his shotgun. He signaled Vail to continue along the snowshoe trail that led toward the stream and he cautiously approached the cabin, calling out.

Vail and Kimball did not have far to go. They found David delirious in a slender stand of paper birch, curled under the blanket and tarp on the moose sled. They brought him back to the forester's cabin in Kimball's arms, stiff and cold.

He opened his eyes. There was Grampa Kimball looking down at him. Someone else, whom he could not see, was taping his side. He felt hot and sweaty. His throat was parched and raw, his entire body tingled with a fever. He pushed feebly at the heavy covers. Kimball took his hand to restrain him. David jerked free and turned away. The pain brought a cry to his lips.

"Easy, boy."

David avoided his grandfather's eyes and watched Vail wind another wide strip of tape across his side. "That should hold you 'til the chopper gets here," Vail said.

"There's this fellow," David croaked, "name is Gary. He's downstream—"

"They've gone after him, Davey."

"You knew—?"

"You told us."

"Me?"

"You've been muttering and mumbling nothing else since we picked you up."

"I started back. I went to get him."

"We figured that when we found you."

"Is he—okay?"

"Don't know yet." Kimball took the boy's hand. David stiffened. "You're running a fever, son. Try to take it easy."

"My side hurts something awful."

"Figured that, too, the way you howled each time we touched you."

"Mr. Sewall had this shotgun, see—?" The words would not come. He turned away.

"Easy, boy. Help's on the way." He squeezed David's hand and joined Vail at the far end of the cabin and spoke softly so David would not hear. "Could you reach Greenville?"

"They're passing the word. I told them we have the boy."

"How's Briggs?"

"Couldn't make it out. Too garbled."

They heard Morrison's snowmobile climbing the bank below the bluff. Vail went to the door. "They've got him," he said and went outside to help.

Kimball sat on the bunk alongside David. "We've sent word back to Mother and Dad, Davey. You'll be seeing them soon."

David was silent. Kimball glanced over his shoulder to see how close the rescue party was. "David, I need some answers to a few questions before they get back. Feel up to it?"

David shrugged. Kimball went on. "Did Tatum have a knapsack full of money with him?"

"Who?"

"Tatum. The man who kidnaped you."

Tatum, the boy thought. Gary Tatum. Pal of Sydney Briggs.

"David?"

"I wondered what his name was."

"Quickly now. Did he have the ransom money?"

Ransom? Oh poor Gramp. You still don't know. "Yes," he whispered.

"Where's the knapsack?"

"Last I saw, it was on his back."

"Too bad," Kimball muttered and thought: If the heart doesn't end Sydney, this will.

"Why is it bad, Grampa?"

"That money, Davey—well—" Kimball hesitated. How do you tell a beat-up, pain-racked fourteen-year-old that his father who's in the hospital critically ill is also a crook?

"If it's the money that's bugging you," David whispered, "forget it."

"I'm afraid it's not that simple."

"It's gone, Grampa."

"What do you mean, gone?"

"We burned it."

"You—*what?*"

"We had to. To stay alive. The night of the blizzard."

"Burned the ransom money?"

"To ashes."

"All of it?"

"Every last dollar." He saw the strangest look in Kimball's eyes. "That's all right," he said fiercely. "Serves Dad right, for what he tried to do. Serves him damn right!"

"What on earth are you saying?" Kimball, bewildered, searched the boy's face.

"I don't care," David said in a choked voice.

Kimball patted his arm and turned away, deeply affected. He went to the window and watched them unload Tatum.

God moves in a mysterious way. His wonders to perform . . .

David stared at his grandfather's back. Money, he thought bitterly. All they ever give a damn about.

They were bringing Tatum in. David closed his eyes. Alive or dead no longer mattered. Nothing mattered any more.

CHAPTER THIRTY-THREE

Clean, he thought.

He had never felt so clean. Scrubbed, hair trimmed and brushed, the linen sweet-smelling, fresh and crisp as cucumbers. So clean he could scream for the pure joy of it.

He had never spent much time in a hospital. Funny how he had never noticed nurses before. The way they went about their jobs, cool and neat and so sure of themselves. Like making the bed. Zip, zap, the hospital corners tight, the sheets smooth as glass. Fluffing things up, patting things down.

One of them, Miss Pelletier, was young and pretty. She was the one he watched most. The way she moved. Like a young doe he had seen once, ankle-deep in the Allagash, unaware she was watched. She was the one on duty when the young doctor who was flabby and bald showed up and poked his fingers around the taped ribs just to see if he could make David cry out. Then he asked a few stupid questions and hung around yacking with poor Miss Pelletier who had to stand there and take it. They laughed a lot and the crummy doctor winked at David and said what a brave little man he was.

Little man, my ass. I could tell him a few things'd make his hair stand on end. If he had any.

Mostly, he just lay there alone, thinking about things. His mind was a muddle of hazy images to be sorted out. He could think back clearly to the time at the forester's cabin when the man who wasn't Grampa Kimball or one of the wardens had given him a shot. He had tried to tell them he was okay and didn't want a shot. All he wanted was to see what it was like, looking down on the big woods from the glass cage of the helicopter. That was the last thing he remembered until he woke up in the hospital. A day ago? Two days? He closed his eyes.

Why don't they come? Doesn't anyone give a good goddamn what's happened to me?

Grampa Kimball had said they'd be waiting for him when he got back. He remembered that very clearly. Was his mother worse off? Not up to the trip from the funny farm and her shrink said no? And where was his father? Off on another big deal? Off to skin the natives in Aroostook out of the old family homestead? Too busy to drop by and say hi to his son? Or too ashamed of the deal with Gary and Eddie Michaud that backfired? One thing he knew for sure. If he never saw his father again, it would be too soon.

Maybe it's because I burned up the ransom money. It sure gave Grampa Kimball a turn when I told him. That's it, all right. It *had* to be the money. Nothing else in the world makes grown-ups act so crummy. Not that I give a shit about the money. I can take care of myself. But you'd think . . .

He wiped his eyes. From his bed by the wide misty window he could see across the broad expanse of the snow-covered hospital lawn the road that ran out of Greenville through the junction to Rockwood. Traffic was heavy in both directions. Any minute now, one of the cars would turn into the drive and it would be the white Continental with the BRIGGS tag.

He idled away the time counting deer lashed to the car tops. For pickup trucks where no antlers showed, he counted half of them as having deer. Fair enough, he reflected. I'm not counting the hundreds killed illegally and never registered. He counted twenty-eight before he stopped. Too many, he thought, feeling queasy, remembering the wasted one that morning after the blizzard.

He wondered how a deer felt with a rifle pointed at him, about to explode. He knew that some deer blow and snort when spooked in the woods, but he never heard of a deer making a sound after it was shot. Old Mert told him he once heard a gut-shot buck deer blat like a sheep. It was the only time in all his years of hunting he heard a deer cry. Rabbits and hedgehogs, though, they cry like babies when they're shot, enough to make you never want to shoot a living thing again.

Those dead deer out there on the highway, headed to no-where, had no problem. Their worries were over. But how about the others still in the woods? The fawns and does who stood by or hid or ran while the shot one fell. How much do they feel?

How much do they remember? He could tell them how it felt. He could also tell them what it was like to be leashed and beaten like a dog. He could even tell them how it felt to be dead. Not like those deer out there. Dead like he was. On the inside.

Miss Pelletier came in, all smiles. He had some visitors. His heart leaped and he tried to sound casual when he said to bring them in. But it was Junior Tuttle and a stranger in a dark coat. David could not hide his disappointment.

Junior Tuttle looked like a Northwest Mountie. He had his two-tone blue uniform pressed to a razor edge and he acted proud when he introduced the FBI agent from Bangor. The man asked a lot of questions and David told him everything he wanted to know. Junior told him that Gary Tatum was down the corridor with a police guard outside his door. As soon as his operation was over, they'd be moving him to a prison hospital. David asked about the operation. Frostbite, Junior told him. Tatum would probably lose most of his toes but he was going to live. They were making damned sure of that.

"What about my folks?" David asked as they were leaving. But Junior Tuttle was already through the door and the FBI man only shrugged. Miss Pelletier came in right after that. David asked if he could go down the corridor to say good-by to Gary. He had no hard feelings. Not any more.

Not a chance, Miss Pelletier told him. Strictest orders. But she rumpled his hair and it made him feel so different, he forgot to ask about his mom and dad.

He watched through the window as Chief Tuttle's forest-green Ambassador with the four aerials went down the driveway. Just as it reached the highway, a raunchy-looking pickup truck turned in. For a moment he thought it was Grampa Kimball's. He could almost see his mother sitting in the cab. But he was wrong. David watched it until it was past his range of vision. He buried his face in the pillow.

He thought about what it must be like to have no toes. He remembered reading about an eastern college girl who survived a plane crash with her injured pilot in the frozen wilderness of the Yukon. Because of frostbite, her toes had to be amputated. Yet she went on to say, in the book she wrote about her experience, she intended to lead a perfectly normal life, skiing and even taking ballet lessons to acquire extra good balance. And because of the experience she discovered something she had never known before. She loved life.

It was after reading her book that David learned everything he could to prevent frostbite. Things like tucking his hands under his armpits or between his thighs—anywhere as long as it was warmer than the extremities. And heat, not cold. A temperature of 100° was okay, but you had to be careful not to go too high above body temperature because the rapid change could destroy the fragile tissues.

It was one of the most exciting books David had ever read and he wished right now he had a copy of it to read again. Better still, he would give a copy of it to Gary. Gary was lucky to be alive.

Or was he?

He had a sudden desire to see Gary. I must be out of my skull, he told himself. He got out of the bed and very carefully went to the door and looked down the hall. One of Junior Tuttle's deputies, a local boy named Ben Cyr, just back from navy duty overseas, sat in a chair two rooms away. No one else was in sight. David went to him. The door was open and he could see Gary's head turned toward the window. The deputy had gotten out of the chair and had David by the arm, gently. "You better get back in your room, Davey." His thick body blocked the door.

"Can't I just for a second say hi to him?"

"What the hell for? After what he done?"

"I'll stand just inside the door. I swear to God, Ben."

"If anything happens—"

"Please, Ben."

Something in the boy's tone touched the guard. After all, he thought, the two of them had been through hell together. Like they were war buddies, kind of. Shipmates. He really understood. He stepped aside. "Just for a second or two, now."

David stood a few feet from the bed. Tatum's hands were bandaged and his wrists manacled to the bedpost.

"Hi, Gary."

Tatum turned. David was surprised to see how healthy he looked. Red-cheeked, pretty as ever. He had expected sunken cheeks and damage, some physical evidence of the ordeal Tatum had endured. He found it in Tatum's eyes—lackluster and empty, staring at him without interest, almost without recognition.

David's mind groped for the thoughts he wanted to express—the rescue, the college girl's Yukon ordeal, frostbite, how he would have stuck with Gary all the way, the truth about his father, the ransom money. A million things, now that they both were free, kind of.

The unspoken words were drowned and lost in the vast empty pools of Tatum's unblinking eyes. All David could do was stare back, full of pity not alone for Tatum but for his mother and father and himself. For the very nature of things. Tears welled. Not a word was spoken.

Then Tatum seemed to come to life, not stirring, yet his eyes burned blue. His thin dry lips were barely moving and David bent close.

". . . still make it together, David. I have this plan, see? Foolproof. The key to these handcuffs are in that idiot guard's hip pocket . . ."

David tore his eyes away and backed off. At the door he heard Gary's voice, clear as ice and faintly mocking. "Good-by, Gary."

Past Cyr, the horror of it struck David halfway down the hall. Chilled to the marrow, he crawled under the covers and sobbed. The bastard, he thought. The dirty lousy bastard. He's wrong, *wrong!*

He wished his mother would come.

She bent over and kissed him lightly behind the ear. He turned and looked up at her. She was the most beautiful sight he had ever seen. Even with the strange swelling, slightly purplish round one eye, and the tired lines delicately etched, she was to him all that was serene and lovely and timeless.

Behind her, Grampa Kimball loomed, weary and grim. David could not remember a time when he had looked so peaked and old. His mother's cool fingers traced the pattern of scars, feather light, on David's cheeks. "Tattoos," she murmured. "Like a sailor home from the sea."

"War paint," he said, not trusting his voice. They both had to be careful, they loved each other so much. Miss Pelletier came in, a brisk welcome breeze. The tension eased and they were relieved and grateful. She gave David a pill to swallow and juice to suck through a wiggly straw, and quickly left. In the odd silence that followed, David felt confident now, and strong enough to ask the question that plagued him. "Dad away on business again? Or is he too ashamed to face me after what he's done?"

She sat for a moment stunned, then turned with a helpless expression to her father. "He's dead, Davey," Kimball said. "We just buried him."

He heard the words. He had heard them many times in different ways, always of his own making. In his moments of deep despair, he would wish with all his might they were true. He had pictured it happening at the cottage, a drowning perhaps. Or a bad fall. Or he would be seated in a classroom and a message from the headmaster or principal would summon him to the front office while his classmates stared and sniggered. He would be told in solemn tones to sit down and be strong. A highway accident. A shooting. Hundreds of different wishful ways, but only in those despondent spells, those fantasies. And now it had happened. . . .

He was in his mother's arms. The strain and pent-up emotion locked inside him during the days of terror and pain let go. He fought to control his sobbing, to stem and slow the flood. It was too real, too deep. He went the full distance while she held him and soothed him. She too wept, but not much and only for him. The weeping was out of her by now. Not the grief, though. They would share that for some time to come.

Much later, when it was dark and they had gone and he was alone, he tried to think about how things stood. Like when you're lost in the woods, be calm and don't panic. Like get your head together, Briggs, and figure things out.

Before they left, they had told him what his father had done. The good and the bad. He understood now what had happened, and why. And he had a clear, almost a shining vision of what it was his father had expected of him.

Things always were easier when adults leveled with kids. You'd think they'd know that by now.

Miss Pelletier came in. She was finished for the day and going home. She seemed subdued and did not smile. "I'm sorry about your father, David."

"Thank you," David said quietly. "He was a very unusual man."

She smiled then and fluffed his pillow and pecked him. "You're a most unusual boy, you know."

When she was gone he turned to the window and stared at the headlights of the passing cars on the highway. All those dead deer, he thought.

Novelist, artist, and professional consultant on the arts and education, Martin Dibner began his writing career while serving as a naval gunnery officer in the Pacific during World War II. His novels, often dealing with the dilemma of decent human beings caught up in a world of violence and materialism, have been published in numerous translations world-wide. One, *The Deep Six*, was made into a major motion picture. Mr. Dibner, who lives in Maine, is also the author of *Seacoast Maine*, an affectionate look at its people and places, with photographs by George A. Tice.